She likes Hawaii, but she just might love Boston...

Still stinging from her recent divorce, Emily Buzzly heads to majestic Hawaii to soothe her wounds. But once she arrives on Oahu, Emily discovers that a man she assumes is a beach bum is in fact her personal tour guide, hired by her sister. With his long hair and tattoos, Boston Rondibett is everything Emily detests—despite his sun-kissed surfer body. And with her straight-laced, executive persona, Emily is everything Boston rebels against. But both have a lot to learn about making snap judgments...

As it turns out, Boston's real job, the one he truly cares about, is running his soup kitchen and homeless shelter. Embarrassed by her assumptions, rather than lazy beach days, Emily soon finds herself feeding the hungry, and even involved in the search for an AWOL soldier. And to Boston's surprise, she's loving every minute of it—and he's loving seeing her loosen her chignon and be the admirable, beautiful woman she is. As each works through the challenges of the past, these two very different people just might find their hearts are on the very same page...

I0677570

Books by Roxanne Smith

Long Shot Romance Series
Men Like This
Relapse In Paradise
Running the Numbers

Published by Kensington Publishing Corporation

Relapse In Paradise

A Long Shot Romance Novel

Roxanne Smith

LYRICAL PRESS
Kensington Publishing Corp.
www.kensingtonbooks.com

First Electronic Edition: November 2015
eISBN-13: 978-1-61650-691-9
eISBN-10: 1-61650-691-1

First Print Edition: November 2015
ISBN-13: 978-1-61650-692-6
ISBN-10: 1-61650-692-X

Printed in the United States of America

I dedicate this book to Sergeant Jesse Lain of the U.S. Army in thanks for his service.

Acknowledgements

I'd like to acknowledge Jesse Lain, to whom I've dedicated this book, for his insider tips about life on Oahu. Any mistakes or misinterpretations are mine alone, either by accident or with intent.
Tarran Clack, Spencer Lain, and Dakota Lain have all lent an ear or offered advice as I needed it. Finally, a shout out to my beta readers, Tabatha Frazier and Dani-Lyn Alexander, who provided valuable feedback and lovely compliments.
Thank you.

http://smithrox.blogspot.com/
https://www.facebook.com/roxannesmith.author
https://twitter.com/ThisSmithRox

Chapter 1

Boston rubbed his forehead and let his exasperation show plainly in his tone. "Hani, I don't have time for this, man."

Even doubled over with his head stuck inside the cold oven, the overgrown Hawaiian took up most of the space in the dark galley kitchen. The one narrow window set above the porcelain sink had been scrubbed just last week. Boston had watched Akela bring down the threadbare curtains and take a sponge to the glass pane with his own eyes, but the room seemed to stay gloomy.

Boston blamed Hani's giant body blocking out the sunlight. Or scaring it away.

Hani's head came out of the oven and cocked to one side in annoyance. Despite it, his clear, dark eyes held only concern. Maybe a hint of fear. "Don't push me, *haole*. If we don't get this stove working, we ain't feeding nobody. Akela's bringing plates she made from home, but that won't get us through the day. And if Mama finds out she's helping here, Bos, it won't be good."

Fair point. Hani's sister did a lot around the shelter, without her family's consent or knowledge. Since Hani had left home and landed on the streets, they'd had little to do with him. Less so after he took up running The Canopy with Boston. Except Akela, who refused to disown her only brother.

Boston pulled a wad of bills from the side pocket of his maroon cut-off shorts with tired reluctance. The frayed end of his shorts tickled his shins and got caught in his leg hair, but they were his favorite pair.

Probably because Hani hated them. Boston figured he'd picked them out this morning in a subconscious effort to antagonize his business partner.

He held the fat wad of cash aloft to give Hani a better view. "Relax, big guy. See this? It's my paycheck from the job I picked up last week. Money just came down the wire."

His friend didn't appear impressed. Hani had never much cared for money. It was hard to work up a whole lot of concern for something they never had. "Whatcha gonna do, huh? Hand it out? We're trying to give these poor folks a decent plate of rice, not send them back to the liquor store."

Boston put zero effort into hiding his impatient groan. "Your brain's as thick as your barrel chest sometimes. Hell no, I'm not about to sprinkle cash on a bunch of homeless guys. But I bet I've got enough right here to pick up an old used oven at the appliance yard downtown. Relax, man. We're in paradise, remember?" He gave Hani his best cheesy smile, the one he might use on folks if he ever turned to selling cars to make a buck.

The big man stopped fooling with the lost cause of an oven to put a hand over his large belly and laugh lazily.

Like Boston knew he would. If the famous Chef Hani of The Canopy, Honolulu's poorest and smallest soup kitchen, didn't have a sense of humor, no one did.

He shook his head, a slight smile on his wide mouth. "You're funny, Boston. Real funny. You try that paradise talk on the next straggler who finds his way in here. Wait till I can watch, though, 'kay? It's been too long since I seen you get your ass handed to you. In fact, I think it was Jordan who gave you your last shiner, huh? A girl, even."

Boston's insides seized up in his gut like a bad toe cramp. Not the result of nostalgia, loss, or even heartbreak, but fear. Happened every damn time Jordan's name found its way into a conversation. Or into his head. Or he caught a glimpse of the tattoo in his reflection. He absentmindedly rubbed the spot on his ribcage where the ink etched into his skin, barely visible through the threadbare white T-shirt he wore.

A hui hou, it read. *Until we meet again.*

So much for that.

Hani must've caught his expression. He ran a flat palm over his face as if to wipe away the grin he'd already dropped. "Hey, man. I'm sorry."

Boston waved him off and forced a smile. "Don't be. We've got bigger problems."

Hani was back to fiddling with the knobs of the broken oven. "Damn thing." He sighed. His shoulders drooped. "I like to see the money but hate to see it spent before you even go over the books. Tell me about this new job you got before I call Thompson down here to help me move this thing." He kicked the bottom of it. "Stupid piece of junk."

"What about Kale? Did he finally do the right thing?"

Hani grunted. "Whatever *that* is. Like either of us would know."

They were certain Kale was an AWOL soldier from the army base at the center of Oahu, but neither of them felt any compulsion to turn him in. Boston would be damned before he'd do it.

The Canopy was a soup kitchen/sometimes shelter when weather hit and they brought a few poor souls inside, not a halfway house or rehab facility. They fed people a couple times a day, as many as they had rice for and nothing more. Hot food, no soapbox talk. Guys like Kale and Thompson relied on the place for a safe haven, and Boston relied on them for help maintaining the shelter. Damn hard to make payroll without liquid assets.

Hell, without *any* assets. The building itself wasn't worth the broken industrial oven they were about to toss on the curbside.

Hani's thick, black eyebrows drew together in a concerned wrinkle. "I ain't seen Kale in a while, but something tells me he didn't turn himself in at the base. His face would be all over the news if he had."

"How would we know? You see a television in here?"

Hani rolled his eyes. "I may not get out much, but you do. You would've seen something, heard something. One of the boys would probably know."

The boys. That's what Hani called them even though a few women made their way into The Canopy from time to time. The stragglers, the panhandlers, the bottom-feeders. Sometimes, in his more poetic moods, they were the lost souls or the forgotten.

Boston ran a weary hand through his shoulder-length hair. "Nothing I can do for a street kid on the run from the Army. But I can tell you about the job. About two years ago, when I first started doing the guide thing, this couple came from London on their honeymoon." He scratched his chin. The lady was American, he recalled. "Or was it California? Can't remember. Anyway, great couple. Totally laid back." He snapped his finger. "Jack, that was the husband. Jack and Quinn. If all my clients were as chill as these two, I'd love my job."

Air blew from Hani's lips with a rude noise. They called it a raspberry back on the mainland, but there was probably some Hawaiian word for it Boston didn't know. "Whatever, man. You know you love dragging mainlanders all over the island. Don't lie."

Okay, yeah, so he loved it, but what wasn't to love? Oahu did the work; Boston only had to drive and point. "Well, they called last week.

They're surprising some family member, a cousin or something, with a plane ticket and hired me to meet her at the airport and show her around the island."

Hani finally gave up on the oven dials with a disappointed, thin-lipped grimace. "You'll probably have it easy if you liked Jack and Quinn so much, eh?"

Boston sucked in air through his teeth. "Nah, I don't think so. Quinn booked this lady's room at the Hilton. Right on Waikiki. She and Jack, they were down for the full experience, you know? They stayed in a little cottage on North Shore that didn't have air-conditioning or sealed windows. Given that, the lofty hotel reservation gives me the impression their cousin—aunt, sister, whatever—isn't made of the same stuff. You smell what I'm cookin'?"

"Oh, I smell it, brother. Smells like you got a rough job ahead." Hani stopped short of whatever he'd been about to say next to give Boston a lingering head-to-toe appraisal. "She's gonna dig for spare change when she sees you, man. Then, when she finds out who you are, she's gonna call the lady who hired you and ask her what the hell she was thinking. *Then* she's gonna go straight to the Hilton Village and hire one of them real guides. The ones who wear the mint green polo shirts and have official stuff like clipboards and name tags."

Upper crust business rivals. Well, not really rivals. The people who came to Boston were usually the ones intent on avoiding things like client rosters, preplanned lunch menus, and name tags. *Especially* name tags.

Boston ran a critical eye over his shorts, which were doing their job offending Hani. "She'll get used to me. She'll have to. If Quinn's buddy ditches me, I'll owe her back the deposit. Since I'm about to spend it on an appliance we need to operate this place, I'd better have something up my sleeve, huh?"

An anxious grunt escaped Hani's lips. "Damn right, you better. Hey, you heard what happened to Ryder, didn't you?"

Boston nibbled the inside of his cheek and thought hard. Ryder... Ryder, sure…. Or, wait. No, that was Robert. Wasn't it? He scratched his neck. "Too many, man. Not enough time for me to get to know them all." At the rate their homeless patrons came and went, who but Hani could keep track? He had the benefit of both working and living at the shelter. Boston's part was making the money to keep it going. On a good week, he'd get to The Canopy once or twice. During a bad week, he made it daily, but it meant no money coming in. "Remind me."

"Guy could've come straight from some bank downtown. Like he might be the CEO or something. Suit and tie."

"Oh, yeah, I remember him. Expensive haircut, trimmed nails, tailored slacks. As recent as they come." Boston had spotted him twice. The first time had stopped Boston in his tracks. His heart had thudded in his chest, stupidly hoping some benevolent rich dude had discovered their operation and came to donate. Until Boston saw him chowing on one of Hani's rice plates. The second time, Ryder hadn't looked so fresh. His button-up was wrinkled, his slick black hair a little less slick. "What happened to him?"

Hani's flat gaze stilled on Boston. "He got arrested last night." A pause. "In Kalihi. I was thinking if bail is set low enough, maybe we can pull something together. Ryder's a good dude."

Boston checked a sigh. Hani reminded him of a spoiled wife sometimes, asking for a new car at the same time Boston was breaking his back just to pay the mortgage. He shook his head slowly. "Kalihi is bad news, man."

Hani's plaintive stare didn't waver.

Boston ran a hand over his smooth cheek. Shaving. His only concession to societal niceties. He tended to get more business when clean-shaven, like facial hair was some sort of trustworthiness gauge. "I don't know, Hani. Guy like that, maybe he developed an expensive habit—the kind of habit that takes a man to Kalihi in the middle of the night. If that's the case, I'd just as soon not get involved." Kalihi had no shoreline, no draw for tourists. Just a working-class neighborhood with the crime and drug problems encountered in any city. It had to go somewhere.

Hani didn't let go. "You can't assume nothing. We don't even know what he was arrested for. One of the boys let me know about the arrest, but he didn't have any other info."

Boston hated to let Hani down but couldn't promise the money was enough. "Let me see what I can do about the oven. Maybe I can pick up a used one. If there's anything left, we'll talk about what we can do for Ryder."

Hani beamed. "You'll come through, *haole*. That's what you do." He wiped his hands on the apron tied around his expansive waist and turned back to the stove.

Haole. It had taken Boston years to get accustomed to Hani's familiar use of the word, Hawaiians' not-so-nice name for white people. Whether or not it had prejudice connotations depended largely on who was saying it and how. Hani used it as a term of endearment these days, but that hadn't always been the case.

He hesitated to say it, to give Hani hope, but *maybe*… "I might be able to squeeze a little more out of Quinn."

Hani had started sorting through a shelf of pots and pans on the far wall. He didn't look up but raised his voice over the clunks and clangs. "Oh, yeah? How you gonna do that? Be a *real* guide after all? I got a clipboard 'round here somewhere." He hefted a huge stainless steel pot into the sink.

Boston grinned at Hani's doubtful expression. "Hell, no. This lady's vacation is open-ended. No departure date is set. I got a two-week advance. If she stays longer than two weeks, I get to charge for it. The longer she stays, the more I get paid."

"Why can't you just tell them your rates went up? Insurance companies pull that crap all the time. Inflation, man. I'm just saying." Hani's innocent shrug almost made Boston laugh.

"I'm not successful because I gouge my clients. You know that."

Hani gave the stove a frustrated kick and muttered something unintelligible and probably offensive under his breath in Hawaiian. He smoothed down a long strand of hair that had escaped from his braid. "Don't try to sell me your credo, Boston. I think we both know why you're so damn good at this private guide business, and it ain't nothing to do with prices."

Was Hani about to berate him for giving away Oahu's local secrets to tourists? He thought they were past this.

Hani's grin came slowly. "It's them long, golden locks. Akela knows what I'm talking about. You're like a Barbie doll, man. You're so pretty it's confusing sometimes."

Boston refused to be baited. Hani constantly gave him a hard time about his "pretty boy" looks. Maybe he should grow a beard after all, his clients be damned. "Flattery won't convince me to marry your sister." It might be playing with fire to tease Hani about the mean crush Akela had on him, and the pink hibiscus tucked perpetually behind her right ear, a status symbol declaring to anyone in the know that she was both single and available. Unfortunately, Akela didn't merely resemble Hani—they were practically identical. They even had matching braids, big thick black ones they wore straight down their backs.

He hadn't noticed the blue speckled stovetop coffee urn sitting atop the broken stove until Hani reached for it and poured the dark contents into a mug, disgruntled. "Cold coffee, man. How do you like that? I was gonna offer you some brew, but I guess compliments are all I can afford. You'd make a terrible prince, anyway. Don't know why I bother."

Boston's eye roll didn't do the situation justice, but he didn't have time to groan and walk away.

Hani bobbed his head like he knew what was coming. "I know, I know. You don't believe me, but I'm telling you, brother. We're descendants of the royal Hawaiian family. Kemahameha the Great, man. He's my great, great, great, great something. With the conquest of O'hua in 1795, he became the founder of the Kingdom of Hawai'i. Fifteen years and a few concessions later, *bam!* You've got a unified country, my friend." He poked Boston in the chest with a large, stubby finger. "Until your people showed up, anyway. I'd be living at Iolani Palace right now if it weren't for you *haoles*."

On an island where dialects and languages came in many flavors, Boston appreciated the universal. He flipped Hani the bird. "I have to go. Keep an eye out for the delivery guy from the appliance yard. We'll have rice flying out of here by lunchtime."

Hani grimaced after taking a sip of the cold half-brewed coffee. "Hey, you never said what this lady's name is. How you gonna find her at the airport if you don't know her name?"

Boston dug around inside the outer pocket of his frayed cargos and came up with a crumpled yellow note. He unfolded it. "Emily Buzzly-Cobb. That's one hell of a name."

Another grimace from his friend. "I'm starting to feel sorry for you, brother. She even sounds like a stick in the mud."

Boston smirked. "I'll just have to knock her loose."

* * * *

Some places on the Web described Honolulu International Airport as the busiest U.S. airport.

Emily glanced around and doubted it. A seasoned traveler, she'd seen far worse at LAX, O'Hare, and JFK. Perhaps Hawaiians weren't morning flyers. She checked her watch. Six hour flight plus a three hour time difference in her favor meant she'd only lost three hours.

If she didn't calculate for jet lag.

Which she wouldn't. She could sleep when she went back to California. On Hawaii time, it was seven in the morning. The perfect hour to begin her first official day in paradise. First, she needed to get to her room at the Hilton her sister, Quinn, had reserved for her stay.

Her completely open-ended stay.

No return ticket accompanied the surprise flight to Honolulu Quinn and her husband, Jack, had sprung on Emily out of the blue in an effort to help her escape her post-divorce funk. But that was the point—to break free of deadlines. If she wanted to go home after a week, she'd book the flight. If she wanted to stay, she'd stay. Stay and do what, who the heck knew.

Maybe forget Blake Cobb existed for a few weeks. Forget her failure as a wife and her failure to be true to herself. She should've never gotten involved with her sister's ex-husband, especially knowing what she did about him. How could she be so successful in one arena of life, yet such a miserable failure where it mattered?

Usually, Emily had meetings and consultations to keep her mind from such dour reflections. The lack of a schedule and sense of urgency was like having the floor shift beneath her feet with nothing to hang on to. No tether. No one waited for her at the hotel, no one expected her at a function downtown, and no one clamored for her expertise.

Emily caught herself smiling, despite the disheartening thoughts of her ex-husband. No consultations. No meetings. No pencil skirts, panty hose, or sensible black pumps.

She glanced at her pin-striped pencil skirt and slide-on loafers.

Okay, first her hotel room. Then, a gratuitous shopping venture for a vacation wardrobe. She must've gone into autopilot when she dressed for the flight and wore what she always wore. She'd even taken to wearing slacks on the weekend because why buy jeans to wear one day a week? She didn't recall if she even owned a pair anymore.

Emily stopped at the conveniently placed Starbucks kiosk outside the terminal exit and ordered a tall caramel frappe. It was downright decadent compared to the coffee she'd suffered on the plane. With her indulgent coffee in one hand and her luggage handle in the other, Emily navigated her way through swarms of travelers to a cabstand outside.

A native woman greeted Emily with a friendly welcoming smile and a lei of white, heavenly-scented flowers. She inhaled deeply and let the floral aroma take over her senses.

Her shoulders relaxed. This must be the island vibe people talked about. An ocean breeze from the west blew the fine hairs around her face into a playful dance. Even the humidity enticed her. Such rich air. So *tropical.*

She came to a dead halt that nearly sent the scalding contents of her coffee flying. Without blatantly staring, Emily recovered herself and tried to get a better glimpse of the man standing near the cabstand with her name on a sign.

She double-checked the placard.

Yep. Emily Buzzly-Cobb. That was her name. Pretty unmistakable except for the time she'd gone down on a reservation list as Buzzing Cod. Or, more facetiously, the time she'd been addressed as Fuzzy Knob at a school fund-raiser with her nephew.

She regarded the man holding the sign.

Definitely homeless. His unwashed sun-streaked blond hair was a few tangles away from becoming dreadlocks, pulled back into a ponytail at the nape of his neck. His ragged red shorts were hacked off so the hem frayed around his shins, and he wore a tight-fitting faded T-shirt of indeterminable color. It might've been tan or even a light blue at one time. His heavy-duty black hiking sandals with tread like a tractor tire appeared to be the only thing on his person of any value.

His smooth face surprised her. Where did a homeless guy get a good shave?

And why would Quinn hire someone like this to drive her to the Hilton? The last bit of the unsettling image came from the tattoos on the man's arms and legs. Several more on his torso were noticeable through the worn fabric of his shirt.

Emily suppressed a shudder and smoothed her hair into place. Merely examining his made her want to run a comb through hers. Luckily, he hadn't seen her yet and wouldn't recognize her. She made to walk past him.

He pinned her with pale blue eyes the size of half dollars. "There you are."

Her body froze mid-stride. "Excuse me?" The flat question came out sounding like an accusation. She inwardly cringed.

The man didn't seem fazed by her tone or dumbstruck manner. He was probably used to people reacting strangely to him. He stuck out his hand. "Emily, right? I'm Boston. Your ride."

She took his offer of a handshake like she would any CEO's and silently thanked God for the automatic responses her career had ingrained in her. "Boston." This time she was careful to keep her tone neutral. "That's an interesting name. How did you know what I looked like?"

"Quinn sent a photo." He gave her a sort of cockeyed half-smile. Not the genuine article by a long shot, but not quite a smirk, either. A pair of aviator sunglasses kept hair from falling onto his face. He slid them back on his nose, and his cornflower blue eyes vanished behind the reflective lenses.

Cornflower? Really? It was some nonsense Quinn might use in one of her books. Didn't make a lick of sense. Corn didn't grow flowers and if it did, they certainly weren't blue. "Very thoughtful of my sister," Emily mumbled.

At least she wasn't the only one sending out prickly vibes. She blamed Boston's unfriendly bearing, which she gauged by his forced smile, on her choice of attire. It gave away everything about her.

She was one of *them.*

Suits. Working stiffs. Nine-to-fivers.

Otherwise known as someone who worked for a living.

She didn't much care for him, either, which made his dislike easy to stomach. Indeed, the feeling was mutual. Emily only had to survive the ride to the Hilton, and they could dust off their hands and part ways.

Boston offered to carry her bag, and she let him. He could do something to earn his tip besides harbor barely contained displeasure with his fare.

Wordlessly, Emily followed as he guided her though two levels of the parking garage, and her thoughts turned to Quinn. How best to tell Quinn and Jack they sucked at making travel arrangements? They obviously hadn't done their research on cab companies, or they wouldn't have sent a homeless man to pick her up from the airport.

Eventually, Boston pointed them toward a late model white van with a simple logo pasted on the passenger door.

Wonderful. A ride in a nondescript white van with a total stranger.

Emily hadn't realized she'd come to a halt until Boston paused one stride away from the vehicle. He made a lazy about-face with an amused grin lifting one corner of his mouth. "What's the matter? Does my van creep you out?"

Heat flew up from her chest like a rash and spread over her face. Boston had to notice the furious blush on her pale skin, which made it worse. Didn't he know anything about tact? "No, no. Of course not. I was, uh, admiring your company motif."

He gave a doubtful glance at the circle drawn with *The Island Experience* printed in bold maroon script inside. "Whatever you say. You can sit up front if you prefer."

She hitched her chin up a notch and started for the van. "I believe I would, yes. Thank you."

The polite response irked her. She used manners to diffuse social awkwardness, an old defense mechanism. The more dismissive Boston became, the stiffer she'd get. It had worked so well during her marriage she and Blake were on the same sickly sweet polite terms as two soccer moms at a bake sale by the time the lawyers were called in.

She rolled her shoulders in an attempt to loosen the tight muscles. Why'd she care what this bum thought of her, anyway?

"*Mahalo*." He tossed her bag in the backseat of the van.

She paused in opening the passenger door. "What?"

"It means 'thank you,' among other things."

Boston smoothly navigated the twists and turns of the airport with the practiced ease of a veteran driver. At least he knew his way around, and they wouldn't waste a lot of time getting lost or turned around. Before long, they were sailing down a highway rife with morning commuters in strained silence.

Well, at least on her end. Boston didn't strike her as the type to possess the honed social sense or level of self-awareness necessary to notice something so subtle as an uncomfortable silence.

However, her job had taught her to combat bubbles of discomfort like this one. She walked into businesses and tossed out ideas managers didn't always want to hear with one hand while smoothing their ruffled feathers with the other.

She really ought to be able to handle one lowly beach bum. She keyed in on the only interesting thing about him she'd learned so far. "Are you from Boston, then?"

He kept his gaze on the road. "Would you believe me if I said I was?"

He didn't appear to have come from particularly creative stock and had no discernible regional accent. He could be from anywhere.

"Sure."

He chanced the quickest of glances and flashed his first genuine smile. It stunned her to discover it changed his whole face. He almost didn't look homeless anymore. "Well, don't. I'd be lying. Boston Rondibett from Mesa, Arizona at your service. And I'm never going back to that dry, windy hellhole unless God himself is tugging me by the ankles. Or my mom says please."

"I'm from southern California. Similar climate."

She'd meant to present common ground, but he surprised her. "I know."

Her head snapped in his direction. "How do you know where I'm from?"

He shrugged one shoulder as if the question didn't strike him as relevant. "Quinn told me. How else would I know? I was her and Jack's personal guide when they honeymooned on the island. She asked me to show you around while you're on vacation. Besides, you flew in from LAX on a non-connecting flight. See?" He slipped into an intentionally idiotic accent. "Even a scruffy dude like me can did math."

Normally, Emily would've bounced back with a scathing comment, but her jaw hung loose. "You're my *vacation guide?*"

"Did I stutter? Although, now you mention it, 'vacation guide' makes more sense in terms of a title, but it's kind of a mouthful."

"So, you're not dropping me off at the Hilton and going on your merry way? I'm spending my entire vacation with you?" Emily winced. She might've tried harder to disguise her derision. Still, the guy needed a haircut and a bath. She hadn't forgotten those atrocious shorts, either. She'd suggest the underside of a sewing machine if they wouldn't be better off in the garbage bin.

Boston didn't say a word. Apparently, he was the kind of man who spoke through action, and his next stunt involved slowing down the van.

She sputtered. They were in the center of a multilane highway with vehicles whizzing past on either side. Emily quit trying to communicate and started praying. If she was going to die, it couldn't hurt to go out with the Lord's Prayer on her lips.

Miraculously, Boston didn't get them killed, mangled to death in a fiery crash of steel on asphalt. He managed to ease over two lanes and come to a stop on the shoulder of the highway.

Emily released her white-knuckle grip on the door handle and seethed. "You're a psychopath."

Boston flicked on the hazards and put the van in park. He swiveled his body toward her and yanked the sunglasses from his face in a quick, agitated movement.

She realized then, regarding him straight on, they felt the same way about each other. Forget disdain. He'd passed judgment and found her lacking.

As she'd done him.

Boston spoke in a measured tone. "I'll put it to you plain, Ms. Buzzly-Cobb, if that is your *real* name. I have a job to do. We don't have to like each other, but it'll make for a better time had by all if we can at least manage to get along. A little mutual respect would go a long way. I'll even give you a reason to try it. I know this island like no one else you're gonna find. Ask your sister if you want my references."

Now, *this* Emily could handle. Directness. "I don't care about your résumé."

"Well, you should. It's impressive."

"Does it include how utterly charming you are? Or mention you've got the hubris of a D-list celebrity?"

He gave her a sad puppy-dog frown. "I'm simple folk. Try to keep the vocabulary at my level."

Something in those great big blue orbs said he knew exactly what she'd said. And some of what she hadn't. "If I don't like you, why should I have to spend the next couple of weeks in your company? Or you in mine, given the feeling is mutual."

"I never said I didn't like you."

"I can read expressions better than you can fake them."

That seemed to catch him unaware. He stared at her unguarded. Finally, the corner of his mouth quirked up. "Me. You." He pointed at each of them in turn and continued with exaggerated caveman speech. "See island. Pretty stuff no one else will show you. Boston good at this." He hooked both thumbs toward himself and gave her a simpleton's grin. "Me already paid. You sit back and get over it."

Good thing she hadn't laughed. Her back straightened. "*Get over it?* No, I don't think I will. Drop me at the Hilton and keep the damn money. I'll pay Quinn back for her trouble."

Boston dropped his goofy act and flopped back against the seat, at the same time gusting out a great sigh. "Man, you don't have any sense of humor at all, do you? Not a shred."

The plainspoken observation was more insulting than anything else he'd said or done in their short acquaintance. "I happen to be hilarious."

He didn't seem convinced by her deadpan delivery. His loss. He wouldn't be around long enough to get to know her unique approach to humor, which tended to run a little dry.

"Fine. If I don't have a sense of humor, it's probably because there's nothing funny about your lack of class or professionalism."

"You basically called me a dumbass. What did you expect?"

Had she? "I don't think you're stupid. Just repugnant."

"Oh, that's *loads* better." He snorted like the whole situation amused him. "I apologize, okay? My mouth does things without permission from my brain sometimes."

He sat up, gripped the wheel, and offered her a small smile. She couldn't tell outright if he meant it as mocking.

"Look at us," he said. "We're a mess and we just met. That means one or both of us have already decided how we feel without giving the other a shot. I have a suggestion, if you're open to hear one."

"Let me guess. You want to start over?" She refused to roll her eyes like a teenager and had to settle for a flat stare.

Boston bit his knuckle as if unsure of his next words. "Anyone ever tell you you're a hard ass?"

A laugh escaped her, unbidden and unexpected. It seemed to surprise them both. "I might've heard it a few times."

"Well, there you go." Relief colored the words like he'd solved a complicated puzzle. "You're a no-excuses kind of girl, and I'm a guy with a pocket full of 'em. No wonder we didn't hit it off."

Great. Now, good-looking surfer dude wants to play Gandhi.

Whoa. Good-looking surfer dude? Had that thought really popped from her cranium? Well, his eyes were pretty remarkable. And his smile redeemed quite a bit of his face. "Why don't you start by telling me just what makes you so special, Mr. Rondibett? Then, maybe we'll discuss second chances."

Boston blew out a stream of breath through pursed lips and slowly shook his head. "You strike me as a tough sell, but I've got faith in the product. First, I gotta know something about you, though. See, there are two types of tourists. You're either a traditionalist or you're an explorer. Trads, they want what everyone wants—the brochure version of Hawaii. Diamond Head. Dole Plantation. Pearl Harbor and Waikiki Beach. Beautiful, special places, for sure, but there's so much more to Oahu. And that's what a real explorer wants to see. The soft underbelly. They want experiences no one else has, pictures no one else takes. *That* is what I can do for you, Emily. So, yeah. I'm mouthy, but I'm worth it."

Natural-born salesman, this one. "You would say that."

His mouth formed a flat line, some of the lightheartedness gone. "Know who else? Your sister. She hired me. I'm guessing not because you'd find me charming, but because I've got something to offer."

Emily had to concede Boston's point. Quinn definitely hadn't chosen him to accompany her based on their likelihood of having anything in common. It left a single alternative. He might actually be something special as far as island guides went. "Okay, Mr. Rondibett. I'll give you a shot purely based on faith in my sister's judgment. Perhaps we can both try to be somewhat less abrasive to one another."

"Does that mean you'll relax a little?"

She cut her eyes to him, a warning not to push her buttons. "If you pretend to have some semblance of professionalism. Now, take me to the Hilton. I have a six hour flight to wash off."

Boston saluted and flicked off the hazards. As he checked his mirrors, engaged his turn signal, and prepared to merge back onto the highway, he flashed Emily a lopsided, dimpled grin that made her question her decision to give this another go. "One thing, miss. We aren't going to the Hilton."

Chapter 2

Oh, man. That face was priceless.

Emily's mouth fell open in a perfect little *O*. She might pass for adorable if she weren't so snooty. And that was saying something, considering she was at least near his age. Late thirties, possibly even forty. The bun clinging for dear life on the back of her skull was Snoozeville, but she had nice, creamy brown eyes.

Creamy eyes, huh? Nothing weird about that. Still, they made him think of smooth milk chocolate, and right now they were about the size of Maui.

"I'm sorry. We're *not* going to the Hilton? Did I hear you correctly?"

With his hands at ten and two, and eyes on the road, Boston couldn't glance over to give her a *chill out* stare. "This is our first test of trust. Explorers don't stay at the Hilton. That place is a bumper cushion between you and the real deal. You need four swimming pools? Penguins behind glass enclosures and parrots in cages? Me, I prefer the ocean to a pool and sea turtles at my feet as opposed to a zoo outside my window. But, hey, that's a personal point of view." He shrugged, careful not to overdo the nonchalance. Every word was sincere. He didn't want to come across as some hammy showman.

A bubble of silence lasted several beats. Boston waited for Emily to wrestle with the pull of curiosity. Finally, she caved like a bad soufflé. "Real sea turtles?"

Boston grinned. "Do they make fake ones I don't know about?" Wait, a minute... Wasn't she from California? "You're not much of a beachgoer, are you?"

"Gee, what gave it away." She didn't even bother to disguise the dry response as a real question.

However, had he been pressed for an answer, he'd have to say it was probably the high-flying CEO costume she had on. Who dressed like that for a vacation to the tropics? It wouldn't surprise him if she had pantyhose on under that calf-length skirt or owned a pair of shoes that weren't sensible lady loafers in every shade of boring.

"Point taken," he conceded. "On North Shore, which is where we're headed, there's a damn good chance we'll run into one this time of year. The waters are too rough for swimming but ideal for surfing. Obviously, this brings a lot of folks out, but nothing like the crowds you'll find at Waikiki."

Judging by her studious expression—brow drawn, lips pursed while she nibbled the inside of one cheek—he might have an easier time with Emily if he kept her mentally occupied with island trivia. "Did you know Hawaii outlawed billboards? Don't want ads funkin' up the view, you know? Kinda wish the Internet would take a hint. Also, it snows here. How's that for incredible? Hawaii's elevation is through the roof, so some of our highest peaks get snowfall when it gets cold enough." Was it working?

She faced him at the same time he chanced a peek her way, and he was caught again by her countenance. She was like a wise old owl, intelligent and watchful. "How far to North Shore?"

"With traffic? An hour, maybe. We're going clear across the island. See here." He pointed toward her window and the towering buildings blocking a full view of the ocean. "That's south. We're heading east. If we keep going, we'll eventually run smack into the Waikiki area, but we're going north. Hence the name. *North* Shore."

Emily aimed her pointer finger at his face. "Let's make one thing clear." Her voice had the same quality Boston had used on his students once upon a time, back when…

Never mind that. He imagined Emily used it on executive blah-blahs or slow interns, or whatever context it might be needed doing whatever the hell her job was. He'd throw money down on anything involving PowerPoint presentations and strongly worded interoffice memos.

"I'm the only one of us who gets to be a sarcastic jerk, got it? Because it's *my* vacation, and I didn't come here to put up with a surly guide talking down to me because I don't know which way is up. Do I appear to be in possession of a compass? A smidge of respect will go a long way toward you keeping your job, Mr. Rondibett. I may not know the great underbelly of the island, whatever that is, but I can drive around and get lost with the best of them."

Well, hot damn. Color him chastised.

He tried to hide his grin. "While we're doling out the complaints, I might as well mention I don't much care for the mister and missus, polite as it may be. I'm Boston. You're Emily."

"I'm sticky. Is that normal?"

"The humidity. You don't get much of that in southern Cali, do you? Sometimes it's like drowning in air. It can be hard to get used to, and it's a lot like sauerkraut—people either love it or hate it. But I understand it's good for the skin." Personally, he didn't mind it.

"So, you're a health guru, too?"

Boston stole another peek at his passenger. Arms crossed over her chest, frowning while she gazed out the window. Either the scenery displeased her or he did, and it was easy enough to guess which. His grinned slipped away.

This lady was going to be trouble. He'd known it the moment Quinn texted him a photo of Emily with her severe business bun and the flat, no-nonsense expression. He'd like nothing better than to drop her at the Hilton and let her have her cookie-cutter vacation, but Hani was counting on him.

It'd taken nearly every penny Quinn had paid him to replace The Canopy's busted oven. If Boston was going to scrounge up bail money for this Ryder guy, he needed Emily. Somehow, he'd have to impress her enough to make her want to extend her stay so he could hit Quinn up for another advance. Gas wasn't cheap on the island, either. He was taking a risk on this impromptu trip to North Shore.

"I can be whatever you need," he said in an effort to lighten her dour mood. "Papayas are plentiful on the island and an excellent source of vitamin C. Avocados are also abundant—"

"Tell me more about North Shore." Even the sigh that followed the demand sounded bored.

That sealed it. Emily definitely wasn't getting the number for his emergency phone. She'd be calling every five minutes to complain in that tired, blasé tone and end up costing him his job. "Or I could give you the deets on your accommodations."

That got her attention. She sat up from her slumped position and uncrossed her arms. "Great idea. Maybe we'll be friends after all, Boston. You're starting to figure me out."

He smirked. She didn't know the half of it. By the time her vacation was over, he'd have her strutting around in a bikini with her hair loose around her shoulders, nary a sensible lady loafer in sight.

Some people adapted quickly. Like Quinn and her husband, Jack. They'd danced to the beat of the tropics like they'd been born under a coconut frond. Someone with Emily's particular hang-ups took a little more finesse and time.

And a pinch of rough handling to get the gears moving. After all, you couldn't surf a calm sea. "You ready for this? I'm taking you to a *tree* house. Isn't that nuts? You're gonna love it."

"Turn around."

He almost pulled over again for the sake of another look at her face. He kept driving instead and ignored her.

"I've changed my mind. Turn around, take me to the Hilton. You're clearly insane. Quinn, that.... Ugh. She waited three years to get payback, but she sure did choose her moment."

Payback, huh? Sounded like the sisters had some not-so-sisterly history between them. It didn't surprise him. Oil and water, those two, and in more ways than one. "Calm down. Let me explain before you make any executive demands. I'm not talking about a wooden plank construct some Joe Nobody nailed to a tree."

"Funny, because that's the precise image *tree house* tends to bring to mind."

"This one is special. It's built up high on the side of a mountain. A stone staircase leads you up to an A-frame-style house with a wrap-around balcony on both levels. The view of the beach is outstanding. You're practically chilling in the treetops. The house itself isn't anything special. It's maybe even a little rustic."

The breath rushing in and out through Emily's nostrils made more sound than the air conditioner. "How rustic? Is there at least running water, or do I stand on the balcony and hope for rain?"

The outburst both annoyed and amused him. Since he was used to clients like Emily, he gave in to amusement. Plus, he liked annoying her right back. It beat getting angry. "You'd probably have to walk down to the beach to get enough water for a good scrub down. The canopy's too thick that high on the mountainside. I'd recommend the shower, personally. You do yoga? You look like you do yoga. That's probably a better activity for the balcony. I don't yoga, so I'd sit and have coffee, but whatever."

Emily appeared to turn speculative and chewed her lip while staring forward at the winding road. Traffic lightened as they turned north and away from the hectic motion of Honolulu's morning commuters.

"Sounds kind of nice."

Boston let out a breath he hadn't realized he was holding. It wasn't much, but from Emily it was as good as he'd likely get. "It is. Trust the seasoned guide."

"Not as nice as the Hilton," she murmured.

"Well, it's not the Hilton, okay? Don't worry, though. I'll accept your gratitude, apology, and plea for another two weeks in my company when the time comes. No hard feelings. It's not your fault you don't know any better."

"You're saying my ignorance gives me a free pass?"

"Sure. Why not? I'm the thoughtful, forgiving type."

"Well, then, I suppose I'd better come clean now."

Money, Boston. You need the money. "Hit me."

"I lied at the airport. Your van definitely creeps me out."

Boston bit his lip to keep from groaning. It was going to be a long two weeks.

* * * *

"Wow." Emily hadn't meant to say it out loud but *wow.*

The tree house, which she'd expected in spite of Boston's warnings to resemble the botched plywood attempt in her childhood backyard, seemed like the majestic jungle abode of a lost Disney princess. Most of the house was hidden behind chaotic foliage, but she noted fantastic narrow windows that spanned both stories and created an unbroken view toward the ocean to the north. The view from the balcony had to be incredible.

To find out, she had to survive thirty stone steps and a winding wooden staircase Boston had conveniently neglected to mention in his babbling about yoga. He'd probably been afraid to scare her off with the idea she might have to work to reach her enchanting miniature chateau. As if he knew her well enough to make the assumption.

Emily skirted a bush bursting with skinny, bright pink flowers as she followed Boston higher and higher up the mountainside and into the canopy. The long tube-like petals reached out for her like pink alien fingers.

It was one thing to gaze out a window at a world of green. Quite another when it wanted to get touchy-feely. California's clusters of foliage generally came from the careful hand of a landscaper, or yards were left to their natural desert scrub, which made plain its desire to remain untouched with things like thorns and cactus spines.

She gripped the strap of her purse with both hands and called after her guide. "You might've warned me about the chummy vegetation." She scanned the strange pink flowers a final time. "It's like they want to get to know me."

Boston didn't slow his ascent or seem in any way burdened by her laden suitcase he lugged up the stairs behind him. "They probably sense how friendly you are."

Emily let that one go. "What about bugs? Spiders and snakes, that kind of stuff. Anything I should know?"

"Lucky for you, *Animal Planet* trivia is part of my package deal."

Had it been anyone else, she'd have gone in for the kill. Instead, she let his "package deal" continue unfettered.

"You see," he said in a tone that would do a professor proud, "snakes ain't a thing here."

"What does that even mean? A *thing?* A thing like they aren't poisonous here? Or a thing like people on the island eat them so they aren't considered a nuisance but a rare delicacy."

Boston stopped on the landing before the final set of stairs. "Look, you want an encyclopedia, I'm the guy. But I'm afraid I'm fresh out of dull personality today."

"Should I check back tomorrow?" She glanced up with a smile in time to catch his. He might be sort of cute if he cut that awful ponytail and did a little wardrobe overhauling.

"Snakes aren't a *thing* here because they're illegal to have on the island."

"Huh. Like billboards. Really?"

"No, I made it up. Just now, Johnny on the spot. That's how I'm so good at my job. Keeping the lies straight gets wicked tough, so I log a journal. I'll show it to you sometime. Reads like an *X-Files* episode, but you tourists really eat that shit up."

If he thought to throw her off guard with his response, he failed miserably. No one could compare to Emily's brother-in-law when it came to absurd flippancy. Boston had nothing on Quinn's husband. "The fun never stops with you. Why are snakes illegal?"

"Don't give me the credit. You're the fun one, sweetheart."

"Call me sweetheart again."

Boston paused a beat at her tone, which she'd expected, for it had been her intention. He studied her face carefully.

Emily kept her expression neutral. She'd let him figure out on his own how to decipher the veiled dare in her remark and decide if he wanted to test her or not.

Apparently, he chose not. He smiled thinly and slowly started for the last flight of wooden steps. "Snakes aren't indigenous to Hawaii. I'm not saying there isn't an escaped fugitive here and there. It might be illegal to own them, but people smuggle them in and out like anything else. Since they aren't part of the original ecosystem of the islands, they don't have any natural predators. No population control. Snakes would decimate the local bird species, species known to live only here. It happened like that in Guam. Hence, the legislation."

He was no Encyclopedia Brown, but Boston certainly seemed to know his stuff when it came to the island. As he should, given his job. She tried not to sound too impressed. "All right, no snakes. Great. What else?"

The final set of stairs brought them to a large covered veranda. Big, leafy hands closed in on the porch from every side, on top and underneath, but frightened Emily less now. No eastern green mambas were likely to slither onto her shoulder as she brushed by.

Boston approached the glass front door and fumbled in his pocket. "Only the common sense stuff. Don't play with centipedes, avoid sea urchins, look both ways when you cross the beach so you don't get hit by a jogger. They can be a real nuisance. Unless you jog. Then joggers are delightful." He took a key from his pocket and unlocked the front door. He stood back with a flourishing bow for Emily to enter first. "Welcome to *Kumu Pili.* Literally translated, it means 'tree touch.' Some *haole* like me probably named it."

He sniggered, and Emily guessed it had something to do with the funny island word. She stepped inside the bamboo foyer and huffed at having to ask. "Well? You want to let me in on the joke?"

"It's nothing. Just a wisecrack my friend Hani would appreciate, that's all."

Emily turned back to Boston. His eyes weren't visible from behind his dark, reflective sunglasses, but she stood close enough to behold the crow's-feet collected at the corners, an indication of a smile. "Tell me anyway."

Boston shrugged and seemed to grow contemplative. "I probably should, actually. Living in L.A., you understand a thing or two about how touchy race stuff can be." For the first time in her company, he became something resembling serious. "You'd better invite me in."

"Oh." Emily realized she'd stepped inside and stood as though answering the door while Boston remained on the other side of the threshold. "I have a natural tendency to take point. Sorry."

"No worries." He stepped around her and strutted toward the kitchen. "I'm not a vampire or anything. You just looked poised to send me off."

"Not while I still have questions." She closed the front door. The natural light coming in through the multiple glass panes kept the foyer bright and airy and cast a dappled design across the light wood. "By the way, I do jog but please quit being a suck-up. It's exhausting. I have a dozen assistants back home I could've brought along for brown-nosing."

Boston searched through the cupboards with his head tilted at a curious angle like he didn't know what he'd find. He located a cabinet with a set of six matching tumblers and filled one with water from the tap. "Are any of them as charming as me?"

"No, but none of them have the brass to call me sweetheart, either."

His lips thinned. "I knew we'd come back to that. I'm sorry, okay? It's an old habit."

"It's one you should try real hard to break, Mr. Rondibett."

"Ah, crap. We're back to the mister and missus stuff again?"

She smiled and sat down on one of three barstools set in front of a tall marble bar. "It's an old habit. You were going to tell me something?"

Boston drained his glass, rinsed it, and set it inside the stainless steel sink. He joined her at the bar, taking the stool to the far right and leaving the one between them vacant. "There's a race component to every place on the planet I've ever been, and Hawaii is no exception. Take me, I wasn't born here. Even if I had been, I'm no Hawaiian."

"Of course not. You're obviously Caucasian."

"Not everyone gets it. Hawaiian is not only a culture, it's a race. It's a blood thing, not a location thing." He splayed a hand over his chest. "I've been living here long enough to say I'm a local. Lived here, born here, raised here, whatever, you're a local. *Haole* is widely known as a derogatory term for white folks like us, but most times it's not said as a racial thing. I mean, it can be, it's just—"

"I imagine that largely depends on who's saying it and to whom." It struck Emily that Boston seemed defensive of the term.

"Well, yeah, I guess so. Try to not take it personally if you happen to hear it, that's all."

She almost laughed. "It's takes a little more than pointing out my skin color to offend me, but thanks for the heads up. Or, *mahalo*, I should say."

Boston popped up from the stool and held a shiny silver key in front of her face. "Well, then I'll leave you in your own capable hands for the evening."

Instinct forced her to cup her hands beneath the key to keep it from falling to the floor if he dropped it, which he did immediately into her waiting palms. "You're leaving me here alone?"

"Did you want me to stay the night?" He raised his eyebrows but stopped short of wriggling them suggestively.

"No, I—what if I need to go somewhere? Do I call you?"

Already headed for the front door, he paused. "You can't do that, unfortunately."

"Don't be ridiculous. I get great reception out here. See?" She dug in her purse for her cell phone. She found it and pulled it out with a triumphant grin. "Bars. Lots of bars."

"I'm happy for you. But I don't have a phone."

Neanderthal.

Barbarian.

Lost soul.

A million descriptive terms popped into her head. Emily posed her next question as carefully and non-judgmentally as her self-control allowed. "What kind of person are you?"

"Oh, what, because I'm not all reachable and stuff? How about I'm a person who doesn't care about social networking. I'm a guy who thinks it's creepy to be tied to a device like a robot. Hey, maybe I'm a guy who doesn't like the idea of the whole world knowing where I am and what I'm doing every second of every day. A guy who doesn't live his life 'on the grid.' A guy who—"

"Okay, all right." She held her hands up in surrender. "I get it. You're a conspiracy theorist. Or a hippie. Or a conspiracy hippie if there's such a thing."

His mouth fell partially open. "I'm serious. It creeps me out how they track us, and we willingly let them keep tabs. Science fiction isn't so fiction these days. Also, I'm broke."

That was probably no lie, given his attire. She *had* mistaken him for a homeless person. "Explain to me how my vacation is supposed to work if I can't get ahold of you. I sit in my tree house until you come back to take me somewhere? Are you going to be nearby? Should I venture out on my own? And if I do, do I get to prorate for your services?"

He did an awkward sort of shuffle shoulder dip move—an apology meets needs-to-pee. "I have to return to Honolulu. But, hey, I'm not leaving you without resources. The house is fully stocked for your stay. You've got the necessities a woman of discerning tastes might need. Soap, shampoo, and food. There's even a place to charge the government-issued tracking device of your choice." He swung his pointer finger toward the front door, where the ocean peeked through the canopy. "The shore is to your north. If you venture out, head west. You'll come up on a street chock full of bars and shops."

Her body deflated, and the irony wasn't lost on her. Upon arriving, she'd been less than excited to have a traveling companion. Now, she didn't want Boston to go. The last couple hours had afforded Emily a distraction from thoughts of Blake.

What was he doing right now? Did he know about the surprise trip Quinn and Jack had sprung on Emily less than twenty-four hours ago? Emily imagined her night dragging on as she stared out from the balcony at the great expanse of ocean and tore herself apart with the knowledge she was very likely the last person on Blake's mind. The view might be new, but the story didn't change.

Boston put a hand on her shoulder. His eyebrows came together in concern, and he took off his sunglasses. "You all right, Emily?"

She sniffed and stepped back, forcing him to drop his hand. "Fine. I'll probably eat in. I'm not much of a social butterfly, anyway."

"I'm a guide, not a pocket escort. I'll be here bright and early to take you somewhere special and obscure, then out for some fantastic local fare. But you've got to do a little exploring on your own, too. Honolulu is my grid. I leave this"—he opened his arms wide—"for your personal discovery. Meet folks. Hit a shrimp truck for lunch. Take a selfie with a sea turtle."

"You're giving me homework?" She lifted a skeptical brow. Why did Boston remind her so much of a shifty street performer? He used the right words but smacked of illusion.

He started for the door again. "I always did enjoy assigning essays right before the weekend. Kids hate that. It's worth mentioning most parents do, too."

If she'd had as much as a piece of gum in her mouth, she'd have choked. She marched over to Boston and glared. "You're full of it. Who in their right mind would let you instruct children?"

He whipped his sunglasses back on, but not before Emily caught the hard stare he returned. "No one in the state of Hawaii. Unless this is a field trip gone terribly wrong. Must've packed the wrong mushrooms for lunch."

"I'm serious. You're a teacher?"

"Currently? Nope. Have I been?" He began a slow backward step toward the door. "Well, I do like to imagine myself as more than a mere guide, of course. You might say I'm an educator of sorts." He grabbed the doorknob behind him as if he couldn't escape fast enough, twisted it, and made a beeline for the stairs that would take him back down the mountain. "Tomorrow morning. Dress casually if..." He nodded apologetically at her outfit. "If you can."

"What kind of answer is that?"

A devilish grin—no other way to describe it, without assistance from Quinn and her massive internal thesaurus—spread over Boston's face. He looked like a lazy cat in a patch of sunlight. "A poor one, but maybe I wasn't a very good teacher."

Chapter 3

The refrigerator harbored the usual suspects. Deli cuts, including turkey and roast beef, plus every type of condiment Emily might wish to slather them with. The fruit drawer weighed heavy with green mangoes and what were probably papayas.

Maybe guavas. Couldn't really expect an apples and bananas kind of girl to know the difference. At least she recognized the avocados on the speckled granite countertop.

She guessed the fruit was supposed to pass for breakfast, since there were no boxes of cereal or instant oatmeal in the cupboards.

She put together a sandwich with some of everything and washed it down with a cold Sprite, another courtesy from the fridge. A far cry from the hot breakfast she'd expected to enjoy at the Hilton, but it'd take some nerve to complain about her accommodations.

A bamboo spiral staircase connected the first floor to the loft-style second floor, where a king-sized bed took up nearly every inch of available space. Then again, Emily decided so long as there was a path to the balcony, who even cared what was inside the house?

Emily stepped through the sliding glass door of the upper level. Unlike the downstairs porch, there was no cover. Only the green arms of the trees reaching for a dawn's pink-tinged sky and a turquoise ocean stretching out forever in front of her. She settled into a bamboo chaise and reluctantly tugged her cell phone from the pocket of the lush robe she'd liberated from the bathroom.

A small part of her hated to disrupt the serenity of the morning with the blurp and beep of her phone. Maybe Boston was on to something with his aversion to technology.

Quinn answered in the flat tone, indicating she had her elbows resting on her desk and her face screwed up in concentration as she stared intently at her computer monitor. Her writing tone.

Sometimes it meant Emily would be lucky to get a full thirty seconds of her sister's attention. Emily usually groaned and hung up without bothering, but not today. Today, she'd get answers. "I cannot believe you'd send me all the way to Hawaii to get your revenge."

"Hm...no, that's not it. I decided to call it *Cornered*. Remember? Revenge is more suited to the antagonist's point of view, not so much the victim's. Since it's the victim's story I'm telling."

"Step away from the manuscript."

"What?"

Emily went for broke. "I'm getting on a plane back home this very minute."

"Huh? Emily, is that you? What, you're coming home? You can't come home. You just got there! You left yesterday, for crying out loud. You didn't sleep at the airport, did you?"

Mission accomplished. Emily nestled down into her robe and studied the canopy overhead. The last of the morning's pink color had morphed into a pale blue, not unlike Boston's eyes.

Boston. Her sister's response to a three-year-old wrong. "I'm calling you about the con artist you set me up with."

"You mean Boston. He's so great, Em. You're gonna love him."

"Am I, Quinn?" A moment of clarity rocked her. "Oh, I see. You went off to London after your divorce and found Jack, so I'm supposed to fall for the first hobo I meet and forget Blake's and my failed marriage? You amaze me sometimes, you know? My life isn't some story you can manipulate and bend to your will. Has anyone ever talked to you about your serious case of God complex? Because this would be the ideal time—"

"Slow down. What are you talking about? If you're attracted to Boston, that's...weird. I was going to say great, but I won't lie, Em. It's weird."

"I am most certainly not attracted to that rogue."

"It's been my experience rogues are most attractive. Although, it'd be nice if you gave me *some* credit. You and Boston couldn't be more different. Not in the 'opposites attract' way, either. I'm cringing on the inside at the thought." She let out a small, breathy laugh. "You're so dramatic."

Emily ran her hand across the smooth wooden arm of the chaise. "But you said—"

"That you'd love him? Because you will. First, let's address your initial cause for concern. For the last time, Emily, I'm not out to get you.

Neither is Jack. Once upon a very confusing time, you tried to break up our relationship."

She flushed with shame at the memory.

Quinn didn't give her time to respond. "Your motives were from the heart. We got it then, and we get it now. And Jack and I are together, aren't we? You didn't succeed. It worked out."

Emily bit her lip but not in time to stop the words from spilling out. "Not entirely."

"Oh, Em." Her sister's voice came across as sad but not pitying. "I was so happy for you when you and Blake married. It seemed like everyone's prayers got answered at once. Blake... Well, Blake's an idiot. What can you expect?"

Indeed, what should Emily have expected?

For her new husband to love her instead of hanging onto his feelings for his ex-wife, who happened to be Quinn? "I think I'm the idiot. Two degrees and a resume that shines like gold, yet dumb enough to fall for the old fix-a-guy trope."

"You fell in love, honey. You weren't trying to fix Blake. You only wanted him to love you back. It's the human condition, not some overplayed story arc."

Quinn had been a professional author for thirteen years. Emily had to yield to her authority on overplayed story arcs.

"Maybe you're right." She shook her head and allowed herself a wry smile. "We have the most convoluted family. At least my divorce from Blake is clearing the air somewhat."

"I'll admit we struggled with what Seth should call you." By marrying Blake, Quinn's ex-husband and Seth's dad, Emily had gone from aunt to stepmother. "Also, Jack tortured me with a horrific southern accent for months, but I'm sure there's worse out there."

"Like marrying your stepbrother?"

Quinn groaned. "Oh, hell, you're right. So convoluted."

As if she could've guessed their dad would go to London to visit and end up falling for Madeline, Jack's mother. Emily grinned. "You should write a book."

"I'm cracking up. On the inside." Quinn's dry response was standard-issue. "Since we've addressed the main concern, why don't we get back to the reason you called? What's your beef with Boston?"

Emily's lips moved, but words failed to emerge. What exactly *was* her problem with Boston? Besides, of course, his attire, unwashed hair, and overall smooth-talking attitude. "He's a beach bum."

"He surfs if that's what you mean."

No, but it made sense. "Why him, Quinn?" Since her first theory hadn't panned out, maybe she ought to garner some enlightenment from the source. "What's so great about this guy you'd hire him despite how obviously unsuited we are?"

"Sheesh, Em. How suited do you need to be? His job is to drive and point. When I was in London, Jack taught me great cities have secrets you won't find without some insider know-how. Don't ask me how he found Boston, but I know he's worth every dime. We really hit it off with him. He personifies the island. Relax a little. Give in."

"Are you paying him enough to buy a new pair of shorts? Either half of them were eaten during a surfing accident involving a shark, or he's perpetrating the surfer-dude thing to put on a show for his clients."

Quinn jumped to his defense. "You're reading him wrong. He's the genuine article. No gags or gimmicks."

"Maybe not, but there was something…" Something shifty. Something not quite honest. "I might not know him like you do, but I'm pretty good at reading people, and something's up."

"Maybe he picked up on your dislike."

"I never said that."

"You didn't have to." Quinn paused to sigh. "I realize he's not your usual type of company, but you'll be glad you gave him a chance."

Your usual type of company. The words struck Emily right in the gut. Since when did she have a *type* of company, and how long had her sister thought of her as such a snob? She rose from the chaise, trying not to grunt from the effort, and shuffled to the edge of the balcony, where she gripped the ledge and let the thin silence stretch out while she pondered how to reply and still keep a firm grasp on her dignity.

She realized after the briefest moment of reflection it was impossible. Since she'd met Boston at the airport yesterday morning, she'd been a total snot. To make herself feel worse, she imagined how Jack and Quinn must've greeted him—happily and without a care for what he'd been wearing.

Oh, my God. I'm a stuck-up bitch. She swallowed, pride and all. "I think I might owe Boston a small apology." She still believed he had a shady little secret, but it didn't give her a free pass to treat him like a second-class human being.

"You've got plenty of time to make it up to him. I'm sure his one requirement is you be an appreciative tourist. Not exactly a chore." Quinn stopped talking abruptly before continuing in a quiet, hefty tone. "Em, listen to me. I know divorce isn't something you bounce back from like one of those little rubber balls. I would never send you off in the hopes that a little island nookie might solve your problems. In case you are attracted to Boston, I only want to you stop and recall I'd been apart from Blake for over a year when I fell for Jack. It took time. First, I had to come to terms with Blake not really being the one for me. It felt like a big mistake. For a long time, I clung to these images of our past together, instead of scrutinizing who we'd become. But we're not talking about me, and this trip Jack and I forced on you isn't about a man. In fact, I hereby ban you from men for the duration of your vacation. You do *you,* Em."

Emily gazed down the mountainside she'd climbed yesterday. The dirt-packed parking spot where Boston had parked the van peeked through the web of branches. "And no one else?"

"Right. Thoroughly enjoy Boston, but only in his capacity as someone who can turn your time on Oahu into something magical and special."

"He did seem well versed on an array of trivial facts."

"The guy knows everything. It doesn't surprise me, since he taught high school in a past life."

The teacher thing again. Emily tried to imagine Boston with properly hemmed clothing and a respectable haircut. Nope. It didn't jibe. She caught a glint of reflected sunlight through the trees from below. A black sedan sat parked in the drive. "I'm going to ask you more about that later, sis, but I better go. It seems my magic rental car has arrived to whisk me off for some island adventure."

"Call me anytime. Jack and I are taking Seth back to California in a few weeks to visit Blake. I'm trying to get this rough draft done before we leave. I hate taking work on the road."

Emily mumbled her good-byes and went back inside to find suitable clothes. Maybe if she rolled up her shirt sleeves and sprung for a pair of flip-flops she could get by with her stuffy wardrobe until she had time for a real shopping trip. Perhaps Boston wouldn't mind taking her. Heck, he might like her better when she wasn't trussed up like a corporate monkey. It'd make the impending apology she owed him easier to stomach. If not, she had jet lag and terrible airliner coffee to blame.

She yanked up the zipper on her mid-calf skirt and promised to henceforth value Boston for his expertise, instead of judging him by his shorts. Even as she thought it, she couldn't help but shake her head. "God, but they're some awful shorts."

* * * *

"I don't know, man. That kind of thing can backfire real easy. And if it does, you can kiss your golden reputation good-bye, brother. It ain't stealing, but it's damn close."

Hani's doubtful words lingered in Boston's mind like onion breath, strong and clingy, as he drove through the small village of Haleiwa on his way to retrieve Emily.

Stealing seemed a tad strong for what Boston had done. More like he'd allocated funds and been stingy with the information regarding where they'd gone. Quinn had trusted him enough to let him keep the refund from Emily's room at the Hilton. Why bother her with specifics of what he'd done with it?

Okay, so telling her he'd used it to rent *Kumu Pili* was a small white lie. The tree house belonged to his friend, Mongo, and hadn't cost Boston a dime. But, knowing Quinn, she probably would've supported his humble act of goodwill, bailing Ryder out of jail this morning.

Leave it to Hani to get technical.

They needed the money. Boston had come through, as usual. In fact, he'd daresay Emily benefited righteously from his minor deception. No way the Hilton's manufactured atmosphere came close to what she had to be experiencing at *Kumu Pili*. The tree house was the real deal.

Boston slowed to a cruise and turned onto the dirt and gravel road leading up to the house. As he reached where the path ended at the beginning of the stone steps, he hit the brakes harder than he'd meant to. The sudden stop and moment of panic sent twin jolts through his body.

A black sedan sat parked under an overhanging tree. Boston jumped from the van and walked around the car. It was a rental, given away by the barcode sticker on the front window. Either Emily had a knack for making friends, which didn't strike him as the likeliest option, or Boston was in deep shit.

He hadn't actually told Mongo he'd be bringing anyone to *Kumu Pili*. He'd made the decision on the fly after picking up Emily at the airport and idly doing the math on what an open-ended stay at one of the Hilton's tower suites must've cost. They were high-end. As primo as primo got, literally feet from the world-famous Waikiki Beach. Boston wouldn't have had the stones to try it during peak season, but in February, what were the odds Mongo had booked other clients for this particular guesthouse?

Boston's heart skipped a beat. *Please let me be wrong. I want to be wrong. Tell me I'm wrong, damn it.* He bounded up the stone staircase, slowing once he came to where the wooden switchback steps took over.

Apparently, his good karma tank was on empty. Hani would say he'd used it up robbing Emily of her Hilton suite.

She stood on the veranda with a young, pastel-washed couple and their small child. The kid held a little basket of mangoes close to his chest and looked every bit as strained as Boston felt. Every pair of eyes locked on Boston when he reached the landing.

The man sported a pair of wrap-around sunglasses hanging around his neck and wore a pale orange polo shirt. Boston had a sudden longing for an orange-flavored Creamsicle. The man frowned at him. "You've booked *Kumu Pili,* too, huh?"

His wife in a lavender and yellow plaid eyesore of a shirt, huffed. "Who ever heard of such a thing? We've had our reservations for a month. You expect this sort of confusion in the summer—"

"Which is exactly why we came in February!" her husband finished with a flourish of his arms.

Boston refused to even look at Emily. The relief on her face at seeing him come up the stairs plunged him into a cocoon of guilt, and the worse part had yet to come.

He offered the family his best smile, the one normally reserved for police officers and his mother. "Folks, I apologize for the mix-up. I'll help Mrs. Buzzly-Cobb get her luggage together, and we'll be out of your hair in no time. A simple mistake, I assure you, and the fault is entirely mine."

He couldn't risk pissing off Mongo's legitimate paying clients for the sake of one he put up for free. Forget burning a bridge—it'd be more like packing that sucker with C4 and filming the explosion over a soundtrack of gleeful laughter.

Friendships didn't come back from that.

Emily's face went round all over, from the perfect *O* of her mouth to her quarter-sized eyeballs.

He sucked in a breath and took her hand. "C'mon."

She followed him as though dazed.

He lifted a finger to Mongo's guests as if to ask for a moment while he pulled Emily behind him. They didn't look happy, but they weren't shouting or throwing mangoes.

Boston and Emily slipped inside the house, and Boston started snatching up items he assumed were Emily's; a half-empty can of Sprite and a silk-lined black blazer tossed over the back of the couch, among other things.

Once out of earshot from the unexpected company, Emily rounded on him with gritted teeth. "What's going on?"

Pretty damn obvious, wasn't it? "I screwed up. Hurry. Get your stuff together." He bounded for the spiral staircase. "If we're quick, Mongo will never have to hear about this. More importantly, I'll never have to hear it from Mongo."

Emily didn't budge. "Who is Mongo?"

Boston bit back an impatient retort. *Finesse. Don't piss off any more people today than is absolutely necessary.* He breathed through his nostrils. "Help me pack your things, and I swear, I'll explain everything on the way back to Honolulu."

She took a few steps toward the stairs. Progress. "Honolulu? What happened to leaving this to my *personal discovery?*"

He didn't appreciate how she slipped into an unflattering impression of his voice. "I don't sound that dopey when I talk."

"Yes, you do."

"You're upset right now, and that's perfectly understandable. However, I can't do anything to fix it until we get out of here."

With her jaw clamped together like an angry vice, Emily finally ascended to the second floor and started tossing her scattered clothing into the open suitcase on the bed.

It was hard for Boston to imagine she had a hard time picking out what to wear this morning when all her clothing was practically identical. Was it so difficult to choose between black and dark gray? Maybe the pinstripes came in different colors, and he lacked the discerning eye to tell them apart.

What in the hell was he going to do? The deposit for the room at the Hilton was long gone. He couldn't afford two weeks at a Motel 6, let alone any of the resort hotels. He ignored the bullets of sweat already forming on the nape of his neck.

C'mon, Boston. Don't lose your shit now. Figure it out. It's what you do. He had the one-hour drive back to Honolulu to come up with a plan.

* * * *

"I apologize, sir. We're booked solid through the next week, I'm afraid."

Boston glared at the young lady's placid face behind the tall, gleaming black counter. "What about the tower suite reserved up until yesterday?"

"It appears one of the wedding guests had been on standby for a suite and was offered the upgrade once it became available. Again, sir, I do apologize."

He wanted to scratch his eyes out. Emily's steely gaze burned into his back. She could probably guess by his body language it wasn't going well.

"This is one of the biggest hotels on the beach. There are four massive towers, and you're saying not a *single* bed is available?"

She offered him a pitying smile. "The wedding party. Without giving out personal details, it's for a celebrity of some renown. Normally, this time of year we always have a room open, which is exactly why the wedding was scheduled this way. We could never accommodate an event like this in the summer."

Boston rapped his knuckles on the counter and chewed his lip. He'd call Quinn and explain. He didn't have any other choice in the matter. Emily would have to downgrade to one of the lesser resorts, perhaps farther from the beach.

Hell, maybe he should call Mongo. Usually, he had something to trade for using his friend's properties, but he didn't have a damn thing to offer, which is why he'd slipped Emily in at *Kumu Pili* under Mongo's nose. Maybe he'd do it for one of Hani's rice plates. Or a date with Akela—

A muffled ringing emanated from his shorts.

He turned around in time to catch another one of Emily's wide-eyed expressions of surprise. Well, at least he was keeping her on her toes. He started for the hotel exit with Emily hot on his heels.

"No phone, huh?"

He ignored her angry growl and dug the most outdated camera phone in existence from the side pocket of his khaki cargo shorts, still moving. "It's not mine, okay? It's the business phone. Emergencies only."

"Oh? And if I'd had an emergency last night whilst stranded in the middle of the jungle?"

"It's for my other job, your highness."

"As what? A drug dealer?" She mean-mugged him a final time, crossed her arms, and waited like she expected him to confirm or deny the accusation.

Boston breathed in through his nostrils and slowly un-gritted his teeth. *She's not worth the worn enamel.* Her uppity, demanding attitude was starting to wear pretty damn thin.

"Excuse me." He barked a greeting into the cell phone. Only Hani had the number, and if he was using precious minutes, it meant something serious.

"Boston, I need you here. Ryder's been processed. He'll show up any minute."

"That's great, man, but why can't this wait?" He lowered his voice and moved to the other side of the parked van, away from Emily, not without some measure of relief. Her fixed stare could crack granite. "I screwed up at the tree house. Mongo booked legit clients, and the Hilton doesn't have a single vacancy. Once I get Emily settled, I'll swing by."

Hani became urgent. "Bos, you should come now. It's about Kale."

Boston waited until Emily had wrenched the van's passenger door open and climbed inside. "I can't bring Emily to The Canopy. You're out of your mind. I told her I'd show her the underbelly of the island, but I damn sure didn't mean that. Besides, this lady... I might strangle her, Hani. If they find her mangled body floating in one of the harbors, do me a favor and assume I offed myself shortly afterward. I wouldn't do well in prison."

"That's not funny, man."

"It wasn't supposed to be. Kale hasn't been gone long. He's probably hiding out or trying to find passage to the mainland."

Hani's voice grew heavier, into a tone Boston never ignored. "I told you, Kale hasn't been around for a while. He has a room here, man. He's not some in-and-out straggler. He *lives* here. You tell me, Bos, why a man on the run from the United States Army would leave a safe haven once he found one? There ain't no sense in it. He was safe here. He's missing, and I think he's in trouble."

Boston groaned and pinched the bridge of his nose. "Goddamn it, Hani. I can't believe I'm gonna do this. I swear, if I lose this client, we're screwed. You understand me? There's no way I can pay Quinn back her deposit or money for the hotel room."

"That ain't even the biggest problem you got, my friend."

"Oh? You have something else for me? More broken kitchen equipment or missing residents? Have you checked on Thompson lately?"

"Worse. You had a visitor this morning. Jordan Stacey came by to see you. There's a message, but I'll give it to you in person. I prob'ly don't need to tell you this, brother, but I ain't too happy to see her showing up here. I thought it was done."

"It is done." Boston ended the call and slumped against the van. What the hell had he done in a previous life to deserve this? Robbed banks? Drowned pretentious corporate mules?

Jordan Stacey, the last person on the planet he wanted to ever see again, showing up at the one place Boston considered a refuge. The last time she'd cropped up at The Canopy, it had almost cost him everything. On the upside, with each passing minute he had less for her to take.

Chapter 4

Boston slowed the van as he traveled along a narrow side street sandwiched between the Alo Moana district and the outskirts of downtown. He stopped across the street from The Canopy and prepared for the shit storm when he explained to Emily where they were and what they were doing.

"We're in Alo Moana. It's a hodgepodge area on the fringes of both the beach and downtown, home to a fabulous outdoor mall and some not-so fabulous areas as well. Normally, I'd never dream of bringing a client to the shelter, but if it's important enough for Hani—that's my partner—to use the emergency cell phone, I owe it to him to find out why."

A bloated pause filled the air.

Ice-cold words stabbed the humid air in the van cabin. "Did you say *shelter?*"

People like Emily were part of the problem. Boston bit back a sigh. If more people offered a helping hand, instead of an upturned nose, places like The Canopy wouldn't be so damn common and necessary in the first place. How easy to look down on someone from the glass-encased high-rise office Boston imagined she inhabited.

"It's called The Canopy. Pretty simple set-up."

She stared at him with perfect blankness. "You're serious. We're visiting a homeless shelter."

The hint of awe in her voice incensed him. He whipped off his sunglasses and fixed her with some naked judgment of his own. "That's right. Though, technically, it's more like a soup kitchen. This is the other job I mentioned. This might sound nuts to someone like you but, of the two, it's the one I actually enjoy. The people I work for here might not be able to pay for my services, but they damn sure appreciate them more. You're welcome to stay in the van and douse yourself with hand sanitizer if you're afraid the condition is contagious."

He abruptly shut his mouth. The last thing he needed was for Emily to fire him. Somehow, he had to get her to stick around another two weeks. That, or immediately find another client.

Her gaze narrowed. "You run a guide service and a shelter. Why both? Why not commit to one or the other?"

At least she didn't rail or sound disgusted. Only curious.

"One of them pays." He slid his sunglasses back on. "Usually enough for me to afford the other." He yanked the keys from the ignition. "You want to come in or wait in the van?"

Emily lowered her head for a glimpse through the driver-side window. She wrinkled her nose. "This is it?"

The two-story, condo-style building sat squished between a Japanese restaurant that donated their leftover rice every day and a consignment jewelry shop, which had a perpetual "For Rent" sign in the second-story window. A small eave sagged over The Canopy's entrance, and three crumbling concrete steps complimented the scarred front door. Some long ago occupant had painted the whole thing a hideous eggplant hue with forest green trim.

The outside wasn't even the worst of it. The toilet leaked. Hani's industrial cooking equipment took over both the kitchen and formal dining area, so they'd converted the living room into a dining hall, thanks to major donations of picnic tables and plastic lawn furniture. Boston's office was a broom closet off the kitchen, hardly big enough to hold a desk. The two bedrooms upstairs barely held three twin-sized beds between them. The living room-come-dining hall had a hole in one corner of the old wood floor from a suspected termite problem and yellowed wallpaper from a bygone era.

From roof to foundation, it was a mess. But it had been a damn cheap mess.

Boston scratched his ear. No need to tell Emily all *that*. "The location is ideal, even if the color scheme sucks."

Normally, he went out of his way to treat his clients to a piece of Paradise they could call their own. Not often did he find himself intent on bursting their illusions with a heap of reality. But if anyone deserved a strong dose of realism, it was the lady sitting next to him. "In the last five years, homelessness has surged thirty-two percent. I mentioned Alo Moana's mall, the largest outdoor mall in the country, but what you won't hear anyone tell you is how the beach park across the street is littered with tarps serving as homes for dozens of people. Those lucky enough to own a tarp, at any rate."

Emily chewed her lip. "I didn't realize it was such a problem here."

"Our number one civil issue. It's a crisis. Anyone who says otherwise has an agenda, is ill-informed, or plain has blinders on."

She nodded toward The Canopy. "Tell me about this place. What exactly do you provide?"

Why did the answer always seem so small and lacking? "Food. That's it." Did he imagine the disappointment flitting across Emily's face? "There are a hundred places around the city for these guys to go, and yes, they are overwhelmingly male. Some shelters offer housing, meals, jobs, even rehab. For many, it's a lot of pressure. They won't go looking for help where there are strings attached. Hani and I, we only feed people. No sermons, no judgment. If someone is ready for more, we send them to one of the bigger outfits with more resources."

"You feed people and send them back out to the streets?"

"I don't send anyone anywhere. They leave." He stopped and tried to dial back his defensiveness. "We have beds upstairs and take on a couple semi-permanent residents who're interested in working. One of those residents, a guy named Kale, might be in some trouble, which is why we're here."

Emily sat there emotionless. Her blank gaze gave nothing away and compelled Boston to explain further.

Not because he gave a damn what Emily Stuffy-Pants thought. He merely appreciated the opportunity to talk about the shelter. It never hurt to spread the word. "You know, one day maybe Hani and I will have a huge spread. One day is a fickle bitch, though. For now, we do what we can. My end is executive. I make the money, pay the bills, pick up food and supplies from donation boxes around town, and get our name out in the community. We're always in need of new benefactors. Hani is the chef."

Emily still hadn't flinched. No movement beyond an occasional blink.

Boston had no clue if she was disgusted, intrigued, or a mix of both.

She finally met his eyes. "So, you're like the CEO."

He shrugged. What the hell. If she needed to put it into familiar terms to grasp it, sure. "We tend to think of it in restaurant terms. I'm back of house, Hani is front of house. I operate the ledgers, he's daily operations. He's here twenty-four-seven. One of the three beds I mentioned is his."

Ah. There it was. A reaction. Emily's face fell in undisguised bewilderment. "He *lives* here? But I thought…"

What? That Boston worked from a fancy corner office, Hani wore a pristine white chef's coat, and they both went home to nice two-bedroom middleclass homes every night? He opened the van door and jumped out. "Yes, Hani *lives* here. Before you ask, I don't. My place is a few blocks away."

To his utter amazement and instant uncertainty, the van's passenger door opened and slammed closed as Emily made her decision.

Boston was torn between admiration and gall that she might only be feeding a morbid curiosity.

Inside The Canopy, Akela made the place welcoming, despite the disrepair and deterioration. The dining hall always seemed inviting with its tin-can vases holding fresh hibiscuses she brought from her garden. Might also be the warm aroma of rice floating from the back of the house where Hani prepared lunch.

Emily wordlessly followed him past the foyer, pausing only once to scan the dining hall and its array of mismatched furniture.

"I'll introduce you to Hani and Thompson, his helper. They both—"

"I don't care what that *kepolo* says about me, it ain't true." Hani's booming voice thundered down the tunnel of a long hallway connecting the kitchen to rest of the house.

Boston explained in a lowered tone. "He called me a devil, but it's perfectly normal. We're friends, I promise. Don't be scared."

"Scared? Why would I be—"

Hani's massive form ducked under the low-hanging archway between the narrow hallway and the dining area. With his greasy apron, a large wooden spoon in one chubby fist, and a gut to rival anything pot-bellied within a hundred miles, he certainly dressed the part of soup kitchen cook. "Unless he says I'm handsome. Or charming. Or I make a mean Spam sandwich. Anything else, definitely a lie."

Boston would be risking his life to say it out loud, but sometimes Hani reminded him more of a Japanese sumo wrestler than island royalty. He surreptitiously surveyed Emily for her response, strangely pleased she didn't seem overly concerned about the giant, ink-covered Hawaiian barreling toward them, despite what she must think of Hani's tattoos.

They were more extensive and colorful than Boston's. They covered every available square inch of skin, stopping abruptly at his wrists, ankles, and neck—sacred body parts, according to Hani.

If Emily ever got one, Boston imagined it'd be a barcode across the nape of her neck. Or "Corporate Barbie" stamped across her lower back in Times New Roman typeface. Fantastic ideas he'd be sure to mention should she ask for his advice on the matter.

For now, her only reaction was the quizzical lift of one brow. "Spam? I heard that right?"

Boston ignored her and made introductions.

Emily offered her hand, and Hani accepted it.

Then he rocked back on his heels in an exaggerated assessment of their new acquaintance. He scrutinized her from head to toe. The merry twinkle in his eye was probably the only thing keeping Emily from taking offense.

Instead, she seemed amused by his open study. "Like what you see?"

A warm smile spread over his generous lips. "I'm jus' trying to figure out why you ain't got no flower in your hair. Boston, get this girl a flower! Inquiring minds want to know."

"Flower?" Her confused gaze swung to Boston.

"Women sometimes wear flowers in their hair to display their marital status. Left ear, like the left ring finger, denotes you're taken. A flower behind your right ear means you're single and available."

"I'm divorced. Would I use a dead flower?"

Hani laughed and clapped his hands in approval. "Oh, I like her. Can we keep her, Bos?"

Boston suppressed his annoyance when Emily smiled back at his partner. Two days, and she'd only scowled at him. Two minutes in Hani's company, and she was *Miss Congeniality*. "You'd probably just put it on the right to show you're single. Or not wear one if you're off the market."

Hani slapped him on the back. "Flowers—they're kind of a sensitive subject for my friend here. See, my little sister has quite the crush on Boston. She never comes to The Canopy without her flower, just in case."

Emily cooed. "That's adorable. If she can stand those red shorts of yours, I'd say she's a keeper."

Hani threw up his hands in surprise and looked at Emily with round eyes. "Oh, my goodness, you, too? Thank God! See, Boston? I told you, man. They're awful. Don't even give them away. Just toss them in a shredder."

"They're pretty terrible shorts, I have to admit." Emily punctuated the statement with a sincerely apologetic frown.

The last thing Boston needed was his partner and his client bonding over their mutual dislike of his fashion choices. Didn't they have more pressing concerns? "I didn't come here for a lesson in what not to wear. Can we—"

Emily spoke over him like he hadn't said a word and put a hand on Hani's meaty forearm. "I'm sorry, I have to ask. Did you say Spam a minute ago? As in the canned meat?"

Hani gave him a wide-eyed look of reproach. "What the hell kind of crackpot guide are you, *haole?*" He turned around, his long black braid swinging out behind him, and headed back the way he'd come toward the kitchen. "C'mon, Miss Emily. How do you explain it, brother? Spam is a culinary wonder. It's magical. You can eat it any time of day. With eggs for breakfast or with rice for dinner. Or with rice for breakfast."

Boston motioned for Emily to follow Hani as his voice began to fade with his passage down the hallway. He murmured as she walked past. "They sell it at McDonald's here. It's kind of a big deal."

Her nose wrinkled. "No way."

"Yes way!" Hani's shout rang from the kitchen.

Boston entered the cramped galley kitchen behind Emily. Thompson had his arms elbow deep in sudsy water, washing plates from this morning's breakfast crowd. "Thompson, this is Emily. Emily, Thompson. He's another resident. He's Hani's protégé and also mute, so please don't take offense if he doesn't say hi."

She surprised him once again by offering Thompson a wide, genuine smile. "At least you've got an excuse. People think I'm rude when I stay quiet."

Thompson went back to working with a grin where there hadn't been one before.

Hani already had a skillet down on the hot surface of the new griddle-top oven. "You're lucky, both of you. It's a nice day out. The panhandlers won't come for a shady place to get a hot meal till full noon, so I've got time to whip you up something real special. You ain't never gonna look at Spam the same again." He used his chin to point in Boston's direction. "I heard this *kepolo* tell you something-something McDonald's, but forget that. Take apple pie. McDonald's will sell you an apple pie, right? But it ain't like Mama made. My Spam is like your mama made it." He grinned, his big face shining like an olive moon.

Emily's features morphed into unmasked doubt. Her mama probably didn't make Spam. "This is the fantastic local fare you promised me?"

Boston's stomach growled. He didn't dare pretend he didn't love Hani's cooking, Emily and her uppity refined taste buds be damned. He'd eat her plate, too, if she didn't like it. "Believe it or not, my itinerary for the day did not include lunch at a soup kitchen."

Her creamy brown eyes crinkled in amusement, and she laughed.

It stunned him into perfect stillness, unable to respond in any way but to stare with his mouth agape like an idiot.

Her laughter tapered away. "Is there something on my face?"

He shook his head.

Her eyebrows went up. "Did I speak Mongolian?"

"No. You haven't laughed before. Not since we met. That's the first time I've heard it. It's very nice. Perhaps we can salvage this vacation of yours, after all."

The laughter had gone, but an iota of amusement still glowed from behind those chocolaty irises. "Doubtful. I don't even have a place to sleep tonight."

If he thought her sense of humor could withstand it, he'd suggest Kale's empty bed upstairs. But it seemed a damn shame to piss her off now she'd finally loosened up. "This might sound like my *hubris* talking"—he winked—"but you'll forgive me after you eat."

Please, dear God, let her like Spam.

* * * *

Emily hadn't known the extent of her talent for acting until now. She'd kept up her visage of unimpressed, stone-cold statue, despite feeling about an inch tall ever since they'd pulled up in front of The Canopy and she'd been taught the lesson of her life.

Saint Boston. Go figure.

The jerky guide, who'd effectively ruined her vacation a mere two days in, had a heart of gold. He put up with snobs like her for the sake of feeding a handful of people a day in a building Emily wouldn't hesitate to call condemned in a city where the work he did amounted to a single grain of sand on the beach.

While she, the sniveling privileged vacationer, had been nothing but a God-awful snot since they met. She'd been so far off the mark it embarrassed her. Never again would she tout herself as a good judge of character.

She definitely had to apologize now but, heaven help her, pride had its place among her finest qualities, and she wasn't ready to beg his forgiveness yet. He still needed to find her a place to sleep tonight.

First, she took the opportunity while picking the last sticky grains of rice from her tin plate to offer hers. "Okay, I forgive you. I've never had Spam before, and I have to say it's pretty good."

Boston glanced up from his nearly empty plate with a downturned mouth. His lips glistened with grease. He licked them. "Never?"

It took her a beat to move her gaze back to safe ground. "Do I look like someone who eats conspicuously labeled meat product from a can?"

No hesitation in his response as he bobbed his head in a *point taken* manner and went back to polishing off the last of his rice.

Emily flopped against the plastic lawn chair, pushed away her empty plate, and dropped her hands in her lap. With her head hung low like a sorry dog's, she ground out the words. "I owe you an apology." She raised her gaze.

Boston's eyebrows gathered in a puzzled stare, and he froze with the plate halfway to his mouth. He'd been about to lick it clean.

Gently, she took the plate from his hands and offered him a napkin. The fact that he appeared genuinely flummoxed, instead of arrogantly expectant, only made it worse. She stacked the plate on top of hers and forced herself to sit up straight.

If she was going to do this, she could at least try for some dignity. She'd faked it up to this point, hadn't she? "I said I owe you an apology. I made some very base assumptions when I met you. It's not an excuse, of course, but I didn't expect anyone to be waiting. Quinn could've said something. And you...well, you..." She closed her eyes and spit out the words. "I thought you were a bum when I saw you at the airport. Even with the nice shoes and close shave." She forced herself to peek at Boston through one eye.

An amused smile lit his narrow, dimpled face. He wore his hair loose today. It fell to his shoulders, straight and sun-streaked. "This won't be the most shocking thing you've ever come to terms with, but I have been homeless. I guess the fashion stuck."

"Really, how can it be my fault when you dress like a bum? You remind me of a guy I met on the subway once. He had a neon green Mohawk and wanted to know what I was staring at."

Finesse wasn't exactly a part of her skillset. She could converse, break ice, and find common ground, but not without being her forthright self. At work, people respected it. In social situations, it often proved a hurdle. "I'm sorry. That's all. I made some rash judgments based on your appearance, but also, let's be honest here, Boston. You're not exactly the most professional person I've met. I understand that's apparently what makes you unique to your market, and doing what I do for a living, I ought to have recognized and accepted it instead of holding you against an imaginary ideal of what I thought I should expect."

"Man, these big words again."

"You're being intentionally difficult." She sat back and crossed her arms. She noted the defensiveness of the posture but was unwilling to pretend she wasn't feeling somewhat defensive. "I'm trying to say I'm sorry."

He leaned forward. In doing so, he came close enough for her to take in the deep lines around his eyes and the faded freckles on his cheeks. He was older than she'd first thought. "If only to make you feel better, I'll admit I made some judgments of my own. I decided right away you were an awful snob. Though, to be fair, you were dressed like one." He made a point of glancing at her clothes. "You still kind of are."

"Yeah, well, I *am* an awful snob. You weren't far off the mark."

"Nah." He shook his head and rose to take their plates. "A real snob wouldn't have stepped over the threshold into a place like this. You'd still be waiting in the van."

Hani came barreling into the dining hall with a large tray. "Give me them plates, Bos. It's lunchtime, and you know what that means. This place is about to exceed its occupancy limit. I need you two well-fed folks to clear out. Make room for the hungry people."

Boston handed over the dishes and rubbed his belly. "Thanks, Hani. We'll get out of the way."

"Oh, no, you don't. I didn't invite you back to base camp for a lunch break, remember? We need to talk before Ryder gets back. C'mon." He waved them toward the kitchen. "Unlike you, I can work and move my jaw at the same time. Take notes, eh?"

Boston snorted. "More like you have Thompson to churn out plates for you."

"Having an assistant don't hurt." Hani glanced back long enough to sneak a wink at Emily.

She'd fallen into instant like with the giant Hawaiian. Even his nonsensical jumble of tribal tattoos hadn't been enough to put her off. If only he'd teach Boston to be so charming.

She followed the men back to the kitchen, where Boston struggled to open a thin, warped wooden door on the far end of the galley she hadn't noticed earlier. Somehow, it didn't surprise her it turned out to be a broom closet, but the desk wedged inside the small room certainly caught her off guard. They'd managed to wrestle in a small filing cabinet with a few office staples resting on top. The office, she'd wager, where Boston executed his end of the business.

She spared a thought for her spacious seventeenth-floor window office back home with its panoramic view of downtown Los Angeles. Another pang of guilt hit her square in the chest. A cushy reclining desk chair and top-of-the-line laptop were a few of the things she took for granted.

Boston managed an entire soup kitchen from a broom closet and, judging by the evidence, entirely by hand. A large paper ledger book sat on the desk, but there was no computer in sight.

Saint Boston.

He insisted she sit at the desk in yet another plastic lawn chair. When she got home to L.A., she was going to ship him a real chair. She'd send a desk if anything larger than what he had would fit.

She twiddled her thumbs while they carried on a conversation she had no place in.

Boston leaned against the doorjamb with his back angled toward her, folded his arms, and addressed Hani. "What makes you think Kale's in trouble? And what does it have to do with us, and how, exactly, is Ryder involved?"

Hani's hands seemed to operate on autopilot as he moved through the kitchen, even while his gaze remained mostly fixed on Boston. He measured out dry rice from a large bucket into a massive metal stockpot, dented and dinged from use. "From the top, Bos. Thanks to you, we got Ryder bailed out. Dude didn't even wait to leave the station this morning before he called asking if Kale showed up while he was in lockup. I say, come to think of it, Kale ain't been here in days. Ryder gets real agitated like Kale shoulda been here."

Hani paused to transfer the pot of rice to the sink. He flipped the tap and raised his voice over the sound of water gushing from the faucet. "Ryder told me Kale is his cousin or something. Turns out we were right. Ryder does work downtown."

Boston's face wasn't in Emily's view, but she heard the smile in his reply. "Smooth hands don't lie."

"You said it, brother." Hani issued a small, disappointed shake of his head. "Ryder tells it like this. He's having sushi for lunch at the beach park and swears he saw his cousin, the one his whole family must be talking about, Kale, hitting up a tourist for change. Ryder starts asking around, handing out the rest of his California rolls for information. This goes on for a week before anyone opened up. He finally learns Kale was supposed to be in Kalihi last night."

Boston nodded once. "Ryder went and ended up getting arrested."

"Wrong time, wrong place." A grunt as he lifted the pot from the sink cut short his sad reply. He hefted it onto the industrial stovetop. "Cops thought he was part of a deal going down. Ryder is still looking for

Kale, and he ain't gonna stop till he finds him. With the rumor about Kale having business in Kalihi, Ryder's afraid, man, and I can't blame him. Kale might be in with some bad folks. Real trouble. Like he ain't in enough as it is."

"What do *you* think, Hani? Where's your gut on this?"

Emily didn't know why the respect in Boston's tone should cause her to gawk suddenly at the back of his head. Probably because she figured respect was something he doled out sparingly. What would it take for her to earn it? She silently snorted and hummed the *Mission Impossible* jingle in her head.

Hani stirred the rice and water together with his big wooden spoon and didn't glance up. "I dunno, man. If you're Kale, what do you think? Family's a strange thing, ain't it? Ryder wants to help, but could be his idea of help ain't what's Kale's. Ryder might think turning him over to the base is the best thing for him. I can't say I blame the kid for running."

To the base.

Emily blinked. They were harboring an AWOL soldier? Were they *insane*?

Boston sighed and pinched the bridge of his nose. "Okay. We got us a runaway homeless kid and a family member with mysterious motives. What exactly do you expect me to do about it, Hani? How am I supposed to track down a kid who doesn't want to be found?"

Hani stopped his stirring and pointed the wooden spoon at Boston. His eyebrows went up, and he waggled the spoon, sending flecks of water into the air. "Don't do that, Bos. The people who come in here trust you, man. They know you ain't about to do that kid dirty. If you're asking, it's 'cause you're gonna help. It ain't like there's a whole lot of places for a guy like Kale to hide, right? See, Ryder's coming back here, and he ain't leaving till his cousin comes back, which means—"

"Kale won't return so long as there's a chance Ryder might turn him in."

"Exactly, and by now, Kale will have heard Ryder's been looking for him…." Hani's voice came to a slow halt as both he and Boston realized Emily had been the one to speak.

They appeared to have forgotten she sat there listening to the whole exchange.

She shrunk under their scrutiny. "Sorry."

Boston gave her a hard, fearful stare.

"I'm not going to tell anyone." She tried to keep the defensiveness from her voice.

He had no cause to trust her, of course, but it still stuck like a burr to her sense of pride. Just because she'd never harbor a fugitive didn't mean she'd run to tattle to the first officer she saw.

Hani smiled at her. "He knows. He's just an ass."

Boston turned away from her. He put one hand on his hip. The other ran across his smooth jaw. "So, we have a new guest. I'm assuming Ryder intends to take Kale's bed till we find the kid, then?"

"You'd be correct in your assumption." From the hallway beyond the three of them, a tall man with black gelled-back hair and clean-shaven face strode into the kitchen like he owned it. He wore a clean white dress shirt, though wrinkled, and slate gray slacks with shiny loafers gleaming beneath the tailored hems.

Emily immediately recognized him.

Not by name, of course. She'd never met him before. But she knew men like this. Ryder was a powerful man—the kind of man who had the authority to walk into a room and command it based on his intrinsic belief it was his to command.

She stood, refusing to smooth her hair or give any indication she lacked for self-assuredness, confident introductions would be made.

Her confidence was ill-placed. They were not. She berated herself for forgetting she'd left nice society back at LAX.

Ryder, however, followed etiquette protocol. He greeted Hani with a friendly nod, shook Boston's hand with a short introduction of himself, and turned to her. Custom dictated women made the call regarding handshakes. She'd decide to offer or not, but a man never did.

Emily held out her hand. "Emily Buzzly. Nice to meet you." She'd decided to drop the Cobb ever since seeing her full name spelled out on Boston's card at the airport. It was a ridiculous name to begin with, and her name change would be legal in a matter of weeks, anyhow.

"Ryder Chastain." He smiled in a knowing fashion, as though they were alone in some shared secret. He recognized her, too. "Likewise."

Emily breathed a little easier with Ryder in the room. He didn't intimidate her like he might some others with his assumption of authority. Quite the opposite. He granted her a reprieve from feeling so terribly out of place.

He returned his attention to Hani and Boston with an expression of expectation. He slid his hands—smooth hands, like Boston had said—into the front pockets of his slacks. They were wrinkled, too, but Emily wouldn't hold that against a man who'd spent last night behind bars.

"What's the plan to find my cousin? He's been living here, correct? Mr. Palakiko here doesn't seem to have any clues, but perhaps you do, Mr...."

Why Emily had expected Boston, of *all* people, to cringe or bow under Ryder's weighty tone, who knew. She was a slow learner, maybe.

Boston did neither. He slid his hands into his pockets, perfectly mimicking Ryder's authoritative stance, despite practically wearing rags by comparison. He appeared one part irritated and one part nonchalant. As if Ryder was an annoying fly he was almost too lazy to swat at. "Plans aren't my thing," he answered in a bored tone. "Plus, I'm not convinced this is my problem. I don't run a daycare. My concern runs more toward filling the empty bed I've got upstairs." He examined Ryder up and down, judging and condemning in a glance. Then he smirked. "You can have it, but you'll work for it." In the very next instant, giving Ryder no chance to reply, Boston whipped toward Hani as though the conversation was over. "Didn't you say I had a message from Jordan?"

Ryder's mouth formed a tight, thin line, but he seemed accepting rather than indignant. He rolled his shoulders as if to gather himself and responded before Hani had time to answer Boston's question. "You can't ignore your job for a week and expect to keep it. This search for Kale has cost me my income and more. I'd appreciate the bed, and I'm not afraid to help in any way I can."

Boston slowly turned around and offered Ryder a bland smile. "I'm glad. Because there are others who'd jump at the opportunity to have a bed to sleep in tonight—and have far more need of it than you."

Emily put a hand on Ryder's shoulder, both in an effort to comfort him and get his attention.

Boston's gaze snapped to where her hand rested.

She ignored him. "Why don't you let me buy you a cup of coffee, Mr. Chastain? I think perhaps Boston and Hani need a minute to confer, though I'm sure they can help." She gave her guide a sidelong glare, knowing full well he'd read it loud and clear. *You're being an ass.* She smiled at Ryder. "I'd like to hear more about Kale."

Deep brown eyes lined with long, dark lashes zoned in on her. Ryder pressed his lips together while he searched her face. Finally, he exhaled and offered her a small smile in return. "I can't say I'm in a position to turn down free coffee. I'd like that very much."

On their way out, Emily caught Boston's gaze. "After coffee, I'll get a cab and find accommodations. Tomorrow, I'll stop by and let you know where I'm staying."

Ryder waited for her at the end of the hallway with his hands still deep in his pockets. Relaxed but powerful. Like a lion at rest.

Before reaching him, Emily regarded Hani and Boston one last time with a glimpse over her shoulder. She caught Boston's smirk and halfhearted eye roll. The response hardly puzzled her. It must look like she'd found the missing piece to a matching set. No, it didn't mystify her at all.

Hani's drawn expression of concern, however, made her wonder if she'd been rash in leaving her guide for the company of a perfect stranger.

Chapter 5

Emily didn't know where they were, let alone where she intended to purchase Ryder the promised cup of coffee.

At least she'd freed Boston to address his message from Jordan, whom Emily had to assume was a girlfriend. Boston's sun-kissed long locks didn't do it for her, but some other woman with less discerning tastes and lower standards might find him attractive.

Okay, *lower* seemed kind of rude even for her. Merely *different* standards.

Emily peeked at Ryder as he checked the street for traffic before crossing. She realized he'd taken the lead without her notice. She followed.

Familiar, if unknown, company beat hanging out with Boston. He made her unsure of herself and the ground shaky. He challenged her honed instincts and deep-rooted opinions of things. Like homelessness. And charity.

Ryder didn't seem the charitable type, but thoughtful enough. He paused for her to catch up with a slight lift of his lip that might've been a grin. "I've worked downtown for years. There's a nice little coffee shop not far from here. Closer to Alo Moana." A few blocks later they entered a small café close to the outdoor mall Boston had mentioned.

She allowed him to order their drinks and waited for him to break the ice. He would, of course. Men like Ryder were leaders, and no leader waited for someone else to take the initiative.

His smile radiated relief. He folded his hands neatly in front of him on the small, round table. "Thanks for this. I've had a rough week."

"I can only imagine." In truth, she kind of could. Boston hadn't made such a good start of her vacation. "Tell me about your cousin. I understand he's…" Should she admit she had most of the story already? "Perhaps in some trouble."

Kale's plight genuinely interested her. She'd been in Ryder's shoes once, interfering in her sister's life with only the best intentions. Intent didn't always dictate outcome, however.

What were Ryder's intentions?

His smile disappeared, and his gaze darted toward the glass window with a view of the bustling street. "Who knows with Kale?" He groaned and crossed him arms. "He's hiding from the Army. Definitely in trouble."

She was no actress. "Oh. I see."

Ryder didn't seem to notice her lack of astonishment. "The whole family's in knots. He's homeless, lost, and confused. He needs help. I need to find him."

She expected Ryder's dark eyes to hold some fear or sadness, but she met his gaze and forced herself not to react to the hardness in his glare. It belied his worried sentiments. Of course, anger would be a perfectly acceptable emotion for him.

Emily understood that and much more. She sipped her coffee and swallowed. "Ryder, I know a little something about family in trouble." She remembered Quinn three years ago, living abroad with a foreign film star, winding up on the front page of tabloids. "It's easy to think we know best, but sometimes we don't give our loved ones enough credit."

Like trusting them to know where their heart is.

Emily bit her lip. Not much she could do about it now except try to pay it forward. She'd help Boston uncover what Ryder had planned for Kale.

Emily didn't possess the skills of an interrogator or a player. She didn't have much of an excuse for asking personal questions that might or might not render an answer—let alone promise a truthful one—but she had to try. "What happens when you locate your cousin?"

Ryder took his time studying her.

Tired of waiting, Emily shrugged and took a gamble. "I am, above all else, a law-abiding citizen." She couldn't act worth a damn, but reading people was a specialty.

A slight nod from Ryder made her stomach dip. He approved. Then he frowned and turned away. "I haven't decided yet. I may not know what's best for Kale, but my family has had more than enough heartache over his choices. Maybe it's my place to get involved and force him into doing the right thing."

Ryder was right. Kale's actions were thoughtless, not to mention illegal.

So, why didn't she agree with him?

* * * *

After coffee, Emily decided to go back to The Canopy. She'd rather get Boston's opinion on nearby hotels before having a cabbie drive her around aimlessly while she looked up prices and vacancies on her phone.

Ryder offered to walk her with her. They arrived and she started up the crumbling steps into The Canopy but stopped when she noticed Ryder had fallen a step behind her.

He stared past her head, up and to the right. The small eave blocked her view of whatever point of interest had drawn his attention.

She waited. "What is it?"

He hesitated, peering at her through eyes squinted in consideration. "You need a place to stay, right?"

Hardly a secret. "For two weeks, yes."

He pointed to what he'd been focused on, and Emily left the steps to see for herself.

Preposterous. The ability of speech left her. She gaped first at the "For Rent" sign, then at Ryder.

He had no trouble deciphering her unhinged jaw and wide eyes. He steadied his dark gaze on her and breathed in. "I'll be frank, Emily. Hani, the cook"—he cocked his chin toward The Canopy's withered front door—"has practically grown into the walls of this place. He can't help me find Kale. It took me an entire week of asking around to get a single rumor out of the homeless community at Alo Moana park. Since my arrest, I've wondered if I wasn't setup. Someone warning me off. I'm an outsider. No one's going to talk to me, and I wouldn't trust the information now even from some brave soul." He issued a breathy, humorless laugh. "C'mon, look at me. I'm the enemy."

Emily's attire didn't differ much from Ryder's. "I'm not any better."

"No, but Boston is. However, his primary concern has always been his clients. You take priority over Kale. I know it's hardly fair to impose this way…." He left room for Emily to respond.

"You're saying my vacation is something of an inconvenience for you?"

A one-shouldered shrug accompanied his earnest expression. She had to give him points for honesty. "I'm not suggesting you ditch Boston. Not at all. By all accounts, he's one of the best. However, consider my take. If you're nearby, Boston's bound to spend more time at The Canopy. He's my only hope."

And hope was about the only thing he had, wasn't it? Regardless of Ryder's motives, Kale needed help. It'd be best for Boston to find him first, and if Emily discerned Ryder's motives in the meantime, they'd even have a clue as to what they ought to do once they found the poor kid. The idea of helping warmed Emily. Maybe she'd become something of a snooty elitist, but she had the power to do something worthwhile and useful. Something *good.*

She regarded the apartment windows and tried not to chew her lip off. It didn't appear promising. Or pretty. Or structurally sound. "I'm not sure about this."

Ryder's stretched smile struck her as forced. "Doesn't hurt to ask." He put a hand on her shoulder and steered her toward the storefront of the consignment shop.

A sign so faded she'd missed it earlier hung from a post next to the door. "Second Chances. Fitting name." The grime on the opaque windows blurred the displays of jewelry inside.

Emily truly wanted to help Boston find Kale. Of course she did. But stepping inside the small dimly lit store stuffed with counters and cabinets jammed in at awkward angles had her doubting her degree of dedication to the cause. "Ryder, I'm not sure—"

"Come on in! I'm Wendy. Y'all holler if you need help or a look-see inside one of the locked cases. Twenty-five percent off bracelets today!"

Judging by the southern drawl, Emily surmised the shopkeeper was no more a local than her. It was impossible to catch a glimpse of the woman between the maze of product and the furniture housing it all.

Ryder stood on his tiptoes. "We're here about the apartment."

A shuffle of paper. A squeak of plastic on plastic. The tinkling of metal and the creak of floorboards announced the approach of the shopkeeper. Wendy peeked around a tower of earrings directly in front of them. "Did you say you're here for the room upstairs?"

Room? There was a world of difference between a room and an apartment, but Ryder nodded easily.

Wendy came into full view. High-waist jeans and a button-up top with the tails knotted at her belly button didn't quite match the glittering chandelier earrings draped from her earlobes. She was barefoot, which shouldn't have surprised Emily. More than anything, her eager expression gave Emily pause.

Had no one else asked about the rental? Emily clamped her mouth down on another protest. *Can't hurt to look. We're only looking.*

Loose reddish-brown curls fell from Wendy's haphazard ponytail balanced precociously atop her head. Gray blossomed at her temples, but her face held little evidence of age. She kindly smiled. "What can I tell you?"

"Is it available?" Ryder's query left his lips in a haughty, impatient tone.

Emily stilled. *Dear God, is that how I sound to people?* She and Ryder seemed to have everything else in common. Surely, though, she was more polite to strangers, even bare-footed, hick-sounding ones.

Wendy went from welcoming host to defensive landlord. Her smile faded. "Sign's in the window, ain't it?"

Emily stepped around Ryder. "I'm the one considering the rental. May I see it?"

Wendy recovered a little. "Why, sure. Come with me, sweetie."

Emily held up a palm to Ryder, telling him to stay put. He didn't have to be wildly observant to have caught on to Wendy's dislike.

He shifted his feet and glanced away, clearly annoyed, but didn't budge.

She followed Wendy's winding path to the back of the store where she began an ascent up the narrowest, most rickety staircase Emily had ever seen. She took a breath, prayed for courage and light feet, and started up behind the shopkeeper with a death grip on the handrail.

The staircase butted up against the wall on one side, and she kept her hand out flat against wallpaper matching The Canopy's in age, if not in pattern.

"May I ask if I'll be expected to sign a lease of some kind? I'm afraid I won't be here long enough to satisfy a full-term rental agreement."

Wendy didn't pause to answer but spoke over her shoulder. "A monthly agreement would suit fine."

Emily halted. An entire *month*? Four whole weeks? A sensation like drowning came over her. Two days ago, she'd been packed off to Hawaii without a moment's notice. This morning, she woke up in a tree house, was confronted by terribly dressed strangers, and got booted all before lunch.

Now she attempted to rationalize renting an apartment she had to traverse the Stairs of Dread to access in order to help some kid she'd never met.

Wendy blithely continued, "Financial reasons are the only reason I bother renting it out at all. I tell you, honey, keeping a business going in this part of town ain't easy any more than it's cheap. We don't get the same tourist flow this far inland, but dang if we don't get charged about the same rent as some beachfront property. I suppose I should thank the Lord I'm next door to a soup kitchen." At the landing, she paused and regarded

Emily. "That don't bother you, does it?" Her stern expression said she'd have no qualms passing judgment depending on Emily's answer.

"I, uh, sort of know the proprietor." She waited to see if the response pleased Wendy.

The older woman beamed. "Oh, good! Boston's the sweetest, ain't he?" Her smile turned mischievous. "And a sight for sore old eyes." She made an *mmm* sound like they were talking about pie. "The Canopy's something of a detractor for most renters."

Under normal circumstances, it would've been one for Emily, too.

The two doors at the top of the stairs were wooden and warped as many of them seemed to be on Oahu. Emily guessed it had to do with the high humidity. One led to a basic bathroom—sink, toilet, and shower stall. Outdated and dingy, but clean. Wendy swung the other door open to reveal the bedroom and stepped back for Emily to enter.

She did with no small amount of trepidation. She expected to be horrified, but her shoulders relaxed.

Some of the wooden floorboards and wall panels were as warped and curved as the door. A twin bed sat under the window where the "For Rent" sign clung to the clouded, aged glass. The thin blanket on the bed matched the drapes. The bright white sheets and single pillow appeared brand new. A three-drawer dresser with an attached vanity had been pushed back at an angle into the far corner, and...

And nothing else. No rugs, no pictures on the walls, and no ornaments adorning the small bureau.

Emily held on to the straps of her purse with both hands to keep from wringing them together. Holy cow, she was entertaining the notion of staying here. *Living* here. "Probably doesn't come with room service, huh?"

Wendy didn't smile at the quip. "Rent's eight hundred a month. Two hundred deposit."

For a split second, Emily took it as a joke. A little retaliation for her room service jest. She stopped scanning the room and stared at Wendy.

The shopkeeper's deadpan expression didn't waver.

Emily continued to ogle the woman. Her difficulty in renting the unit had nothing to do with its condition and everything to do with the price tag stamped on it. Emily hated to think what this crazy old woman charged for her jewelry.

"You're serious? That's exorbitant. And completely unreasonable. You're charging what I'd pay for several nights at an upscale hotel right on the beach."

Wendy put her hand on her hip and dipped her chin in a nod. "It ain't a hotel, though, is it? This is permanent lodging in a desirable area, even if it ain't Waikiki. The street we're on is Alo Moana, and it's the next best thing. And, frankly, darlin', I need the money. The rent's got to cover my losses plus my mortgage. But sales will pick up in a month or so. If they do, I can charge less for this place."

Emily rubbed her forehead where a headache was forming. "I can't justify—"

"She'll take it."

This time, Ryder earned Emily's agog expression. "No, I won't. I'm sorry to have wasted your time, both of you." She hitched her purse strap higher on her shoulder and stalked toward the door. If Ryder didn't move, she'd knock him over.

He didn't budge. "I'll pay."

She glared at him. Then, struck by a thought, she took a step back.

The same guy who'd needed bail money—money provided by a shelter with little of it in the first place—had the means to offer up a thousand dollars, Johnny-on-the-spot?

"Please, Emily." He held out his hands in appeal. "How else will I find my cousin? You can't tell Boston about the money. He'll ask me to leave the shelter."

"He'd be right to."

He closed his eyes. "I know. I know. I'm going to pay it back—the bail money, the food I eat, all of it. Every last penny."

Hide information from Boston. Aid in Ryder's deception. For what? To keep Emily nearby, which, in turn, kept Boston nearby? Whatever Ryder's motives, they were strong ones. And she'd find out more by playing along.

"Fine." She turned to Wendy, who'd witnessed their volley of words with rapt attention. "I guess I'll take it."

After the money exchanged hands, Ryder offered to retrieve her luggage from Boston's van and also inform her guide of Emily's new lodgings. He'd be shocked to learn they were neighbors.

Sitting in the bare room, Emily had little to do but twiddle her thumbs and sweat under the collar of her dress shirt. She undid the top two buttons. It didn't help.

Stuffy clothes for a stuffy woman.

She banished the self-degrading thought. She didn't have a car or a guide, but she had a fine pair of legs and an intense desire to trade in her polyester and wool for something more island-friendly.

Emily picked up two keys from Wendy, one for her room and one for the store, which would allow her to come and go as she pleased, and set off on foot with a smile on her face.

Bring on the sunshine.

* * * *

Boston hadn't had time for Jordan's message when the call came in of a significant donation at one of the drop-off locations in Kahala. Furniture, something they could always use and apt to go missing before Boston had time to retrieve it if he didn't scoot.

It didn't bother him a bit. Relief came closer to the mark. Delaying bad news was sort of his specialty. He'd been doing it since he'd turned twelve and realized his parents were the same age as the other kids' *grand*parents. Most people his age had parents in their sixties. His mom and dad had celebrated their eighty-first birthdays this year.

Won't be long.

Don't think like that.

He tried not to most of the time. For the second time today, he pulled the van to a stop across the street from The Canopy. The old streetlamp usually took forever to flicker on well into darkness, but tonight it glowed dim orange against the purpling sky.

He rubbed his eyes and jumped when he opened them to Akela's round, beaming face mooning at him through the window.

She backed up, allowing him to open the door and abscond from his chariot.

"Hey, Akela. I owe you for saving our butts yesterday when the oven died."

She shrugged, but her smile told him how much she appreciated his acknowledgment.

He treaded warily around Akela, careful to be kind but not give her any ideas. The last thing he needed was a misunderstanding involving Hani's kid sister. "You really saved the day. Hani better make it up to you somehow."

She didn't head back into The Canopy, even after he moved to unload the three chest-of-drawers he'd pick up from the drop.

"Did you, uh, need something?" Oh, God. Was she gonna ask him out? *Please don't. Please don't.*

She tucked her hair behind her ear, subtly drawing attention to the flower there. "Ryder took Emily's bags from the van while you were with Hani earlier. He asked me to give you a message, but then you got the call for the donation and took off before I had the chance."

"A message, huh?" *I'm Mr. Popularity over here.* He grunted with the effort of hefting the first dresser. Hopefully, Hani wasn't still so busy he couldn't help Boston make light work of the rest of the load.

"He said Emily rented the room over the jewelry store next door."

"Wha..." Surprise loosened his grip. The corner of the dresser slid from his grasp and dropped onto the asphalt road with a loud *crack*. It narrowly missed the toe of his left foot. He hardly noticed. He jabbed a finger in the air toward the window above the shop—the window now devoid of its "For Rent" sign. "*That* apartment? My client rented *that* apartment?"

Akela wrinkled her nose.

He didn't blame her. He caught the doubtful scorn in his voice. Still. "My Emily? You're sure?"

She affirmed with a nod. "Hani also gave me Jordan's message to pass on."

A hot flash of anxiety jolted aside Boston's incredulity. *Well, shit.* He swallowed and tried to maneuver the dresser into a position that would allow him to pick it up again. "What the hell does she want?"

Akela's cheeriness faded. She knew the whole sad history between Boston and Jordan. She pressed her lips together and studied fingernails flecked with pink polish. "Nothing new. Boyfriend dumped her." Akela shrugged and met his gaze with visible sadness. "Same as last time, Boston. She needs you."

Chapter 6

The knock on Emily's door startled her. She hoped Boston had decided to start his job as a guide in earnest. In three days, she hadn't done any sightseeing or adventuring, let alone anything special to make him worth her time and her sister's money. Ryder had at least showed her a new café.

She opened the door to a strange woman, yet had no problem placing her. "You must be Akela."

Had to be. She was a shorter, squatter, prettier version of Hani with a beautiful pink hibiscus tucked behind her ear.

The girl grinned. "That's me. Boston's cleaning the van for some trip you two are supposed to take today. I brought you breakfast." She had a soft voice. A young voice. She offered up a plate covered in tinfoil, and Emily realized she was starved.

Upon closer inspection of the bikini she'd purchased at the mall last night, she'd ordered a small salad and diet soda for dinner. This place did terrible things to her grasp on reality.

Emily took the plate with a grateful smile and moved to the bed.

Akela came inside and shut the door. "Don't ask me where you're going. Boston's kinda tight-lipped this morning. I didn't ask." She offered a small, apologetic shrug as though it was her job to report to Emily.

"I like surprises, anyway." She didn't, but the poor girl's shoulders slumped, and Emily didn't want to be the cause of it. "Thank you so much for the food."

"Boston's, uh…" Akela appeared to search the ceiling for the right words. "Well, he's a little upset about you staying here. Not because it's not great," she rushed to say. "It's because of your sister."

Emily paused in sniffing under the tinfoil on the plate. "Quinn? What's she got to do with anything?"

"Oh, you know." The young woman blithely shrugged and sat on the opposite end of the bed from Emily. "She hired Boston to give you this great experience, but I guess it's been one hiccup after another. He never brings clients to the shelter, let alone feeds them one of Hani's rice plates for lunch." Akela eyeballed the little room with a disappointed frown. "You should be in some fancy hotel, not a shabby place like this. Boston feels like he's failing. It bothers him a lot." She sighed, the weary wistful kind. "He's so dedicated."

The words swam in adoration. Emily's mouth quirked up. She remembered now. Akela was half in love with the guy.

Emboldened by the girl's open nature, she dared a personal question. "How old are you, Akela?"

She grinned at Emily's interest. "Twenty-one. I'm the baby of the family."

Not a girl, after all. A woman. "And Boston is what? Thirty-five?"

"Thirty-nine."

Older than she'd thought. Something to be said for a life in the tropics. "That's quite an age difference, don't you think?"

"Yeah, I know." Her dark eyes, almost black, searched Emily. "He's such a good guy, that's all. Even *I* know how rare that is. I mean, I know he ain't interested in me. He's not too old for me, but I'm too young for him." She gave Emily a small, sad smile. "If that makes sense."

It did, actually. Perfect sense. "I imagine he's also afraid of your big brother." Emily peeled the cover off the plate of eggs and rice, still steaming. A strange combination for breakfast, but when in Hawaii…

Akela scooted closer like they were two friends having a sleepover and gossiping. Hani's sister had a warmth and a certain naiveté Emily liked. "Nah, Hani would love to see me with someone he trusts. My parents wouldn't like it, but they're—what's the word? Like, when someone decides they know everything without the whole story?"

Words were Quinn's forte. Not Emily's. "Um. Judge-y?"

"Yeah! Coming to conclusions or whatever. They think because Boston was homeless and had a drinking problem that he's still that same person, but that's not him at all. Some people get better and then go back, but not Boston." Her face said she wholeheartedly believed it.

Emily nearly choked on her rice. Why did it shock her to find out Boston had an ugly past? His involvement in a homeless shelter plus his prior homelessness, which he'd admitted to her firsthand, should've clued her in.

But still. She swallowed the lump of food. "You're saying Boston's an alcoholic?"

For the first time, Akela seemed to weigh her words. She gave Emily another measuring glance. "Well, he *was*. But it wasn't even his fault. Everyone knows Jordan's the reason he got caught up in a bad lifestyle. Boston didn't have a problem in the world before he met her." Akela's gaze went distant, and her expression turned bitter. "She turned his whole life upside down and left him sitting in the mud when she was done with him."

Jordan. Emily heard that name yesterday. "Why would Boston still have contact with her if she messed him up so bad?"

Akela's eyes went round. "He wouldn't! Boston hasn't had anything to do with her for two years now." She lowered her lashes. "Anyway, it's his story. I probably shouldn't tell it."

Emily forked eggs into her mouth and went for lighthearted. "Oh, c'mon. You've told me this much. My sister already mentioned he taught school before…. Well, before things changed, I guess. Jordan's doing?"

Akela was young but not as malleable as one might believe. She shook her head, even as her face expressed an apology. "I'll tell you about Jordan, but I can't talk about Boston's history. It's too personal."

"That's okay. You're a loyal friend. Nothing wrong with that. So, Jordan. She's a drinker, too?"

"Oh, yeah. A real party girl. Not the dedicated type. I mean, I guess she played the part. And, of course, you know Boston." She ended with an eye roll.

Emily didn't, actually, but she was getting quite the education from Akela. She hazarded a guess. "He *is* the dedicated type?"

Akela's shoulders fell again. Did Boston have a clue how deeply this young woman felt his pain? Maybe that was Akela, though. Maybe she was profoundly empathetic and couldn't help it. "Boston gave Jordan his whole heart. She doesn't care about love, though. She dragged him down and took everything from him. Then, when he didn't have nothing left to give, she left him. He fell apart. But wouldn't you know it, someone like that ain't satisfied doing it once. So, she came back and did it again. Every time she left, he crashed and burned, then got it together in time for her to show up again. The last time, he didn't get back up again. That's how he met Hani. They were on the streets together. I guess Jordan didn't have no use for a homeless guy. It wasn't until right after Boston and Hani opened The Canopy she showed up again."

Emily forgot her breakfast. "What happened? How did Boston keep from losing the shelter like he lost everything before? Did he finally refuse to cave?"

"Hani." Akela shrugged. "Hani was there to keep Boston from totally going up in flames. Eventually, he recovered. Jordan ain't been seen since. Maybe she knows he's got a support system now. Or maybe she's found someone else to destroy."

What a God-awful human being. Worse yet, apparently Jordan had returned. Far more discomfiting now that Emily had the whole story. Or at least the bones of it. She had to admit it seemed odd. Boston didn't seem the type to be so *taken*. Manipulated. How powerful did a woman have to be to have that kind of sway over a man?

Emily couldn't imagine having such dominion over another person. "It's difficult to see Boston as someone easily taken advantage of. He's so—"

"Stubborn?" Akela offered.

Emily had to smile. "Yes, definitely stubborn. And carefree, like nothing gets to him."

"*Everything* gets to Boston. You renting this place is enough to ruin his whole morning. He takes everything personally."

Again with the obvious adoration.

Emily took the sentiment with a grain of salt. Stuff seemed to run right off him like a rain slicker. He had the offhand manner of someone with not much at stake in anything.

Just the person to be in charge of her month-long vacation.

Unless, of course, he didn't stick around to finish the job. "Akela, what would happen if Jordan returned now? What would Boston do?"

The young woman didn't appear confident. Her reply came on a soft breath. "Sometimes, Hani asks the same question. Without Boston, there's no Canopy. There's always hope he'd do the right thing, but addiction is funny like that. It's not the alcohol he fights. It's her. It'll always be her."

* * * *

Akela stepped back to admire her handiwork at the same time another knock sounded on Emily's door.

This time, she expected the caller. "Took Boston long enough to clean the van."

Akela had spotted the bags from her shopping spree last night, and they'd spent the last hour playing dress-up, which amounted to Emily trying on every one of her new outfits while Akela *ooh*ed and *ahhh*ed and ultimately chose Emily's ensemble for the day.

Emily's newest gal pal beamed and clapped her hands. "You're beautiful! I hope he's taking you somewhere *super* special."

Boston knocked again but didn't wait to let himself inside. He shut the door and took in the mostly bare room in his casual, couldn't-care-less demeanor. "Nice digs."

Ah, sarcasm. She'd missed it while in Ryder's company. One thing she had to give Boston credit for: he had a sense of humor.

Akela shifted into a state of unbearable shyness in his presence. Emily's heart went out to her as the young woman nervously toyed with the end of her long black braid, identical to Hani's, and smiled at Boston with such admiration it made Emily choke back a giggle.

It wasn't funny, really. A crush could be devastating, as she well knew.

Akela grabbed Emily's empty plate. Even on her rich, brown skin, the blush stood out. "I'll take this back to The Canopy for you. You guys probably have big plans for the day."

"Thanks, Akela." Boston said the words before Emily had the chance.

For whatever reason, she'd expected him to be dismissive, even rude. Because Emily had to face the truth; Akela wasn't a pretty girl. And she had a crush to boot.

Instead, Boston was respectably polite. Warm, but not too personal. Distant, but not in an *ew-don't-touch-me* way.

Emily managed a quick thank you before Akela scuttled from the room. No other way to describe it—head down, feet shuffling.

"So." She clapped her hands together. "I hear we have big plans."

Boston had his hair tied back in a high ponytail more at home on a girl, but she could hardly deny he wore it well. A little Beckham-ish, she'd admit.

"We do." He paused and glanced around the room once more. "You, uh, sure about this? About staying here? I'm sure we can find—"

"The lease is signed. Wendy gave me a key to the dead bolt. I'm able to come and go as I please. And if anyone were to break in, what would they bother coming up here for? The goods are downstairs."

His pale blue gaze made a lazy trail over her, down to her sandaled feet and back.

She realized she was dressed quite differently from the last time he'd seen her. Gone were the corporate duds. Akela had dressed her in a white dress with big, red flowers. The bodice fit snugly, the skirt swung out around her hips and made them appear more flared than they really were. The hem fell modestly to her mid-thigh.

Heat crept up her neck. She hadn't acclimated to her new dress code yet.

Boston ended his perusal with a lopsided grin that made him look like he had some dastardly plan up his sleeve. Maybe he did. "Nice dress."

"You like it?" She smoothed down the skirt. "It's the most scenic thing I've seen on my vacation so far."

"Hmm." He licked his teeth. "I do like it. It's a damn shame you'll need to change. Those sandals are nice, too, but you'll want some hiking boots."

How did he always find the perfect words to get under her skin? He did it on purpose. Nothing else accounted for it.

"My first real outing, and we're hiking?" She cocked her head to the side. "People actually pay you for a good time?"

He slowly crossed his arms. "What's wrong with hiking?"

Wrong?

First of all, she'd have to expose thighs that hadn't seen the light of day since 1996. Second, though she might *want* hiking boots, it hadn't crossed her mind to purchase a pair. "I'll have to go shopping again."

That seemed to give him pause. "I bet Akela can loan you a pair."

Emily patiently reminded herself why she'd come. This was supposed to be a time of self-discovery and de-stressing. If that meant hiking a mountain instead of strolling white sandy beaches, then fine.

Go with the flow. "Okay. You win. Whatever. Ask Akela about boots, and I'll change. Do me a favor and tell Hani I said thanks for breakfast. A strange but yummy breakfast." She snatched up one of her shopping bags from the mall.

"Actually, I made it."

She stopped searching for the khaki shorts she'd bought yesterday and squinted at Boston. "Akela said—"

"Hani gave her the plate and asked her to bring it up, but I cooked this morning." He shrugged. "Hani wasn't feeling well. I'm a terrible cook. Just be glad anything was edible."

She went back to digging through her new wardrobe. "Well, well. Is there no end to your veritable talents?"

He astounded her by shuffling his feet and clasping his hands behind his back. "I am sorry, Emily."

Her mouth probably gaped wide open. "For what?" She'd been the judgmental snoot. What had he done besides go out of his way to help a confused soldier and his desperate cousin? She wanted to kick herself for making the joke about the scenery on her dress. "Listen, I get it. Things happen—"

"You shouldn't be staying here. The right thing would've been to take care of your needs as my client before addressing personal business. There's no excuse for it. I'm on the payroll, and this is not what Quinn had in mind when she asked me to take care of you." He offered her a grim smile. "This place doesn't even have room service."

His observation came so close to the joke she'd made yesterday, she snickered. "Look at it this way, Boston. You can walk to work."

The slightest tug on the corner of his mouth. Almost a smile.

"And I don't mind. It's…" She peered around. She had a bed with clean sheets, a private bathroom, and a window to gaze out of. "Different. And different's okay with me. Everyone comes to Hawaii dreaming of the ultimate island experience, right? I'm in the trenches. Isn't that at the very heart of what you advertise?"

His eyes narrowed like it hurt to consider the idea. "Yeah, but I don't usually mean it so damn literally."

Finally, she located her khaki shorts and yanked them from the plastic shopping bag. She stood up straight and shook them out. *God*, they were short. "I want to make the most of the time I'm here. Help me and we both win."

He smiled in full, his dimples deeper than ever. "Keep wearing dresses like that, and I definitely win more than you."

* * * *

Boston had made a poor bet with himself.

He'd counted on Emily in slacks and a colorless button-up top and a lengthy lecture on why she'd need a different ensemble for hiking. At most he expected her to have swapped out the mannish loafers for a pair of low heels.

The dress—and Emily inside it—had blown him away.

Those legs.

Miles and miles of legs. He recalled Quinn being tall, but she'd been a wispy thing. Emily shared the legs-forever trait, but with a little more *oomph.*

Her bun thingy had vanished, along with her corporate uniform. She'd been hiding loose waves of chocolaty brown curls in that bun of hers, identical to the shade of her eyes. It fell long enough to caress her milky white shoulders.

And she hadn't seemed any less confident, despite the change in attire, which had rocked him as much as the dress had. In his experience, women like Emily wore their pantsuits like armor.

It'd taken a great deal of control to stifle the urge to ogle her body this morning and ignore the mesmerizing sway of her dress sashaying around her full hips—hips a man could get a grip on.

Thank God they were hiking. He'd have to swipe any beach-going plans off the agenda. If a modest dress made him drool, Emily would kill him in a bikini.

And if Ryder ever caught sight of her in either, he could probably kiss his client good-bye.

Boston frowned. Had their instant connection truly bothered him? Did he care if they probably had matching briefcases sitting in their walk-in closets lined with wrinkle-free gray slacks and stiff, white button-ups starched to perfection?

Maybe. Yeah. But for only Kale's sake. As a matter of trust.

Ryder had the world-owning attitude every prick with an office in a downtown high-rise seemed to perpetrate. A classic chicken-egg scenario. Did the corporations only hire people with a deep sense of entitlement, or did it culminate after they took the job?

Boston would never know. Before operating The Canopy, he'd been a lowly teacher and a homeless beggar. He'd never had any power to begin with.

Keeping pace with Emily and convincing her they were on equal footing tested his ability to fake it to the max. Once upon a time, he might've been close. He'd been respectable, at least. There'd been an office and a laptop. Some okay clothes. A socially acceptable haircut. Presently, however, he bobbed around the murky bottom of the societal barrel while Emily sat square at the top.

She hadn't put him at ease with her casual acceptance of lunch at a soup kitchen or her undaunted undertaking of less-than immaculate living quarters. To the contrary, he felt *observed*. Emily witnessed his life through a protective barrier courtesy of her lofty station on high, mingling without putting her toes in the water. Like a scientist studying a contagion from behind a microscope. Safe. Unaffected. Then she'd go home and convince herself she was a better person for it.

The idea both pleased and prodded him. It indicated an open mind. And yet she'd gone off with the first corporate douche she ran into.

But did it bother him?

Not as much as hijacking Emily's vacation again to pursue a personal motive. Though, to be fair, it was a "two birds, one stone" situation. They were halfway across Oahu, and Emily had blessed their journey with ponderous silence as she took in the sights.

Finally, he pulled into the entrance of the Schofield Army Base. He didn't attempt to get through the guarded entrance. After all, one didn't waltz onto a military base without the proper credentials. Instead, he ignored Emily's confused examination of their destination and parked in the visitor lot. He also pretended not to notice her much meaner stare when he reached across to the glove compartment and popped it open to grab the phone.

She arched a brow. "Emergency?"

"Sort of. We can't get in without calling for help."

Zachary Lionel picked up on the first ring and promised to meet them at the gate in ten minutes.

"An old friend," Boston explained, returning the phone. "He'll get us onto the base."

Five minutes later, Sergeant Lionel hopped into the back of Boston's van, flashed his identification at the gate, and they were welcome onto the base.

Boston took the opportunity, while driving through the compound, to quiz his friend before dropping him back at his apartment. "Hey, man, I heard the craziest rumor yesterday."

The sergeant leaned forward and gripped the back of Boston's headrest. "Yeah?"

"I heard they found the AWOL kid. You know, the lettuce dude."

Zachary laughed and prepared to open the door as Boston pulled up to the curb in front of the sergeant's condo-style dwelling. "Kale. Yeah, man, I knew him. Good guy, but I don't think they found him. It'd be big news on base. Personally, I think something happened to him. He didn't seem the type to skip." He shrugged, pulled open the sliding door, and launched himself out of the van. "Enjoy your hike, guys!" He took off at a slow jog.

Boston pulled away from the curb. "Always in a hurry, these guys."

Emily's arms and legs crossed.

Those damn legs. The shorts were far worse than the dress, revealing several more inches of flawless pale skin. "I see what you did there. You should've told me. I want to help Kale as much as you do."

He hit the brakes about a yard before the stop sign required him to and stared at her. Since when had Kale become *her* concern? "Why do you care about helping a homeless kid you've never even met?"

She innocently lifted her shoulders like the answer was obvious. "Since I had coffee with Ryder and heard a bit about him. And why shouldn't I care? I might be stuffy, but I'm not an ice queen."

An idea struck him. Emily might be in the perfect position to help them ferret out Ryder's motive. Hell, she might already know it. All he had to do was a little asking. He'd best tread carefully, though. He didn't want Emily to confuse his interest with any other emotion. Like jealousy.

With the van back in motion, he rubbed his cheek. "Ryder's a conundrum to me. He gives up his job and home to move into a shelter to find his missing cousin. Sort of extreme, isn't it?"

Emily seemed to chew on his words. "It would depend on how close they are."

"They can't be that close. Kale's been living at The Canopy for a while. Never mentioned having family on the island. I don't want to intrude on your budding relationship with Ryder, but do me one favor."

She cast him an annoyed glance.

"Just keep in mind we're not sure of his motives. He might mean to turn Kale in. It's exactly the sort of thing a well-meaning family member might do."

Her lips pressed together, a sign she was about to make a highly intelligent point he'd need something extremely clever to argue against.

"You're saying hiding Kale from the authorities, which I'll remind you is illegal, is the more honorable course of action?"

Man, this woman got under his skin. "It doesn't have a damn thing to do with honor. It's about freedom. Maybe Kale came to a point where he didn't agree with what's happening anymore. He bolted. It's not my place to hand him over to anyone. It is my duty, however, to support a man's freewill. I feed people. I don't tell them how to live. I'm damn sure not about to turn Kale over to some stiff-neck like Ryder until I know exactly why he wants Kale so bad."

"And if he finds Kale before you do?"

The thought had occurred. "At least I tried."

"What if Ryder doesn't intend to turn Kale over to the Army?"

Boston let out a sigh of frustration. "I want to trust Ryder, but I don't. Something about the guy strikes me as cagey. He's determined but not in the way you'd imagine a loving relative to be." He let out a breathy, humorless laugh. He had no siblings and his parents were so old they were practically comatose. "Then again, what the hell do I know about loving relatives."

A beat passed. "Jordan seems to have loved you. In one of those unhealthy, dangerous ways. But still."

The comment came so hard and fast from left field, Boston's foot slammed down on the brakes a second time. He'd compared Emily to a scientist peering down a scope into his life without realizing how accurately he'd pegged her. She had no right to bring up the most painful part of his past with some blasé, bullshit insight.

"What the hell do you know about Jordan?"

Emily looked at him full-on and seemed taken aback by his response.

Good. He never thought he'd have to set boundaries with a client, but he'd damn sure establish some now.

She mumbled an explanation. "Akela mentioned her in passing this morning. An offhand comment. Nothing important."

He bet Akela had said a lot more than nothing. Boston raised an angry finger. "My past isn't a topic for discussion. Unless you want to harp on yours? Didn't you marry your sister's husband? Talk about a messed up relationship."

Damn it. He dropped his hands in his lap, thrust his back into his seat, and shook his head. How were they supposed to move on from this? One day Boston would learn to keep his cool when it came to Jordan.

But not today. He eased the van back into motion. They weren't far from their destination now.

Emily's arms were still crossed, and she faced the window.

"Emily, I'm sorry. That was uncalled for. It's just—it's a button, okay? My least favorite and most trigger-happy button is named Jordan Stacey, and it's for the best if we don't talk about her. Ever."

He expected a bland apology or for the silence to continue.

Instead, she faced him with a small, sad smile. "I married my sister's *ex*-husband, if you want to get technical. Unfortunately, career success doesn't necessarily transfer into success in every arena of life. You think *you've* got touchy history?" She laughed drily and went back to staring out the window. "I knew Blake still loved her. I married him anyway. Quinn's like that, though. People like her. I can't even blame him."

Boston stared dumbly ahead, but focusing on the road leading them to Waianae Range became a struggle. He wanted to gape at her and ask *why*? And how? He'd have taken an angry explosion over her quiet surrender to her fate any day. He definitely hadn't counted on the uber-confident and worldly Emily to have the same deep-rooted issues he did. Didn't rich people have affairs to settle their scores? "Hey, it's not a battle of the exes. I shouldn't have snapped at you. Point taken. Can we agree to not talk about either one of them?"

She analyzed him from the corner of her eye. "You don't have to talk about Jordan, but I do hate to see you feeling so darn special over there. See, not only did I force Blake into a marriage he wasn't ready for, I also came very close to letting my guilt over my feelings for Blake ruin Quinn's relationship with Jack. I tried to break them up. In fact, I succeeded for a while."

Boston recalled her comment the day he'd picked her up at the airport. Something about Quinn getting even.

Emily issued another dry laugh and clasped her hands together in her lap. "That's not even the saddest part. The real shame is that I'm over forty, and the only person I've ever loved is my ex-husband. Late bloomer over here." She poked her chest with her thumbs. "No high school boyfriend. Didn't date in college. I've never known love. Not the real stuff that flows back and forth between two people like it's supposed to. As much as you might hate your ex-wife, as bad as she may have been, as much heartache as she must've caused you, Boston—you can't say she didn't love you. And you loved her."

Boston loosened his tight grip on the steering wheel. Why was Emily doing this to herself? To teach him a lesson? To prove a point? Should he say something? Offer comfort?

Emily's eyebrows creased as she stared straight ahead at nothing, and her voice fell to a near-whisper. "I wonder how it feels. I want to hand my heart over to someone who wants it—not reluctantly or out of some sense of obligation—and will offer me theirs in return. Just to know."

When she finally met his eyes, hers were red-rimmed and swamped with emotion but as dry as sand.

"Go ahead and keep your sad stories about Jordan," she said. "I can't relate, anyway."

Chapter 7

The first half of their hike up the rugged mountain path went by in stony silence. Emily hadn't even remarked on the warning signs posted at the trailhead. Boston didn't exactly go out of his way to point out the glaring "Dangerous Trails Ahead" signpost or the sign plainly suggesting they not proceed past the parking area.

He attempted to draw her to attention to the beheading rock of Kole Kole Pass, which had some creepy lore surrounding it.

She hardly peeked at it as they passed.

Whatever. Boston shrugged and kept going. He only had to get her to the end of the dirt path, the place where the trees opened up and they'd have an unobstructed view of the peak of Pu'u Hapapa and Lualualei Valley beyond.

Experienced hikers could reach the summit and back in four hours or less, but Boston wasn't equipped for the full hike to the peak, and Emily was a beginner. The warning signs at the trailhead existed for a reason. Things got a little hairy past the meadow.

Didn't matter when the meadow was the destination.

He stopped and shrugged off the backpack containing the lunches Hani had packed for them, along with extra bottles of water.

"That"—he broke the skin on their cone of silence and pointed at the craggy mountain face rising up in the distance—"is Pu'u Hapapa. Don't ask me what it means because I don't know. It's too dangerous for us to attempt, but the view from this meadow is one of the best on Oahu. Kole Kole Pass is right over—"

She gawked at him, wild-eyed. "People climb *that*?"

The magnificent vista hadn't pried Emily open up like a springtime flower the way he'd hoped, but at least she was speaking again.

"Sure they do. At the top, the trail ends at an old helicopter pad. Hell of a view." Boston made a seat from a suitable rock and laid his windbreaker out over a pad of grass for Emily. "You hungry?"

She wiped the sweat from her brow and observed Pu'u Hapapa another minute. "It's really something up here."

Boston unpacked the paper sacks. He peered inside one of them and offered Emily a grim smile as she joined the makeshift picnic. "Fresh fruit. Rice. Spam. No meal's complete without Spam."

"Not if Hani made it." She took her plastic container and bottled water without further complaint.

A ponderous silence went by while they pushed rice and papaya chunks around in their plastic containers. At least until Emily let go of her fork and pointed at his left bicep, bared by his sleeveless gray T-shirt. "Your tattoo. What's it mean?"

He followed the line of her finger, even though he knew the tattoo well. "It's says *hema.*"

Emily tilted her head. "You're sweet, Boston, but I can read. What does it *mean*?"

Each one of his tattoos meant something personal, beyond what the words translated to. But what the hell. Emily had bared her soul back there in the van. He supposed he owed her. "It's supposed to mean 'unprepared' or 'clumsy.' I don't speak Hawaiian, so I had to take the tattoo artist's word for it."

"Ah." She peered at him. Her eyes squinted against the brightness of the day, despite the cloud cover. The sun reflected off the haze, illuminating the sky like a sunny day. She did her wise owl thing again, considerate and watchful. "That is, what does it mean to you?"

The truth? The tattoo pinpointed his fears during the most trying times of his adult life—getting sober for the first time. His answer came as close to honest as he'd willingly get. "It represents my fear of the unknown. The concept is timeless. Trying something new is scary, whether it's moving to Hawaii or learning to surf. You never feel ready for change. I needed to wrangle my insecurity into something physical. Tangible."

"And the other one? On your right arm?"

"*Ma'ema'e ola.* Clean life." He mustered up a flat smile. "Island living is pretty damn clean."

Her face went still. Again, she studied him. Did he have rice clinging to his face? "Akela told me you used to drink. I'm guessing the first tattoo came before sobriety. The second after?"

Damn you, Akela. Anything Emily doesn't know about me at this point?
He rubbed the nape of his neck and had a hard time meeting her gaze. The
stark face of Pu'u Hapapa seemed no more welcoming, perhaps, but less
condemning and lacking the judgment he expected to read on Emily's
face.

"Very clever. You always this interested in your guides? I should warn
you I'm a leg man." Despite his fear of judgment, he couldn't resist a
glance to catch her reaction.

She grinned and responded to his leg comment with only the slightest
blush on the apples of her cheeks. "I'm the observant type. And I can't
help but be fascinated with your tattoos, considering I don't have any.
Neither does my sister. Or anyone else in my acquaintance."

"Hmm. Not even Jack? He seemed the type."

"Not that I'm aware of. I have noticed yours, though. You have a
yellow hibiscus on your hip, which I believe is the Hawaiian state flower.
The Arizona state quarter on one wrist, another hibiscus on your calf, and
one more. It's on your ribs. Something in Hawaiian, but I can't read the
typeface any more than I can translate the words."

Boston inhaled and let fresh, muggy air fill his lungs.

A hui hou.

Once again, Jordan's ghost butted her head in where it no longer
belonged. "It means *until we meet again*. It means different things at
different times. These days, it's a reminder of my folks. In a few years,
when I'm back home in my native desert wasteland, caring for my really,
really old parents"—he swallowed—"or sorting through their stuff once
they've passed on, the tattoo will probably be my ode to Hawaii."

Emily brushed her hands together as if dusting off crumbs and set
her "lunch box" on the grass. Nothing remained of her fruit, but she'd
hardly touched the rice. "I'm pretty sure my scene in the van covered our
'uncomfortable display of emotion' segment of the tour. I won't ask about
your parents if you'd rather I didn't." A loaded pause. "But I am curious."

He'd sort of asked for it, hadn't he? "Eh, it's nothing, really. They're
old. They've always been old. So old my friends thought I lived with my
grandparents. Mom turned forty-two the year she had me. She and Dad
are both in their eighties." He recalled the last time they'd seemed young
to him. "We came here on vacation when they retired. I celebrated my
eighteenth birthday a few months before."

The island had practically pulsed with freedom. He'd been a studious
kid. Worked hard, earned a free ride to a teaching degree. He was headed
for the University of Arizona the next fall. But Oahu snagged his heart

and imagination and never let go. "I graduated, taught high school in my hometown for several years. And then something happened." He snorted and scratched his chin where he'd nicked himself shaving. "Actually, it's more accurate to say *nothing* happened. Dry, stuffy parents in a dry, stuffy town. I had a dry, stuffy life." He scraped up the last of his rice. "So, when I hit thirty, I left. I came here and started living."

Started hiding.

Sure, maybe a part of him was hiding out. His parents kept getting older, and the longer he stayed away, the faster time seemed to fly. Any day now, he'd be called home, but he wouldn't leave until he had to. No way he'd witness his imminent loss firsthand. Only his experience with Jordan waltzing in and out of his life, elusive as smoke, rivaled the sense of defeat and powerlessness his elderly parents inspired. He'd face the regret when it came rather than fight a losing battle.

Boston cleared his throat and popped the lid back on his lunch container, his appetite gone. "What do you think of the view? Throw me some adjectives. Stunning? Remarkable? A small pat on the back for finally getting something right on this vacation of yours."

Emily smiled and regarded the valley beyond Pu'u Hapapa. "It's incredible. In fact, if I lived here, I'd build a yurt on the mountainside and forget the beach."

He chuckled at the image of Emily sporting furs and holding a spear. "You'd hunt wild pig to survive, huh? Pick seeds and berries?"

"Oh, gosh no." She managed to look sincerely shocked by the question. "I'd send my butler to the grocery store once a week."

A little dig to remind him of her place on the totem pole, as if he'd forgotten. He paused. Or maybe some self-deprecating humor? Hard to tell with Emily and her oh-so-dry sense of humor. "Or you could hire me. For a small daily fee, I'd be your personal hunter-gatherer."

She frowned. "I can't imagine I'd have many resources living in a yurt. I probably couldn't afford you both. I'd have to choose between you and my butler."

"I'm the obvious choice. Being nonfictional and all."

Emily wasn't the bowl-over with laughter type of girl. Her small grin and quiet snort was as good as a hearty guffaw. "You've nearly made up for the last two days, but there's one tiny thing you could do to bring it home."

Emily would be his neighbor for four weeks. That didn't, however, guarantee she'd be willing to put up with him past the two he was contracted as her guide. His need for money hadn't gone anywhere. Emily had to continue wanting his services.

He'd do whatever it took.

He placed their containers in the backpack and hitched it over one shoulder. "Anything." *Please don't ask to do something boring. Or, God forbid, expensive.* If she asked for a spa day, he'd fling himself off the side of the mountain.

"Feed me something without rice."

"Oh, man." Relief hit him first. Then the impracticality of her request sunk in. He dropped his chin to his chest. "You're never gonna make this easy, are you?"

She chugged the last of her water and licked her lips. "Not if I can help it."

* * * *

Boston could've bounced a rubber ball off the tension in The Canopy.

He spotted Hani, hands on hips, in animated conference with Akela and Thompson across the dining hall. Talk from the late dinner crowd prevented him from catching snatches of the conversation, but he had a damn good idea of the subject matter.

Jordan.

Being mute, Thompson lacked the ability to respond with words, but his body language told the story well enough. Strain deepened the worst of the wrinkles on his weathered face. Akela, too, gave plenty away with her lips pressed so hard together they were almost white against her almond-colored skin.

He scanned the room and spotted Ryder tucking into a plate of rice, noting how the man kept one wary eye on his fellow down-and-outers. "Hey, Em, look who's here. Why don't you go say hi? Ask him if he had any luck tracking down Kale today."

She left his side so easily he might've been the one dismissed.

Hani's face lit up when he caught sight of Boston headed toward them, but not in a happy way. He clasped Boston's shoulder and pulled him closer. "Oh, man, it's about time you showed up. I'm about to go into conniptions. I need smelling salts or something."

Thompson bobbed his head in worried agreement.

Akela wore an identical expression.

Boston searched their distressed faces. Maybe this had nothing to do with Jordan, after all. "What's going on? Did you get news of Kale?"

Hani's eyebrows snapped together. "Nah, brother. Worse than that. Phillip called."

Boston let out a low whistle and crossed his arms. Phillip Stacey, Jordan's big brother and polar opposite. He'd never met two siblings more different. While Jordan had lived it up, Phillip had gone the college route, earned a law degree, settled down with a nice girl shortly after, and lived a squeaky clean life.

So clean, in fact, he refused to have anything to do with his sister. One of those "helpful" family members, he'd be the first to drive Jordan to rehab but, in the meantime, he drew a hard line between them.

It was all or nothing with some people.

Boston's personal association with the guy ran along similar veins. Back when Boston had been Jordan's loser, drunk boyfriend incapable of keeping a steady job, Phillip refused to acknowledge his existence in a room. These days, things worked a bit differently. He'd been one of the first people to shake Boston's hand when he bought the dilapidated building that had become the shelter and remained one of The Canopy's most generous benefactors.

Still, they weren't exactly pals. Boston wouldn't call Phillip the friendly type. One reason would compel Phillip to call The Canopy directly, rather than send over a courier or have his secretary make the call, and Boston had guessed it the minute he'd walked in the door.

Damn if it didn't always come back to Jordan.

Hani, Thompson, and Akela stared at him.

Boston guessed what had them so distraught. He kept his arms crossed. "You think I'm going to ruin everything because Jordan had another bad breakup? You can tell Phillip I appreciate his concern, but I already got Jordan's message."

Hani's stare went from anxious to animal. He pointed a fat finger in Boston's face and pitched his voice low. "You don't get to act like it ain't happened before. I've got every right to worry. We all do, because it ain't just you, man. We're tied to you like a damn fishing line. If you get yanked out of the water, we all fry."

Akela put a hand over her brother's arm. "Boston, she's coming. It's what she does. And if it were Jordan alone, we wouldn't worry. But she has a way of—"

"Dunking your ass in a bottle. Let's be straight." Hani was never one to mince words.

Boston nodded and considered his friends. "You're right. So, I won't drink. Problem solved."

Doubt clouded their faces like a spring storm.

Their reactions incensed him even as he understood them. "Guys, I've been sober for two years. I don't even think about it anymore. That's not lip service, Hani. You'd know if I'd been pining away for a drink this whole time."

Hani tilted his head back and chewed his lip. "Maybe. But last time Jordan came sniffing around, you were sober *and* had a girlfriend. What's different this time?"

"Last time I'd gone from homeless panhandler to business owner in the space of a few months and was seeing a woman for the first time since divorcing Jordan. Jordan spilled the beans about my past and convinced me this place would fail. It didn't take a whole lot to talk me into a few shots of Jack, I admit it. But like I said—"

"Two years. I hear you, man." The pity in Hani's plaintive gaze got to Boston worse than any amount of anger. "But this is Jordan we're talking about. She *is* your addiction."

Boston shook his head and stepped back. Their lack of faith filled his mouth with the sour taste of the past. Like his parents saying he'd stayed in Honolulu after achieving sobriety was an excuse to fail, an excuse to stay within reach of the lifestyle, keep the toxic influence near at hand. In case. Like keeping a six pack in the fridge.

They'd been wrong. Like Hani was now. "I busted my ass for this life. I saved every penny I begged for and gave every last cent for this place. Since we opened, I've slipped up once. I let Jordan sabotage a frail relationship and used it as an easy excuse to indulge. She led me like a puppy on a string. How can you believe I'd let her do it again?" His arms fell to his sides, and he looked at each one of them in turn. "How can you have so little faith in me, guys? I work harder than anyone to keep us going. Hell, I've lied to my client."

A few heads turned, and Boston remembered they weren't alone. He lowered his voice. "I turned into a common thief to help someone who needed it. I've taken every advantage of my situation, risked the very income that allows us to operate to help one guy. You're right, though, Hani. If I go down, you're going with me."

"Like a damn ship."

"Well, a storm's coming. Batten down the hatches, splice the main brace!" He chuckled with more humor than the joke warranted. "Unfortunately, it's too late to decide whether or not you trust the captain. But, hey, thanks for having my back. It means the damn world."

Hani closed the distance between them with a dangerous gleam in his dark eyes. "I will *always* have your back. You did this and that, but you ain't done a damn thing alone. You remember that. When Jordan wipes the floor with you because your pride won't let us help, I'll have my mop bucket ready, brother."

Boston's edged reply died in his throat.

Threatening, towering Hani and his promise to be there for Boston no matter what... What the hell could he say to such infuriating loyalty? There was beauty in knowing he could say anything and be forgiven. Maybe not trusted, but at least forgiven.

From the corner of his eye, Boston caught a glimpse of Emily happily taking Ryder's arm as they strode toward The Canopy's exit.

He deflated. He'd planned on surprising her with gyros for dinner after they changed from the hike. He'd missed his chance, and Ryder hadn't hesitated to dive in. In a way, it seemed like Jordan had already asserted herself and made his life twice as difficult as it had been two days ago.

I could say the same of Emily. He clapped Hani on the shoulder. "I'm going home. We'll talk tomorrow."

Hani sniffed. "No so fast, brother. Jordan ain't our only problem. C'mon, let's move this party to the back."

Oh, right. Because they hadn't hashed out some personal history mere moments ago for anyone paying attention to notice? Boston followed Hani down the hallway.

Hani didn't quite make it to the kitchen before he stopped, leaving Boston to skid to a halt or crash into his massive form. He put a meaty arm around Boston's shoulder. "While you been busy with Miss Emily, I've been asking questions. Quiet-like. I ain't trying to draw attention. I got my ear on something, man. And it ain't good."

"Well?"

"I hear Kale owes money. Don't know who he owes, why he owes, or what he owes. But that's a damn good reason to hide out, ain't it?"

Ryder. Boston bit the inside of his cheek. "Yeah. Especially if the collector got wind of your home address." He raised a brow and waited for Hani to catch on.

"You saying Ryder's appearance right around the time of Kale's *dis*appearance just got a lot fishier?"

"Yeah. I'm also not surprised money's involved. The one thing already promising to get my ass in trouble. Because I know what comes next, don't I? You think we should pay off Kale's debt."

Hani's expression turned horrified. "No way, man. You crazy? Kid wouldn't run from a twenty dollar debt, would he? Nah, he owes *real* money if he's hiding from it. If there's one thing we never have around here, Bos, it's real money. But maybe we can come up with some kind of…payment? Enough to buy him some time."

Hani's heart rivaled his belly in size. It'd be nice if his wallet would catch up.

Boston pinched the bridge of his nose. "Okay. Discreetly look into who Kale owes and how much. I'll see what I can find out about Ryder."

Hani's brows came together. "How you gonna learn anything about a guy who popped up out of nowhere?"

Boston didn't bother hiding his weary sigh. "I'm going to ask the woman he's dating."

* * * *

Boston gave a small shrug of concession. "I'm not saying she doesn't make me nervous."

Hani grunted. "Well, how you gonna be mad at us for being nervous, too?"

"I'm not mad, I'm… Shit, I don't know what I am. Offended, maybe."

The entryway of The Canopy afforded a small opening up to the dining hall, exactly the right size for concealing a person from view. Emily decided she better make her entrance now. If the conversation between Boston and Hani got any more personal, she'd have to retreat back to her apartment rather than announce herself. And she didn't want to because Ryder's idea of dinner last night had been sushi—more rice—and Emily had an immediate need of a plate of Hani's eggs.

Emily whisked around the corner as if she'd just entered the building. "Good morning, fellas. How *does* one offend you, Boston? I've wondered."

Her sudden emergence didn't hamper his seamless comeback. "Suggest a hair product."

Actually, his hair looked sort of nice today. He had it pulled back into a low ponytail, much like how he'd worn it the day they met. Even in the dim morning light, it had the gleaming quality of blond only the sun had the power to bestow.

She joined the two men at one of the long picnic tables and pointed a finger at Boston, pistol-style. "Did Hani recommend conditioner? Because I was going to but didn't want to seem forward."

Boston appeared to fight the grin before it stole over his mouth. "Somehow, I don't think seeming forward is an issue for you."

"Actually, we were talking about Jordan."

The hard set to Hani's jaw caught Emily off guard. She'd never seen him so serious. Almost angry.

Well, except last night when he'd been in a deep hush-hush conference with Boston, Akela, and Thompson. Their little group huddle had practically hummed with tension, and she'd jumped on Ryder's offer to take her to dinner. She needed to spend time with him, anyway, if she was ever going to sort out his motives.

She slowly started to rise from the table. "I'll go get myself some breakfast and—"

Hani's dark gaze landed on her. "Nah, you should stay, Emily. Boston's ex-wife has some nasty habits. One of them is showing up out of the blue and messing his life up every time he has it together."

Boston's pale blue eyes lit up like the sun hitting the surface of a pool. "What the hell is your problem, Hani? Emily—"

"Is already involved, brother." Hani sat back, sniffed, and readjusted the long braid lying over his shoulder. "You'd do better warning her about Jordan instead of pretending they ain't coming face to face at some point. Because you know what Jordan's gonna think." He grumbled unintelligibly and started to stand. "You know what, Bos? Ain't my job to sit here and be your damn conscience. I got breakfast to cook. Place'll fill up in another hour."

Emily's stomach grumbled. She had to escape somehow. She'd counted on the two of them moving on to a safer subject, not bringing her into the fold. Not that she didn't already have an idea about Jordan, but it hadn't been made her business until now.

In fact, she recalled Boston's explicit advice against mentioning Jordan.

Before she came up with the perfect excuse to get away, Boston pinned her with an annoyed expression. "Ryder left early this morning. Can't tell you where he went, but I can take a message for him."

His eyes got bigger and bluer every day. What did they remind her of? Something had danced in the back of her mind for days, and it finally hit her.

Light-washed denim. Not the searing white-blue of acid-washed, or the dark blue of unwashed denim, but middle-of-the-road light denim she'd get on a pair of Levi's. No hint of green to turn them aquamarine or teal—just a pure light blue.

She refused to smile. He might ask her to explain herself. "Last I checked my sister hadn't paid Ryder a handsome fee to escort me around the island."

"Yeah, well, last I checked, I told you I had a plan for dinner last night."

Guilt swamped her, along with some mild surprise. Was he *hurt?* "You were having a heated discussion I didn't want to intrude upon."

He peered at her. "Have you noticed your speech turns oh-so-proper when you're on the defensive? When you're relaxed, you speak like a regular human. Once your back's up against a wall, you turn into a damn English major. It's the darnedest thing."

What a bright, florid mind he possessed to be so utterly observant. Yes, she was aware of the quirk. "Perhaps I expect intelligence to aid me in explaining myself. However, as noted early on in our acquaintance, big words are wasted on you." She leaned in. "But I'll get on your level, *bro*. Like, you were arguing with your friends, and I *totally* didn't want a piece of that, know what I'm saying? So, like, when Ryder asked if I wanted dinner, I was all like, *yeah*."

She had other reasons for wanting to spend time with Ryder, but Boston wouldn't approve if he cared.

Boston rolled his eyes, but an apology was coming. She saw it in the lines of his mouth. "I'm—"

She held up a palm to stop him. "Don't. I'll explain in my uppity terms if you can follow. I decided I want to help your friend, Kale. You've been wondering about Ryder." She shrugged. It seemed rather childish out loud. "He likes me. I'm in a unique position to learn more about him."

Boston froze and contemplated her through wide eyes. "You're *undercover?*"

"Something along those lines. Maybe." Leave it to Boston to make a great idea sound stupid. "So far, Ryder's been friendly but boring. He asks a lot of questions about you, like what you're doing to find Kale. Sometimes he seems convinced you know more than you're telling him. He's desperate to find his cousin, but the urgency is different than you'd expect from family. There's a lack of concern, a lack of fear."

Boston ran a hand over his face. "You're a double-agent. That's great. You know, I was going to suggest the idea myself."

"Why do you always have to be such a smartass? I want to help, and this is what I can offer." How did every conversation with Boston turn into some kind of battle? And why did she kind of enjoy it? "You and I are one misunderstanding after another. Let's try an upfront approach and maybe we can come to some kind of…"

She made a rolling motion with her hands, words bouncing around her head and refusing to stick.

Boston quirked a brow. "Understanding?"

"Accord. A permanent one. We need to 'get' each other. I'll go first." She cleared her throat. "Boston, I want to go to the beach. Waikiki Beach, specifically."

He didn't roll his eyes or seem disappointed at her request to visit such a commercialized spot despite his endeavors to avoid them. Rather, he chewed his lip and blinked at her.

She cocked her head to the side and studied him. "What's your weird frown supposed to mean? I didn't ask to swim to Maui. It's such a famous spot, I'd hate to come all this way and not at least stroll the beach. And don't you surf? What can you possibly have against swimming?"

He squirmed in his seat. Scratched his head. Checked his watch. Cleared his throat. "Sure, I surf. I guess if you want, we can hit the beach today."

All resignation, no enthusiasm.

Fine with her. He didn't have to like it. Today there'd be no long vans rides, no miscommunications, no Spam, and not so much as a single grain of rice. Besides, her muscles ached from yesterday's hike, but she didn't want to admit it to Boston. He'd think her stuck-up *and* a wimp.

"Your turn. Tell me about Jordan." As his eyes went hooded, she held up her hands in defense. "I'm not being nosy"—a small lie—"but I'd like to know what I'm dealing with. I assume Hani meant she'll suspect we're involved? If she pops up out of nowhere, how do I handle it?"

With a sigh, he yanked the elastic tie from his hair. The ends swung forward over his shoulders, and he brushed the strands back from his face. "If there's opposition, Jordan eliminates it. To her, you're a roadblock on her path and she'll do whatever to remove you, whether you're my girlfriend or my client, so it kind of doesn't matter. She'll assume we're together because you're hot, but we should still try to explain you're a client."

Emily squirmed. *He thinks I'm* hot?

She wasn't hot. She had dowdy hair, wide hips, and a pretentious sense of style. "What exactly does she want with you, anyhow?"

"She went through a bad breakup recently. She needs someone to take care of her while she licks her wounds."

"You mean someone to party with while she drinks to forget?"

"Probably, yeah."

"Okay, what can I do?"

He rested his elbows on the tabletop. "Help me stay sober, I guess. That's her in. That's how she gets to me. First, she takes something away and gives me a reason to suffer with her." His gaze slid sideways to

Emily. He blinked like coming to terms with this for the first time. "Then she offers the cure."

And down the rabbit hole they went. Astoundingly calculated.

Emily patted his shoulder. "I'm an extremely positive influence. You'll hardly be tempted in my company. I'll also remind you, should you be enticed to have a drink, of the people here at The Canopy who care about you and count on you to do the right thing." Damn, emotion really did make her wordy.

Boston covered his face with both hands. "I'm going to need a beer just from hearing you talk."

Chapter 8

Have I lost my mind? It has to be the heat.

Emily grimaced at the skimpy, pale blue string-tie bikini and went over her options.

She wanted to swim.

They were going swimming.

Maybe she should tell Boston she forgot to buy a bathing suit during her shopping excursion. They'd make a side trip to the mall, and she'd purchase one of those full-bodied contraptions with the wrap-around flouncy skirt and thick supportive shoulder straps.

She frowned at her image in the mirror.

Or a wet suit. That wouldn't be strange, would it? She'd always wanted to snorkel.

She leaned in closer to study her reflection. Her dull brown eyes seemed dimmer and more lifeless than usual next to the brilliance of the gorgeous bikini. Flat, boring, and dull, dull, dull. Like her. Brown and more brown but with none of the glowing olive tones that made it seem striking and exotic on ethnic women.

Akela might not be pretty in a conventional sense, but she had soft, luminous skin Emily envied, and her nearly black eyes were like onyx pools.

The reason for choosing a light blue bathing suit eluded her now. It washed out her fair skin. She ran a hand over the fabric. It was lovely, though, the exact shade of—

Oh, no.

Had she really picked out a bathing suit that matched Boston's eyes? What if he noticed?

Akela burst into her room without giving notice, a floppy straw hat in one hand. She stopped in the doorway. "Oh, *my*. I thought you were the conservative type, Emily."

Roxanne Smith

"I am, but I think I had this idea of trying to fit in. I'm so pale and starched, I stick out here like a donut at a farmer's market."

Akela's bright smile seemed genuine. No doubt she laughed heartily on the inside. "Forget fitting in. You're gonna stand out. Whew, girl. I wish I had me some legs like yours." She bit her lip and tilted her head to one side. "Boston's gonna have a hard time concentrating."

She brightened. "I ought to cover up then. I'll get something new at the mall. Maybe a suit a little more my speed." She glanced from her cleavage to her hip, bare except for a frail little bow of material. Shiny silver beads threaded onto the ends of the strings made a gentle tinkling noise when she moved, like a wind chime in the distance. "This isn't me. It's the wrong color, on top of everything else."

Akela shut the door with a giggle. "You aren't what you wear, girl. You look *amazing*. I didn't expect it, you know, because your other clothes are kinda plain. Anyway, I brought you some stuff."

She walked a circle around Emily and stopped to pull away the clip holding her hair in place.

Waves of untamed partially curled brown hair flopped onto Emily's shoulders.

"Hey!"

"Trust me, you don't want to swim with your hair up. The salt in the ocean water will make it stiff and crusty and create a big tangled mess. Leaving it down makes it easier to comb through. Now." She plopped the floppy hat onto Emily's head and gave her a quizzical appraisal. "You might be from California, but I take it you don't go to the beach much?"

Emily responded with a petulant sniff. "Not sure why you're bothering to phrase it like a question."

"I've been wrong before."

"Fine. Never, okay? I never go to the beach. The water is brown and gross, and there are always a million people."

Akela nodded. "Sunblock. Boston better have some in the van. If not, you make sure he stops to get some, okay? Hawaii is a lot closer to the equator than California. Even if it doesn't feel hot, you're getting tons more UV rays than you're used to on the mainland." She stood back and examined Emily from head to foot. "As for your bikini, you chose the perfect shade. You got a real eye for color. The light blue on your pale skin is almost angelic."

Emily blinked at her. *Angelic. Sure.*

Next, she held up a small red silk bag held closed by a drawstring. Emily hadn't noticed it in her hand. "Now, we're gonna pick out jewelry."

Emily crinkled her nose. "Who wears jewelry to the beach?"

"Everybody." At Emily's doubtfully raised eyebrows, Akela paused and searched the ceiling with an air of concentration. "Imagine a swimsuit as another outfit you gotta accessorize. Those little beads on the end of your ties are silver, so we'll go with that. Oh, and the white sandals you had on the other day are perfect." She handed over small, glittery silver hoop earrings the same circumference as a dime.

Not so bad. Emily hooked them through her ears.

"Last thing. Did you buy yourself a cover-up?"

Shoulders drooping, Emily pulled a wadded plastic bag from the top drawer of the dresser and removed from it the sheer white mini-dress that was supposed to act as a bathing suit cover. She handed the ball of material to Akela. "I tried it on this morning and decided I'd wear shorts and a tank top instead. This thing is almost inappropriate."

Akela sighed. "For the office, maybe, but the people where you're going will have on thong bikinis, their butt cheeks out for everyone to see." She shook out the garment, tsked at the few wrinkles, and handed it back. "Go on. Let's see."

After five minutes of adjusting the sheer jersey-style cover, Akela put an end to Emily's fussing and stood back to admire her handiwork. "You look like a model."

Emily gushed. "Oh, Akela. You're a sweet girl."

"It's the legs. I'm telling you. You have the longest legs I've ever seen. And so muscular. You work out?"

She twisted her knee to one side to study her calf. "Uh, no. I wear heels on Fridays, though. I guess they do more than make me taller, huh?"

Akela smiled like a mother sending her daughter off to prom. "Your chariot awaits. Boston's in the van."

Oh, great. She'd been playing dress-up for a half hour while he waited. She pulled Akela into a quick hug. "Thank you. I mean it, I'd be lost without you." She ran for the stairs, conscious of the fact she didn't have a beach towel.

She needn't have worried. A stack of towels were piled next to a large handwoven basket in the backseat of the van when she crawled into the passenger seat. She buckled her seat belt and hooked a thumb at the covered basket. "What's in there?"

Boston didn't answer.

A quick glance told her why not.

His mouth hung slightly open, and he stared at her like a stranger had hopped into the van and asked his opinion on the opera. At least his ogling didn't concentrate solely on her breasts.

"Yoo-hoo." She waved a hand in front of his face.

His eyes snapped back into focus. He readjusted his hands on the steering wheel and cleared his throat. "Sorry, I didn't recognize you. You, uh…I expected…"

She didn't blame him for not finishing the sentence. He'd probably expected the very alternative she'd tried to swap her bikini for—a full-bodied suit with a skirt to hide the shape of her hips and one of those long, ankle-length cover-ups.

Emily forced herself to relax. Her confidence wasn't tied up in her dress slacks and blazers. Surely a skimpy outfit didn't rob her of her self-assurance. She shuddered to think what that might say about her, to fathom dependency on her wrapper for affirmation of her worth. No, she wouldn't fall prey to that societal nonsense. She'd be damned if a few dimples in her thighs would stop her from enjoying herself.

"I'm getting into the island groove. I assure you, my bathing suit at home is nothing like this. Your expectations aren't far from the mark."

"Big, big words." He wagged a finger at her, his focus returned, and he pulled the van onto the street. "You do look amazing, though." He nonchalantly shrugged and avoided looking in her direction. "So you know."

The echo of Akela's words almost made her believe it.

Almost.

* * * *

Emily liked Waikiki Beach. Mostly, she liked how the pushy vegetation fell away to acres of pure white sand and miles upon miles of gorgeous aquamarine water beyond. Only a few palm trees sprouted up on the sandy shores once Boston guided them past Duke Kahanamoku Lagoon.

Boston walked on bare feet with his flip-flops in his hand, the other arm holding their basket of goodies, with two of the beach towels crammed inside. "Waikiki Beach stretches from here to Kuhio Beach Park, but this is the iconic spot everyone envisions." He stopped without warning, dropped his sandals, and carefully placed the basket on a mound of sand.

He settled back on his heels, thumbs hooked on the pockets of his ratty red shorts.

Yep, they were back in all their tattered glory.

He inhaled. "What is it you do for a living, anyway? Something in a boardroom with presentations and memos? All that jazz?"

Emily squinted at him from beneath the wide brim of her straw hat. "I haven't even dipped my toes in the water yet."

He shrugged, paused for a brief second, as if considering something, and promptly began removing clothing. He whipped his T-shirt with ripped sleeves over his head with a practiced motion. "Come on." He tugged Emily by the hand, pitching her toward the water so quickly she had to grasp the hat on her head to keep it from flying off.

"Wait! I—"

Boston halted at the water's lapping edge. He rested his hands low on his hips and studied her. "You gonna swim with the gear on?"

She thumbed the brim of her hat—the only thing she'd be able to remove with him gazing at her like that. With a deep breath, she yanked it off, tossed it onto the sand a few yards from where Boston's shirt lay, and gripped the hem of her cover-up. Despite common sense—the cover-up was see-through to begin with, her bathing suit clearly visible beneath— her body hummed from the intimacy of pulling it over her head while Boston watched the fabric slide up her legs, past her torso, and finally over the slope of her breasts. She laid the garment over the rounded top of her hat to keep it off the sand. "Quit staring. There are at least ten other women here wearing bikinis."

Even in the bright sunlight, the blush stood out on his tanned face. He dipped his head. "I'm sorry. I don't mean to be a creep. You, uh, look different." He winked, contrary to his plea, slid his reflective aviators over his eyes, and slowly walked into the waves.

Emily kicked off her sandals and traveled out to where the water licked her knees. She paused and, with a grin, fingered the small waves as they passed. The water was so crystal clear she saw straight to the bottom.

Boston had gone out much farther, to the point where only his shoulders were above the water, turning to watch her follow in his wake.

Emily quickly waded after him. The sunlight bouncing off the waves onto her glowing white skin probably flashed like a lighthouse beacon. Any minute, incoming ships would start redirecting their course straight for Waikiki. She waded close enough for Boston to hear her. "I used to be in software sales. I made the move to the marketing department two years ago, and now I'm an executive marketing consultant."

His face went perfectly blank.

No surprise there. Even her family didn't bother trying to understand her job. She clarified. "Something in a boardroom with presentations and memos. And jazz. Boardrooms always come pre-equipped with jazz."

"That's wonderful. If you like jazz. Do you like jazz?"

"I despise it."

"Work must be a bitch then."

Emily stuck her arms out wide for balance. The water slid over her skin, cool and clear, salty and busy. Had it been so long since she'd been to the beach, or seesawed to the ocean's rhythm? "It's not bad. My job, that is. I'm well-respected. Many women aren't, so I try not to take it for granted. I've earned it, though. I always keep my back straight. Never show weakness, never doubt my decisions once I've made them, and never *ever* compromise when I know I'm right. A man wouldn't."

The irony of excelling in what many deemed a man's world, yet at the same time unable to obtain a man, had never been lost on her. The men in her life were able to respect, but never love her.

Boston sank down until only his head bobbed above the surface. Up and down with the coming and going of the water, sometimes catching some in his mouth and spitting it up and out like a fountain.

Emily copied him, submerging everything but her face underwater, happy to have her body hidden and distorted by the constant motion of the waves.

He grinned when their feet bumped together. "Hook your ankles around mine. It'll keep us tethered to each other. You won't slip away on a current."

She did as he asked, using her arms to balance her body and keep her head above water. A bubble of peace enveloped them. The beach wasn't too crowded. Even the splashing and cries of children mere yards away weren't enough to burst their balloon of tranquility.

Until Boston frowned. A wrinkle of consternation formed on his forehead. "My history with Jordan reads like a Clementine Hazel novel."

Emily didn't know what to say. His comparison to her one of her sister's horror novels tickled her, but his sudden desire to bring up his touchy past didn't. Today was supposed to be about fun. At the same time, maybe he needed to talk about it with someone not directly involved. Someone who, unlike Hani, didn't have enough of the story to pass judgment. "What's her hold over you?"

Perhaps she should've started with a less pointed, personal question.

Boston's head snapped toward her, and his jaw turned rigid. "Not a damn thing."

Men and their pride. "Look, if you want to tell me the story, great. But don't pick and choose the pieces. If Jordan didn't have some kind of power over you, Hani wouldn't be worried."

His lips pursed.

She flicked water at him. "Since you're such a Clementine Hazel fan, I'll draw another comparison. If there's anything I've learned from my sister, it's that a story can't be told without honesty. Sometimes you have to shine a light on something ugly. Quinn doesn't gloss over the stuff she finds difficult to write or refuse to dig into what embarrasses or shames her. Without those moments, there's no glory in the triumph."

Boston grunted. "Is that a line from a movie?"

"Probably. I'm not the wordsmith of the family."

His expression was largely unreadable behind his sunglasses. She had no clue if he'd accepted her logic until he spoke. "Fine. You can have it all, Em—the good, the bad, and the *way* bad. First of all, I'm a teacher." He scratched his neck. "Well, I was a teacher at the time I met Jordan. I'd just moved from Mesa to Honolulu after taking a job at a high school, goo-goo-eyed and so green it hurts to remember. We met at a bar. If you do meet her, the first thing you'll notice is she's completely fearless. Brazen. She slipped her number into my shirt pocket when her boyfriend had his back turned." He paused and rubbed his chin.

Brazen and fearless. So far, Jordan sounded good on paper.

Boston didn't speak with reverence, though. More like sadness. "Jordan's never chill, never calm. When she is, man, you'd better take cover because it means she's thinking, and she's smart. Not book-smart. It's a very calculated intelligence. A superpower she uses to manipulate people. I've never known anyone who can read another human being so perfectly."

Emily was torn from the tale by the feel of Boston's leg moving against hers. Had he noticed? He showed no signs, but his knee bent and brought her closer. She swallowed.

He kept talking, seemingly unaware of their physical closeness. "I've told you about my parents. They're old and stuffy. I'm an only child." He shrugged. "Jordan was alien to me, like a wild thing I wanted to catch and keep in a jar with holes poked in the top. But you can't contain a wild thing. You can only hold on tight and pray you aren't left behind. I was so afraid she'd take her energy and liveliness somewhere else. I guess that's why I proposed. Trying to contain it, keep it locked up. Keep it mine. I had this idea she'd settle down with me. We'd have this grand, traditional wedding and then our lives would change."

"Tell me about your wedding." Somehow, Emily had a hard time reconciling the woman Boston described with a church ceremony.

He smiled for the first time. "She showed up at my place one day wearing a white bikini and a crown of purple flowers on her head like a tiara. We got married on the back porch with my neighbor as a witness. I think I knew then nothing would be as I had imagined." His smile fell away. "Being with Jordan is like trying to hold fairy dust in your hand. In a tornado. With missing fingers." He shook his head. "She didn't change for me, I changed for her. I started living her life. When she went to a party, I went. When she drank, I drank. When she wanted to dance, I danced."

"Not exactly a conductive lifestyle for a teacher." A knot formed in Emily's stomach.

Boston pressed his lips together and nodded. A breeze from offshore sprinkled ocean spray onto his face. The flecks of water glistened in the sun. "Jordan's built for it. I had no hope of keeping up with her. Yet, I tried and it caught up to me. A three-day weekend binge rolled over into a Tuesday morning, and I had to go to work."

Emily almost stopped him there. Because surely...

He rubbed his chin and moved the direction of his gaze to the open ocean. "I remember the day in vivid detail, despite my hangover. I'd assigned an essay over the long weekend." He snorted in wry amusement. "All I could think about was having to grade thirty papers on why Jack London never held down a steady job. I did try to call in, but we had no available subs. I didn't have a choice." A quick headshake followed the deep sigh Boston pushed through his nostrils. "I went to work."

Emily put a hand over her mouth. "You went to a school drunk."

"Wasted." He finally faced her, and she was never gladder for his reflective sunglasses. She didn't want to see his eyes. He ran a hand through loose, wet strands of hair. "Luckily, I never made it to my classroom. Another teacher spotted me stumbling through the hallway, and I was escorted off the property and invited to never return. I haven't taught since. I mean, I could. They didn't report me since I didn't actually have contact with students, but... Well, I don't know if I'm the man for the job anymore."

Again, Emily had no idea how to respond. She didn't want the story to change how she perceived him, but it did. He hadn't always been such a saint.

"Anyway, what good's a guy with no money? Jordan bounced not long after I lost my job. I sobered up, got my act together enough to work. Without Jordan, the party ended. No reason to stay up dancing alone. I had no practical experience outside of teaching, and the odd jobs I picked up didn't cut it. I hit up my retirement savings. I guess Jordan got wind I had money again because she came back. I'm such an idiot. I thought she'd missed me and came back for good. We were in love and everything was all right."

"The drinking started again?"

"As my savings decreased. To exact degrees. The money dwindled down to nothing, and Jordan cut loose again. I got my divorce, but we played this back-and-forth game for years. Her new boyfriend would dump her and she'd crawl home. I'd get a real job, she'd crawl home. Eventually, I lost the house and realized I was *homeless*—"

The way Boston said the word with such distaste struck Emily as perhaps the first time she understood him perfectly. So, how had he become what he'd become?

Boston answered her unspoken question. "That's rock bottom, right there. I figured, why try when she keeps coming back to destroy what I build. I gave up on life, basically. I decided to be like her—float through life in a cloud of blurry drunkenness. I stayed that way for years." His mouth formed a grim, flat line. "Homeless and as high as I could get without sprouting actual wings."

This time, Emily looked away. His past made her uncomfortable. Yet, it fascinated her, too. Boston seemed so...*good*. "How long did you live on the streets?"

"Five years. Give or take. Until I met Hani. His struggle is society and strict parents, not booze. He doesn't fit in anywhere, but he keeps a clear head. Together, we made a plan for The Canopy and worked together to make it our reality. In a way, I owe him my life."

Quiet descended. Emily contemplated. Boston made a show of studying a fleck floating by. They'd moved even closer, hooked by their knees now.

Emily tried to not think too hard about Boston's leg in between hers, or the hairs of his shins moving in the water and tickling her skin. "Jordan never came back?"

"She found me every once in a while at first. Then a year went by, then several. I saw her once or twice when I was panhandling with Hani, but nothing more than a wave or a nod. The last time was two years ago, right after I opened The Canopy. I'm sure you've heard the story by now."

"I understand you were seeing someone."

Boston ran a hand over his face, and the impatience of the gesture wasn't lost on Emily. He didn't want to rehash the tired tale. "Yeah. Pretty local girl. She didn't drink, so what the hell would I have told her other than I didn't either. Jordan divulged a few tidbits from my past, and *boom.*

No more girlfriend. And, hey, once your ass gets dumped, well, why not throw back a couple? Almost *too* easy to get to a guy like me."

A guy with a pocket full of excuses. Exactly as he'd introduced himself on day one.

Emily chewed her lip. How lucky would she have to be to avoid a run-in with Jordan? Normally, Emily arrived at a meeting with pre-established power. Her reputation preceded her. She had a name in her world, and people respected it. But to Jordan, Emily was no one.

Worse, an obstacle.

"I'm getting hungry." Now she'd heard the story, she'd love to put it behind them. "Didn't you say something about a Greek place around here somewhere?" She gingerly untangled her legs from his, without kneeing anything precious, and found the sand with her toes. She dug in and pushed herself toward the shore. She was waist-deep before she noticed Boston hadn't followed.

She glanced back with her hand over her eyes like a visor. "You coming?"

Sunlight glinted off his shades. One side of his mouth quirked. "I need a minute."

"Breakfast was forever ago. Don't tell me you're not starving."

He cleared his throat, and his Adam's apple bobbed. "You have some very long...very *soft*...legs, Emily. It's been a while since I've eaten, but it's been far longer since I've fulfilled other appetites, if you take my meaning."

Emily's entire body flushed as she did, indeed, take his meaning. She stammered a reply without forming a single intelligible word.

So, he *had* noticed their proximity to each other.

He grinned at her obvious discomfiture. "Didn't I tell you I'm a leg man?"

* * * *

Boston had avoided spending an entire day in the over-crowded Waikiki area since his first months in Honolulu, when he'd been afraid to branch out into the unknown. Like many transplants, it'd been his starting point. A familiar face in a sea of strangers. It'd taken him time to discover the rest of Oahu.

Usually, when a client wanted to spend time near major attractions, Boston left them to their own devices. But Emily had become too tangled in his private affairs. It didn't feel right to make her go solo. Besides, she might've invited Ryder to accompany her, and he'd probably have happily joined her, especially once he caught sight of her in that damn bikini.

Where in the hell had Emily been hiding that body?

Yeah, he'd noticed her long, toned alabaster legs, but he hadn't expected the rest of her body to keep up so well, much to his detriment. Even now, with Emily walking ahead of him, he had a hard time noticing anything beyond the shape of her curves, from the proud set of her shoulders to her rounded ass just visible through the sheer cover, offering a languid swaying tease with every step she took. Her hair had dried in rough, wild waves, and the light from the orange lamps bordering the walkway glinted off subtle pieces of jewelry in her ears.

Most impressively, her personality hadn't adjusted to match the new exterior.

Boston appreciated a woman whose confidence came from within. Emily was refreshing in a different way than Jordan had been. More real than frightening. More stable than teetering.

A grown man's idea of refreshing.

A *sober* man's.

His mouth quirked up at the thought. Emily was definitely a sober man's woman. She gave no quarter and accepted no excuses. If he'd been with someone like Emily the last time Jordan had come looking for him—

Forget it.

Boston couldn't afford to slip into old patterns of pointing his finger and laying blame on others. It hadn't been the girl's fault Jordan had succeeded. It boiled down to his insecurities, not anyone else's. He should've been honest, and Jordan wouldn't have had a weapon. At least not one he'd practically fashioned and handed over in a gift-wrapped box.

If he hadn't been wise enough to save himself, why'd he imagine Emily had the power?

She slowed to walk beside him. "This humidity is killing me."

He smiled and slid one hand into his pocket. The other held his flip-flops. The beach was no place for shoes. "Like I said before, sauerkraut."

She smoothed a hand over her feral curls. "Well, I think I'm torn between love and hate. My skin feels great, but my hair hasn't curled like this since high school."

A kinky strand curled around her neck from the nape to rest against her collarbone. Boston stopped walking and gently tugged the curl. A grin cropped up against his will.

Her eyes rounded.

He thumbed over the smooth lock. "Sorry. This curl's been driving me nuts. It's a perfect coil." He dropped the strand, and it fell perfectly back into place. He channeled his gaze on the sidewalk, to keep it from traveling over her body again, and resumed walking.

They kept to the boardwalk between the city and the beach as far as Kalakaua Avenue, where the path bumped right up against the shopping district near the statue of Duke Kahanamoku, the father of modern-day surfing, among other grand titles. Boston offered to take Emily into the more exciting streets teeming with shoppers, Gucci and Ferrari outlets, and world-class street performers.

She didn't want to leave the soothing sound of the surf. Damn if Boston's pulse didn't jump when she said it. Any woman who'd take a quiet night on the sand over the frantic ebb and flow of Kalakaua Avenue was a woman after his own heart.

When the sun settled beyond the horizon behind them, Boston turned them around and headed back toward the beach proper. "You remember the cove we passed where the banyan trees form a canopy over a sitting area? We can take a break there if your feet hurt."

She lifted her sandals, which she'd removed long ago, and beamed. "I've figured out why so many people walk around barefoot. It's a free spa treatment."

He lifted his flip-flops and they thumped their shoes together like a champagne toast. "To the sand between our toes."

"Hear, hear."

During the day, people swarmed this area. Boston had forgotten how hauntingly quiet it became at night, with the sun sinking low and the beach-goers abandoning the waves. They weren't alone—never on Waikiki. They passed other couples and families pushing strollers and dragging small children by the hand. Some folks walked closer to the shore with their feet in the water.

Ahead of them, a figure caught Boston's eye. It walked unlike the rest. Not fast enough to be a jogger and too fast to be another wandering soul.

For an instant, he tensed, imagining Jordan and her lazy yet purposeful stride coming toward them. She carried herself as though late for an important meeting, but never too rushed to put an alluring sway into her movements. He used to call her a tease on the run. At a yard away, he realized his fear had been justified.

Boston stalled and grasped Emily's hand, pulling her to a stop.

She regarded him quizzically, then followed his gaze.

Jordan stood like a regal queen glaring down on her subjects.

Emily tilted her head in a curious fashion and gave Jordan a cursory head-to-toe inspection. "You're late."

His ex-wife's narrow chin tilted up. The half-cocked smile on her perfect rose of a mouth faltered and her large emerald-green gaze carved a lazy trail over them, coming to rest at their entwined hands.

Boston fought the urge to drop Emily's hand as an old guilt instinct kicked in.

Jordan hadn't changed. The bleached tips of her long, straight dark hair still danced around her belly button where it fell over her shoulders. A skin-tight white tank-top stretched across her thin frame, intentionally revealing the neon-green bra beneath and her cut-off shorts were as short as they could get without being a skirt. The frayed denim hem caressed the deeply tanned skin of her matchstick thighs. She'd lost at least ten pounds since he'd last seen her.

Her body, on such obvious display, presented a stark contrast to Emily's filled-out form. He'd been enjoying the view without realizing just how spectacular it was, smooth and rounded in all the right places.

Boston shuffled his feet and gripped Emily's hand tighter when she once again took the lead.

"Jordan, right? We've been waiting for you, though I admit I expected a grander entrance."

It took every bit of control he had not to turn and gape at Emily. At the same time, his body relaxed. The tension eased from his stiff back. He rolled his shoulders. He had back-up. Jordan might finally meet her match with Emily.

Jordan seemed taken aback, but the affect didn't last long. She swept her hair over her shoulder to show off her long, lean neck and smiled. Boston couldn't deny her beauty even as he inwardly cringed from it.

"You must be the new girlfriend. Since Boston saw fit to warn you about me, I guess I'm wondering why you didn't listen."

Emily squinted her eyes and cocked her head the other way. "A warning would imply danger. It's more like we discussed which rehab to recommend when you popped up out of nowhere to do your little routine. You ever get tired of the same act?" Emily stopped talking and made a show of examining Jordan. "Have you eaten today, sweetie?" She snaked her arm around Boston's waist and addressed him while keeping her pitying gaze trained on Jordan. "Babe, I know you want her to stay away from The Canopy, but *look* at her. If ever anyone desperately needed a plate of rice…"

Roxanne Smith

Boston shocked himself by laughing. He draped his arm over Emily's shoulders and brought her closer.

Well, hot damn. Never had such a keen expression of confusion graced Jordan's beautiful face. This was turning out to be less of the nightmare he'd imagined and more like a dream come true.

Emily didn't stop there but took advantage of Jordan's lack of reply. "I have clothes, too. You appear to be growing out of yours." She ran a hand through her hair, and a subtle intake of breath pushed her breasts forward slightly. She chewed her lip in exaggerated concern. "Though, I'm not sure you can fill them out. Maybe after we get you back to a healthy weight."

Jordan sneered at Boston. "Where did you find this psychopath?"

Emily laughed, a genuine laugh from her belly, and nestled tight against him with a coy smile. "We found each other, silly."

He had no idea what did it—maybe seeing Jordan on the hurting end of a head game, or having the body he'd been drooling over for hours tight against him, hot skin on hot skin. Whatever the cause, Boston dipped his head and pressed his mouth to Emily's with a tenderness born of fear—he might be taking it too far.

She might snap her head back, gasp, slap him, and destroy the illusion they'd created.

But she didn't. Her palms ran up his chest and she opened her mouth for him.

He forgot they weren't alone. Emily filled his head, and he crushed her closer to his body.

Both a lifetime and an instant passed before she broke the embrace, breathless. A small smile crept over her lips. With her back to Jordan, this smile wasn't part of the game. It was for him only. He smiled back.

Jordan's snort cut through the delicate moment like a razor through flesh. She took a step closer to Emily and rested her hands on her hips. "I'm gonna go barf in the bushes here in a minute, but first let me explain something for your very real benefit, hon."

Emily turned around with the leisure of a lazy cat while keeping her body snuggled against Boston. "Oh, you've prepared a speech?"

Boston relaxed into the game. He wrapped his arms around Emily's waist from behind. "We *love* speeches."

Emily snorted in genuine amusement, which made his heart light in his chest. Winning felt damn good.

Jordan narrowed her gaze and pointed a long finger at Boston. "That man is an addict. He might've put down the bottle, but there's something important—*fundamental*, even—that you should strive to understand. You're looking at his real habit, sweetheart. I'm the drug he'll never quit." She frowned. "It's kind of sad."

Emily matched her condescending tone. "You're right. It *is* sad. Look at her, Boston. Clinging to a past when she had some modicum of power because she holds none now."

The truth of the statement struck Boston like a hammer. "Sadder still, she can't fix her own life and has to break someone else's to feel elevated."

Jordan huffed. "If you think—"

Emily groaned and pushed away from Boston. The cloying sweetness fell away, and Emily's true personality came out in full force. "Look, Jordan, I don't have a fraction of the patience I'm pretending to possess. It's so sad and pathetic, I can't even play the game anymore. Your ambush, your crazy eyes—you're like something out of a bad movie. And you look terrible. If Boston's supposed to find you irresistible and alluring, you should've done a better job of taking care of yourself. There's nothing sexy about being underweight and unhealthy. I get what you're doing, and I get you're terrified to drown alone, but this? Color me unimpressed."

She shook her head and turned her back on Jordan. "Boston, you said she was intimidating. I've had waitresses with more punch."

Boston regarded Emily with open admiration and shrugged at Jordan, who stared gape-mouthed at Emily. "She contends with Fortune 500 CEOs at her day job. I'm sorry if you thought you'd have it easy this time."

Jordan licked her lips and tried for an impression of dismissiveness, but Emily had visibly shaken her. "You don't need a shield from me, Boston. When your friend here goes back home, I'll still be here. Remember that." She stalked past them.

How did she know Emily was a tourist and not a local? Someone at The Canopy had been talking.

Boston expected Jordan to fill his head as she sauntered away—memories, regrets, fears, old haunting doubts of himself and his resolve. But he only had a mind for Emily.

She watched Jordan strut farther down the path, and Boston watched her. He'd never met anyone who didn't tremble when confronted by Jordan. She had a barbed tongue and a withering stare Boston shrunk beneath. Emily had treated her more like an annoying fly than a real threat.

He had a sudden desire to cling to Emily like a maiden in distress hiding behind the prince who would slay the beast. Hey, if the glass slipper fit.

They started on their way again in silence. Their kiss stole Boston's thoughts and left no room for anything but the small wish it'd be possible someday—that a woman as strong as Emily would ever give a weak man like him the time of day.

Chapter 9

Hani placed the plate of rice with pineapple slices and papaya chunks in front of Emily. "I can't believe you're leaving in a week, girl. You just got here."

She sighed. She'd finally gotten over the rice thing. Sort of. More like she'd accepted her fate. "I've been here forever. I can hardly remember what Cali looks like."

"A blessing if you ask me. That place is ug-*ly*."

She ignored him and bit back a smile, digging into her breakfast. She glimpsed at a man one table over, eating with a gusto she'd only ever seen at The Canopy. His hands were filthy, his scraggly beard unwashed, and his eyes red-rimmed.

Remarkable how far she'd come.

The man with rice in his beard and dirty hands popping the fresh fruit into his gapped-toothed mouth would've disgusted her mere weeks ago. Now she sat down to breakfast only feet away and tucked into her meal without a thought besides wondering if he'd be back for lunch. What would Quinn say about her *type* of person now?

Hani didn't head back to the kitchen like she expected. He sat across from her, blocking the view of the man she'd been observing. He drummed his sausage-like fingers across the scarred wood and pressed his lips together.

"Spit it out, Hani." She forked in a mouthful of rice.

"Boston ain't gonna like you having dinner with Ryder again."

"Yeah? Well, Boston's not here, is he? I've put Ryder off the last couple of times he asked because Boston doesn't trust him, but you have to understand I'm in a position to help. Besides, I've got no good reason to turn down a dinner invitation. I don't have plans."

"It ain't Boston's fault he had to pick up donations today. They're spread far and wide. It takes a long time."

"Which is exactly why he said I should entertain myself. And I will."

His dark eyes settled on her, and she knew what was coming next. She shook her head.

He frowned. "Come on, Emily! Boston's been going on for weeks about how you put the smackdown on Jordan. I wanna hear the whole story. Whatever you said to her, it worked. We ain't seen her since."

"It won't stick. She's like athlete's foot. She'll be back."

Jordan definitely hadn't abandoned her crusade to bring Boston to ruin. Emily had been waiting for her to pop up again, unexpected and meaner than ever.

What had Emily in tangles was the *why*. "Hani, can I ask you something? Boston is your best friend, and I don't want to tread on your loyalty to him."

"Pfft. He's the reason you're involved in this. Ask me anything, Miss Emily."

She pushed a clump of rice across her plate. "Why does Jordan do this to him? When she confronted us, I accused her of not wanting to drown alone, but does she truly love Boston? Is she coming back to fix it? I mean, they've been playing this game for years. He's not over her, and she can't seem to move on from him."

A wide, brown hand smoothed over Hani's chin. "I've always believed it comes down to control. Jordan's brother, Phillip, told us she's been in a relationship with some guy for the last two years. Longer than most. It takes dudes some time to figure out she's more than a hard partier, you know. She's got a real problem. They get tired of it, and they dump her. What can she do but crawl back to a guy who always gives her the power? Once she recovers, she bails. It's like refueling or something."

Emily nodded and recalled she'd mention power to Jordan as well. Turned out, she hadn't been far off the mark. "Do you think she's waiting until I leave to come back for him? My four weeks is almost up."

A guilty flash crossed Hani's face, along with a hint of anxiety.

Emily paused. "Something you want to tell me, Hani?"

He swallowed and beseechingly searched her face. "Yeah, I wanna confess on Boston's behalf. Now you're probably gonna be a little pissed off, but keep in mind his motives."

She sat back with crossed arms as he proceeded to fill her in on the appropriated Hilton funds Boston used to bail Ryder from his jail cell.

"I ain't saying it was right," Hani pressed. "I certainly disagreed with him at the time, but his heart's always in the right place."

What did Hani have to gain by giving away Boston's deceit? "Why tell me?"

"Because, Miss Emily, that's who he is. He walks around here like Mr. Don't Care, but the problem is he cares too much. He duped you because he didn't want to let me down. He didn't even remember who the hell Ryder was when I asked for help. Maybe that's the answer when it comes to Jordan." He threw his hands up and heaved himself up from his seat. "Hell, maybe I'm wrong, but I think she comes back because Boston cares, and he'll do anything for the people he cares about. It's different this time, though."

"How so?"

"You, Miss Emily."

She shook her head. "Boston stole from me, but I'm supposed to be the catalyst that breaks him free of Jordan? The math isn't adding up for me here, Hani."

He chuckled and hitched his apron higher on his rounded belly. "He didn't know you then, and he had a strong motive. But now, you see, Boston cares about you, too. Where does that leave Jordan? Nobody's saying you owe Boston a damn thing, but you might stick around a while yet. Something's gotta break the cycle."

Why does it have to me?

Emily chewed through the last pineapple slice in slow motion. How had she gone from tourist to protector, and why didn't Boston simply grow a pair and tell Jordan to get lost? "Why won't he stand up to her?"

Hani sighed. "He tries, but it's a double-whammy. It's more than his first love and the woman he married. It's also a return to other highs. Hell, it's a mecca of good feelings." He tapped his temple. "Imagine you been on a diet for ten years, right? Then Brad Pitt shows up. You *love* Brad Pitt. It ain't just him, though, because he brought along a buffet of the worst things you could eat, too. And he's smiling and taking off his shirt, waving a donut in your face." He bobbed his head. "Yeah, it's like that."

The image was astoundingly easy to relate to. "Okay, I'm starting to get it."

The conversation came to an abrupt end when Boston bounded into The Canopy.

Okay, maybe Boston didn't *bound* anywhere, but he had a definite skip in his step. He sat next to her, a wide grin on his smooth, lean face, and plucked the last chunk of papaya from her plate. "Morning."

His smile was a certifiable contagion. "Please, have my papaya. It's not my favorite or anything."

"I live to serve."

Hani cleared his throat. He looked from her to Boston and back again with an impish grin. "I'll leave you two alone. You wanna borrow my room, you know where it is, Bos." He laughed out loud and strutted toward the kitchen, sparing them a clever response.

Boston's face appeared as red as hers felt, her only consolation.

He clapped his hands together. "That wasn't awkward at all."

"Not even a little."

"I have our itinerary planned for the day. First, I'm taking you to this amazing waterfall nearby. Tonight, it's back to Kalakaua Avenue because I want to show you some of the landmarks we passed the last time we were in Waikiki. *And* I'm going to take you to a real snazzy joint for dinner that's right up your fancy-pants alley."

His speech slowed as he took in her expression. She'd never been good at hiding her emotions, especially guilt. Boston put his palms flat on the tabletop. "What is it?"

"Nothing. A waterfall sounds neat."

One eyebrow arched in question. "Neat?"

"It does, but I kind of made dinner plans. With Ryder."

Boston's whole face shuttered, like curtains drawing closed on a sunny day and casting shade. He shrugged and leaned back. "That's cool. We can hit Kalakaua some other time. I'll have you home in time for your date."

She shoved his shoulder. "Knock it off. It's not a date. We don't want him to figure out we don't trust him. Besides, he knows something he's not telling."

Ryder taking resources from the shelter and letting Boston pay his bail while he had money didn't make a lick of sense, either, and she was determined to figure it out. She toyed with the idea of mentioning the odd financial angle to Boston but didn't want to bring up the bail money. Once Boston realized she knew what he'd done with her sister's Hilton refund, he'd likely be mortified and jump into a strained apology and needless explanation.

She didn't want to make things uncomfortable when they were finally getting along. They'd finally reached some kind of unspoken agreement. She didn't grimace at his red shorts, and he didn't make jokes about her proper speech.

His pale blue eyes turned pleading as met her gaze again. "I only ask you to keep in mind we have a sound reason to doubt his intentions."

"I know. I know. You think he might turn Kale in. I get it."

It seemed like Boston might say more. His mouth opened, then clamped shut. He issued a half-sigh, half-groan utterance and gave her a halfhearted smile.

All halves. No wholes.

"Family's an odd thing. Maybe he's Kale's cousin, but they weren't close growing up. Doesn't mean he doesn't care, right?"

Speaking of caring... She put a hand over Boston's. "I want you to know, Boston, I think Jordan needs *you*. She doesn't come back to torture you. She comes back to feel good about herself. I believe she's afraid of being alone with her demons. If it's a matter of power, more of it's in your hands than you perhaps realize."

He offered her a tight-lipped smile in response. Silence spread thin between them.

Emily pulled her hand back. She'd probably do better to keep her opinions to herself. Until, of course, Boston needed her to fend off his ex-wife again. Emily would be there in her tights and cape, verbal jabs ready to fly like ninja stars, because she cared, too.

Boston's hand shot out, taking possession of hers. "Know what I miss? Your dire cynicism. And I can help you get it back. Jordan's thing is control. She gets dumped by some loser, feels powerless, and returns to someone who can't say no to her."

"Right. She needs you."

"She needs to *use* me. She needs to tear me apart. She could do it to a hundred other guys, but I make it so goddamn easy, why would she work harder than she has to? As far as I can tell, I'm the only guy too stupid to run for the hills."

"Until now."

Boston slouched. "For how long?"

Emily chewed her lip. Good question. "Was Jordan always like this?"

Boston sighed and, still slumped, put his elbow on the table and rested his chin in his hand. "Nope. At least Phillip says she was totally cool until their dad passed away around the time they started high school. She learned grieving and drinking at the same time and used one to cope with the other. I guess by the time the loss faded, the habit had formed. She was caught up in the lifestyle. I've never known her differently."

Emily frowned. Of all the things Boston could've told her about Jordan, he'd said the one thing that resonated.

She gave him a sad smile. "I lost my mom over a decade ago. Not long after I graduated college. It was sudden. Unexpected. I struggled, even though I was already an adult living on my own. I cannot fathom what it might've been like to lose her during such a confusing time."

Boston studied her, but she gave herself over to memories. Mom and Dad at her graduation. Her mother's pride when Quinn signed her first publishing contract. Emily's heart still skipped beats when she meditated too long on the loss.

"High school was a terrible, awkward time for me. If my mom hadn't been there…" She bit her lip. "Who knows how it would've changed me."

Boston's mouth curved into a doubtful smirk, and he tugged a loose curl. "Every guy in this place has a similar story, a reason he's here. It's no excuse for Jordan."

"No, of course not. But let's say I understand her a little better." Emily watched the man with the rice in his beard at the next table wipe his mouth and cast Akela a grateful nod when she came for his empty plate. "And pity her a lot more."

* * * *

"You only gotta ask her to stay, you coward. She'll do it." Hani's enthusiastic nod underlined his faith in the outcome. "I know she will."

"How can I with an ulterior motive?"

Hani rolled his eyes. "You're dense sometimes, *haole*. Having more than one reason don't make it *ulterior*. It means there're two good reasons for her to stick around."

Boston pulled his hair back and tied it into a loose ponytail at his nape. "I need money. What's the other one?"

Hani's exasperation morphed into a sly grin. "I won't spell it out for you, brother. But the issue ain't whether Emily stays or goes. What matters is can we trust her alone with Ryder? More so, can we trust *him* with her?"

Boston hadn't liked Ryder and Emily's blossoming friendship from the start, but he had no desire whatsoever to delve into the cause. "What can I do? I'm her guide, not her damn keeper. You want me to ground her to her room?"

"Please do. I'd love to see her knock you on your ass."

"My point exactly." Boston covered his face with his hands. "I need her to stay, though. Or I need to line up another job." He peeked at Hani through his fingers. "You find out anything about Kale yet? Like how much he's in for? I'd like to know precisely how far down the rabbit hole I'm trying to go."

Hani toyed with the end of his long braid. "Nothing, man. Weeks of nothing but silence ever since the first report of his debt. Either the info's not out there, or Kale somehow shut down the rumor train once he found out it was running."

Boston leaned back and crossed his arms. His back throbbed from the heavy lifting this morning—though he'd never complain out aloud about the dozens of boxes of canned food donations to Hani or anyone else—and his feet ached from the hike to the waterfall with Emily. They'd passed the day companionably enough, but he'd had a hard time being his usual jovial self, knowing she had a hot date waiting for her tonight.

At the moment, Emily was having dinner with Ryder at some ritzy restaurant, wearing a coral sundress with bright yellow flowers and a gold necklace so thin he only knew she had it on when the light hit it at the right angle to make it glitter against her pale skin.

Boston tried to not imagine them making out like randy teenagers. He failed. "Emily's interest in Ryder may be genuine. Besides, who the hell am I, anyway? Ryder's like her. At the same time, it's probably safest if we continue under the assumption he's been sent to collect from Kale instead of being a concerned family member."

Hani shook his head. "I'll give up Spam for a year if you ain't right, brother."

Boston held up his hands. "Let's not be hasty, my friend. There's always coincidence. Could be Ryder's just a really, really stuck-up douche who wants to help his cousin get his hot mess under control. But in case he's not..." A shrug finished the statement.

"Right. You got it, Bos." Hani planted his fists onto his hips. "Now, you gonna talk to Miss Emily or what?"

Boston rubbed his forehead. The day kept getting longer. "I guess I'll have to. Listen, if you'll wait up for her, I'm heading out. I need to think. She'll have already spent a month here. Oahu's only so big. If I'm going to convince her to stay, I might need to break out the big guns. Like Maui or the Big Island."

Which, coincidentally, he needed money to pull off. It always came back to the money.

Hani cocked his head toward a group of three men across the room finishing off a late dinner. "Thompson and I still got a kitchen to clean. I'll look in on her before I call it a night."

"Thanks, man." Boston stood on tired bones as Hani's huge form disappeared down the dim hallway.

He started for the door and froze mid-stride at the sight of Jordan lounging in the entryway, one hip against the wall and her arms folded over.

Emily hadn't been wrong. Jordan had returned, looking leaner and meaner than ever. And there was no Emily around to save him this time.

It'd be a lie to say Jordan didn't make an impact when the mood struck her.

Her haphazard two-toned ponytail trailed from the crown of her head to rest its bleached tips just below one barely concealed breast. Bright red lipstick glistened on her full lips, and the revealing top showcased bony shoulders and exposed ribs, at odds with the unnatural roundness of her augmented breasts.

She looked like a high-price call girl.

Funny how he used to find it appealing. Now he'd give anything to have Emily walk in wearing a sundress that hinted and teased rather than told the whole story. He was burned out on retina-searing fake jewelry, teetering heels, and shorts that didn't leave a man much to discover about a woman's backside.

He'd learned to appreciate the small golden hoops that glinted through Emily's curls on a bright day. He liked the peach tones she wore to accentuate her milky skin, the flat sandals she never once complained about hurting her feet, and the way she didn't need a scrap of material stretching across her ass to draw attention to it.

Jesus, had he discovered *class*? What the hell had Emily done to him?

He grinned, recalling Emily's concern for Jordan's slightness. "If you came for a rice plate, better hurry. Hani's packing it up."

She gave him a tight smile. "She's a marvel of hilarity, your little girlfriend. I daresay she could stand to lose a few."

Even with the obvious enhancements and model-thin body, Jordan didn't come close to enticing. Not the way the soft suppleness of Emily's fuller figure did. "I daresay you've never been more wrong. Look at you, Jordan. You're almost frail."

"You realize she's no different than the last one, don't you? Once she finds out who you are, you think she'll stick around? C'mon, Bos. We know her type. She's like Phillip and Hani's parents. Too good for us. Isn't that why she's having dinner with the tall, dark, handsome guy? He looks like he knows his way around...."

His brow quirked.

"The stock market, among other places." Jordan blinked innocently.

Of course she'd fly an arrow directly into his weak spot.

"Emily is different. She's not too good for anyone. Except, maybe you. You, I don't think she'd put up with."

Jordan's large green eyes widened. They seemed deeper in color with a line of black drawn across the edge of her eyelids. "Oh, and you're elevated or something? You drive around in your crappy old van, pandering to the moneyed set and believe you're part of the club because one of them followed you home?" She snorted. "Boston, please. Imagine what will happen if it does continue with Emily. Imagine her family when she introduces you. A drunk homeless dude?"

He gritted his teeth. "I'm neither of those things."

"Not now, maybe."

"Not for a long time."

She took a few strides toward him, swaying her pointed hips with each deliberate step. "I need two minutes of one-on-one time with Emily and it's over." She paused and assumed an exaggerated expression of deep thought. "Then again, maybe you're playing her. I overheard Hani. You need money, Boston, but I'd never label you the type to play with a girl's affections to get it."

Let Jordan believe his feelings for Emily were genuine? Or let her assume his interest in Emily boiled down to dollars?

Jordan laughed. A compelling thing, that laugh. It hadn't changed. Merriment lightened her deep green eyes, and her chin slid lazily to her chest, while she peered up at him through a thick fan of makeup-coated lashes. "Babe. You're Honolulu's very own Robin Hood. Hani's Little John. Poor Emily. It'll break her rigid little heart when she finds out."

Boston almost laughed right back. Emily had done a damn good job of acting if Jordan believed that. "She's not the type to scare easily, Jordan. She's not impressed or intimidated by a strung-out bean pole with an attitude."

Jordan's jaw clenched. She hadn't liked that. "I don't need to scare her, only remind her of your differences. Besides, you're the one I'm worried about. Emily may not be afraid of me, but you are."

A spark of anger sizzled in his chest. She probably sensed his fear, and it pissed him off.

"Screw you, Jordan. You don't scare me. You embarrass me. You're a walking reminder of everything I've busted my ass to leave behind." He brushed past her and outside into the moist nighttime air. A storm gathered in the north. The palms overhead whipped in the wind, and humidity clung to his body like a wet rag.

Jordan followed, like a dog with a damn bone, trailing behind him with a steady stream of bullshit spouting from her mouth.

Boston let the wind blot her out as he trekked toward his studio apartment three blocks over. The second floor of an old two-story Victorian, not much different than the place Emily rented, had a private entrance via a rickety outdoor staircase, creaky and narrow, adjacent to the main house. The family who lived below rented it to him for next to nothing because of his efforts to better the community.

Yet another thing he stood to lose by falling into Jordan's poisonous grasp again.

He fished his house key from his pocket, which gave Jordan time to catch up. At least she'd finally shut up. The sharp angle of the roof of the house left little usable space in the upper floor, but Boston managed with a few shabby pieces of hand-me-down furniture and scant belongings.

The sudden quiet when Jordan closed the front door against the howling storm made him uneasy. He didn't doubt his ability to withstand Jordan on a physical level, but a drink was starting to sound damn good.

"We've got nothing left to talk about, Jordan. You should leave. I'm not interested in anything my drunk ex-wife has to say."

It hit him the moment the words left his mouth.

She stood by the door, silent and blinking, giving nothing away.

He squinted at her. "You're sober. You were sober at the beach, too." *This changes everything. Doesn't it?*

Her mouth stretched into a humorless smirk. "A million and one metaphors for sobriety, but comparing myself to a judge or a monk seems wrong on so many levels."

Emily's voice echoed in his mind. The sudden clarity stunned him. "You need me. Emily's right."

Jordan snorted and fingered the open blinds as if to look outside. "No, honey, I'm—"

"Desperate? Scared of drowning alone like Emily said? Let me guess, your last boy toy finally had enough of the nonstop partying? I can't blame the guy. Apparently, I'm the only idiot on this island stupid enough to *ask* for it. To *want* it, to fall apart without it." He came toe-to-toe with her, close enough for her to read him and see he meant every word. "I'm not going down with you this time."

Jordan's arms had dropped to her sides. The mask fell away. Her turned-down mouth, hooded eyes, and slouched shoulders weren't affectations. "My boyfriend left me because I *quit* drinking, actually, but thanks for asking." She hugged herself and turned her back to him.

She faced the window, but Boston doubted she saw anything on the other side. "What's going on, Jordan? Why are you here?"

"Gee, I thought your Emily had me figured out." She sighed and started over. "I'm a wreck. I can't eat. I'm not sleeping. I always loved being younger than you. I turned thirty-five a few weeks ago, but I look like the one turning forty this year, don't I? I don't recognize my face in the mirror. When Lucas and I—" She swallowed and began again. "When Lucas dumped me, I came close to giving in. I'd have him back as easy as that. Then, out of nowhere, I remembered you, Boston. It's been a couple years, but I carry around the guilt when I'm sober enough to acknowledge it. You were doing well, you'd moved on, and I was insanely jealous. How dare you sober up and meet a nice girl? So, I crushed you." She either grew brave enough to face him or wanted to witness his reaction, because she turned from the window to look at him.

If she expected pity, she wouldn't find it. "Hell yeah, you did. If it weren't for Hani, God, I'd have lost everything. Not for the first time, either."

"At least you had someone. Who do I have? Phillip? He's hardly going to be any kind of help. My mom is getting old, Boston. Too old to deal with me."

She had a point. "Trying" wasn't in Phillip's vocabulary. Either Jordan wanted it or she didn't, and he'd write her off with one slip.

"Jordan, I can't help you. I'm barely standing. How can you ask me to carry you? I'm the weak one. If you cave, I won't stop you. I'll be right beside you, holding the damn chaser. That's how we work. It's how we've always worked."

Her bony hands grasped his bare arms in a desperate plea. "I won't cave. I'm sorry for what I did to you, for what you nearly lost because of it. But you *didn't*. Don't you get it? If you're the weak one and you made it, then so can I. Emily is an outsider looking in. She has no clue what this is like. How this feels."

"She understands you better than you think, Jordan."

Jordan's gaze hardened. "She doesn't know shit."

"Her mom died suddenly. Much like your dad. She knows loss."

Her perfect rosebud mouth pursed. "She relates to the cause but has no concept of the effect. Forget her, okay? You and me, Boston. Show me how. Show me what keeps you steadfast day in and day out."

Boston took a step back, and Jordan faltered. He didn't lift a hand to steady her. "You want to know how I do it, Jordan? It's pretty simple." He stalked to the door, gripped the knob, and pulled it open. The storm hadn't calmed, and a chill wind swept into the apartment. "I stay the hell away from you."

Chapter 10

Emily lifted her hand to knock, but before her knuckles came down on the door, it flew open, and her loose fist froze midair. Boston looked like a stone statue, his face a foreboding mask of dislike. For an instant, she took it was meant for her and instinctively stiffened.

Jordan stomped through the open door, and Emily relaxed.

A part of her wished she'd have waited to confront Boston at The Canopy in the morning rather than tracking him down at his home, but then she'd have missed this not-so-happy reunion. Boston had been alone with Jordan and hadn't succumbed to tipping back drinks or—so far as it seemed—falling into bed with her. The war had only begun, but every battle counted.

Emily didn't shy away from the confrontation already in play. She glanced from Boston to Jordan and back again. "Shall I wait outside?"

Much to her surprise, Boston's eyes lit up when they landed on her, a slight smile replacing the scowl. "Don't be ridiculous. Come in out of the storm. Jordan was just leaving."

Emily stepped around Jordan, and Boston stared at his departing guest. "I'm sure you've got better places to be."

She appeared to struggle with her composure for a moment as she shifted from one foot to the other and blinked rapidly while looking at neither of them.

Whatever Emily had ventured into, it had been emotional for Jordan. Probably for Boston, too, but he hid it better.

"Yeah, there's a party somewhere suffering from my absence." Her emerald eyes might've been plucked from a porcelain doll. They glossed over with unshed tears and something meaningful meant for Boston. "Until we meet again." One eyebrow arched, and she left, closing the door against the weather.

Boston glared at the door and muttered something unintelligible under his breath.

Emily put a hand on his shoulder. "You okay?"

He turned on her. "Do you mean am I drunk?"

Her eyebrows snapped together. She dropped her hand. "That's not what I asked."

With his back to her, he breathed a deep inhale followed by a loud exhale. "I'm sorry. It's not easy having Jordan crop up out of the damn blue. But it's different this time. The game has changed."

"How do you mean?" *Please don't say me. Hani's wrong. I can't save you, Boston.*

He turned around, and the strain on his usually relaxed, nonchalant face spurred a rush of concern for him. He rubbed the nape of his neck. "She's sober. I didn't notice when we ran into her at the beach. That last comment of hers about heading to a party was a dig at my conscience. She wants help, Emily, but hell, I can barely help myself. I don't want to be the reason she goes back to it, but I don't want to risk what I've managed to pull together." He shook his head and brushed past her to plop down onto a patchwork love seat. "What do you care, anyway? You're leaving this mess behind in a matter of days."

Emily joined him on the love seat. Besides the single bed in the far corner of the open room, separated by a tacked-up sheet, it was the only place to sit. "Don't be an ass when we're finally getting along. I'm on your side."

He cast her a sideways glance. His normally light blue eyes were dark with strain and stress. "Do I leave her to drown or try to save her, knowing there's a damn good chance I'll drown, too?"

Emily sat back against a flat cushion and gathered her hands in her lap. The truth? Boston might not want the truth. "It's a tightrope situation. One slip, any loss of balance whatsoever, and you're both going down."

He grunted. "Insightful."

"Forget it." Emily stood. If he wanted her to speak her mind, fine. "I didn't come here to give advice regarding a situation in which I have nothing at stake. It's not my future on the line. You want the truth about me, Boston? I don't have the patience or compassion necessary for someone like Jordan. I hold a hell of a grudge and have never been one for tolerating excuses. Either she wants it or she doesn't. That's something you should know about me. I don't make mistakes twice. And while I may understand her grief, I may even pity her weakness, I'd never be dumb enough to put my life in her hands. Because, if she does fail, you won't be on the sidelines watching, Boston. You'll be holding her hand, and it'll be too late to let go. You can kiss everything—The Canopy, this apartment, Hani and the rest of your friends—good-bye. There you have it, my honest opinion. However, I didn't come here to share my intolerant views. I came to tell you something about Ryder."

Boston's gaze snapped to her. So *that* got his attention.

Emily clamped her jaw shut on a nasty insult. They hadn't been this way with each other since her first week on the island. She shook her head and started for the door. "It can wait until tomorrow, granted you're in a better mood. It's one thing going toe-to-toe. It's kind of fun. This, though, this is the opposite of fun."

Boston was on his feet, his hand on her arm, before she reached the door. "Damn it, Emily." He hung his head. "Don't you ever feel like everyone is the enemy?"

Yes, actually. She remembered a time when she'd felt exactly that way. "I'm not your enemy."

"You're not like me, either. You're—"

"What? Spit it out. A snob? Not poor? Let it go, Boston. Do you see what you're doing? You're treating me the way you're afraid of being treated. I'm not the problem here. *You* are."

He dropped his hold on her. "You're right. It's something Jordan said. She's already in my damn head." He sidled back to the love seat.

Emily considered him.

To her, Boston was a fighter. How difficult to come up from the dregs, to elevate himself, and then stick around to help those who grappled with the same issues he had. Most people would've run away upon obtaining the clarity of sobriety, herself included. Boston stayed. He lived on the fringes of his past and toyed with the stability of his future to make an impact in the lives of others.

Why didn't he see himself that way, instead of continuing to believe he was some kind of loser?

Emily padded over to him. This time, she sat pressed up against him and nudged him, in demand for his full attention. When she had it, she bowed her head. "I'm going to swallow my pride, which is large enough to be a choking hazard, and tell you something. I don't go around saying stuff like this, but you need to hear it from someone. Brace yourself. I'm about to shatter every illusion you have left about me."

He frowned. "You actually love rice, and you've been busting my balls for the sake of seeing me sweat?"

"You're too cool to sweat. And no, I'm truly sick of rice and look forward to returning home and banishing every last grain from my pantry. What I want to say is I respect you, Boston. Your red shorts make me cringe and your hair is against company regulations, but I've never once attempted to help people the way you do every day."

She regarded his nearly barren apartment and meager belongings.

Scarred, lumpy furniture, chipped and mismatched cups on a plank of wood serving as a shelf, no window coverings over blinds yellowed with age. "I know what my sister paid you. You'd live better than this if you didn't funnel every penny into The Canopy. This life is a choice, a completely selfless choice, and it bowls me over. For all my money and success, I've made a fraction of the impact you have on the world." She met his eyes. "I admire you."

His pale blue eyes held disbelief and a hint of caution, like she'd told a joke and he waited on the punch line. "You're serious?"

She ignored his incredulity. "Jordan reminds you of a weaker time, but I don't think you're who you used to be. I didn't know him, but he doesn't sound like you."

An eyebrow shot up. "Are you breaking up with me? Trying to convince me I'll be okay when you're gone?"

She shoved his shoulder and refused to crack a smile. "You gave Jordan the boot, which is what you should've done two years ago. I had nothing to do with it."

He grew still and the playfulness fled from the moment. "You had everything to do with it." A beat passed. He blinked. "And Hani, of course," he added quickly. "Akela and Thompson. Kale, even, if the guy ever feels safe to return."

Ryder. Emily almost jumped from her seat. "I almost forgot. I came here to tell you—"

"Tell me the truth." The sudden earnestness of Boston's gaze made her pulse skitter. "Why do you keep going out with Ryder?"

She didn't understand. They'd already had this conversation. "I told you. I want to help Kale." She paused and tapped her chin with her index finger. "It comes back full circle to what I've been saying, actually. I've never done anything useful and selfless for someone else. Not like you do." Why'd it sound so stupid saying it out loud? She smoothed her hands across her lap. "My little apartment here is a novelty. I get it. This isn't my life. Everything playing out in front me—the hunger of the people who come to you, the history between you and Jordan, Jordan and her disease—is like a television show. When I go home next week, it'll be the flip of a switch and I'm back in my nice house, driving my nice car, sleeping on silk sheets—"

"Now you're just rubbing it in."

"I'm only trying to do something real for once. I want to leave behind some evidence I existed here. I didn't passively standby. I made a difference. I *did* something. This desire is new to me. I'm not the empathetic type. Children are the only people for which I seem to have any capacity for compassion. Because kids don't have control, the adults around them do."

Boston's lip curled. "That's the dumbest thing I've ever heard. I saw you with my own eyes relate to and understand Jordan. Not enough to justify her behavior, but that's not what empathy is. Empathy is feeling another's pain. Compassion is wanting to do something about it. You empathize with Jordan. How can you say you have no capacity for it?"

Boston read her wrong and gave her far too much credit. "It's not who I am. Really. Ask Quinn, she'll tell you. Hell, ask anyone."

He cupped his chin and narrowed his eyes. "I don't buy it. You know what else? I think you like going out with Ryder because he's more like you. And less like me." He shrugged and glanced away. "It'd be weird if you *weren't* attracted to a guy you have so much in common with."

Oh, if he only knew. Emily slowly shook her head. "I spend my life, day in and day out, with men like Ryder. Yes, I'm comfortable in his company because I know exactly where I stand. But there's a catch. Nothing is free, least of all respect. There's a tradeoff when you play with the big boys."

"What could possibly be the downside?"

"You become one of them."

Boston trailed a lazy examination of her body. Even sitting, it had the effect of making her feel exposed and underdressed. Though, that could have to do with the new wardrobe she'd adopted.

"You're far from a boy."

What she *hadn't* said to Boston gripped her. Just because the men she worked with lost sight of her femininity didn't mean she liked it. She paid the steep price, but there were times she would've given anything to be seen as a woman. Blake had been her ideal vision of what a man ought to be. Clean-cut, successful, charming, and powerful. Her *equal*. Not a man she had to care for or pander to.

Yes, she usually found herself angling for guys like Ryder, to no avail.

So, what was it about Boston that snagged her attention? His ragged clothes, long hair, and tattoos should turn her off. Only, the better she got to know him, the more winning he became, despite his appearance—or because of it. She tried imagining him in a suit with short hair. The image seemed offensive.

He studied her with questions written on his face. "Most women are happy to hear they don't look like boys."

She patted his arm. "Ryder isn't my type. Maybe I don't have a type." Maybe that was why it never worked out with the kind of men she pursued. "And anyway, there's no warmth between us. Or heat."

"Hmm." Boston nodded slowly and considered her. She caught a glimpse of the scholar he'd once been. "Warmth *or* heat? There's a difference?"

"Of course." For example, Blake had offered her neither. He hadn't loved her enough to be warm. Cordial. Sweet, perhaps, when the mood struck him. But no warmth. Not for her.

As for heat... Her sex life with Blake was an unending source of humiliation. She'd never talk about it. Not to anyone.

Boston leaned closer to her. "When we kissed at the beach, warmth or heat?"

If her lips didn't answer, her body would. Her breath came shallower, and a familiar weight settled low in her belly. The effect of that stupid little kiss was her dirty little secret. She'd been waiting for Boston to torment her by bringing it up. How to explain? As much as she pretended disdain, she'd have clawed his clothes off and done something illegal right there in the sand if Jordan hadn't been present.

The attraction didn't embarrass her. The thought of how Boston might react to it, however, mortified her. He'd been more than clear on his feelings about women like her, and no amount of time on an island would make her another person, regardless of the clothes she wore. If that wasn't enough, she had Jordan on which to base a fair comparison of the type Boston felt drawn to.

She licked her lips and gave him an honest answer. "A little of both, maybe."

He nodded as though pleased. "It's curious, don't you think?"

"What?"

He settled back. "Warmth I get. I like you. We get along and have fun together. But the heat... See, you're not my type any more than I'm yours. You're so *together.* I'm attracted to women a little on the wild side. Careless women who don't wear bras and like to dance without any music. Regardless of what you say about Ryder, I've heard enough about Blake to understand you like 'em straight-laced. The slacks, and the neat hair, and—"

"Together?" she suggested.

"Yeah. The opposite of me."

Emily rolled her eyes. "You haven't heard a word I've said. How can you still see yourself as this mess of a guy? You couldn't operate The Canopy if you didn't have it *together*."

"Okay, fine. Say you're right. Do I have it together enough for, say… *you*?"

They looked at each other for a long minute. His blue gaze gave nothing away. Was he testing her? Teasing her? Trying to prove a point of some kind?

"What are you really asking me, Boston?"

He drew in a breath. "I guess I'm asking why you're attracted to me."

Emily's mouth fell open, and her skin practically caught fire. She cursed her pale flesh and tried for mild indignation. "Excuse me?"

His eyebrows rose in clear challenge, and he swept a lock of hair back from his face, where it fell across his chin when he tilted his head mockingly. "You're denying it?"

Her mouth worked like a fish on land, desperately gulping for life-giving water that wasn't there. "Some conclusion you've jumped to."

"Heat, Em." Like he was explaining himself to a halfwit. "Heat is born of attraction. There's obviously something physical between us. Warmth implies emotion, though." He paused and rubbed his cheek, something he did often. "I guess I'm trying to ask if you'd ever consider a guy like me. I mean, like, *similar* to me. Not me. Not *us*." He closed his eyes and took a deep breath. "I'll be blunt."

"Please."

He angled his body toward her, and his hands gestured wildly as he tried to explain. "If Jordan is the only kind of woman I have a chance with, I'm screwed. But you're different. And if there's heat and warmth and *stuff* between me and someone like you, it means I can aim higher. Despite my shorts, my hair, and my lifestyle. So, tell me the truth. Do I have it 'together' enough for you? Or is Blake the only type of guy you can see yourself with?"

She'd never seen him so antsy. "The answer matters to you?"

"It'll give me hope there's life beyond Jordan. I don't need someone who has the power to drag me under. I need someone tough, someone to kick my ass if I don't toe the line, someone to give me a reason to keep my head above water. I need someone—"

"Like me."

The room seemed to freeze. She noticed for the first time the rain pelting against the slanted roof over their heads and the wind howling outside the window. Suspended in time, Emily took in the words she'd dreamed of hearing Blake say to her.

Of hearing *anyone* say to her, her entire life.

Why now? Why a beach bum in Hawaii? Why a rehabbed alcoholic with more baggage than a Louis Vuitton warehouse? Then again, the things he'd said about warmth, and heat, and their odd attraction to one another were real. She supposed she could do worse than Boston.

Only, he hadn't asked about her, but someone *like* her.

She wouldn't be answering for herself. It'd be for the next woman Boston felt beneath. She wouldn't wear a bra or own a single pair of nude pantyhose. She wouldn't have a closet full of sensible pumps and modest heels. She wouldn't have a plain face with plain eyes and plain hair.

She'd act like Emily and look like Jordan.

"Yes." It came out a half-choked whisper. Emily cleared her throat and tried again. "I believe so. I mean, I like to think there'd be no comparison between us when it came to, uh, you know. Love. One would hope, anyway, right? That warmth and heat would be enough for anyone to overlook the differences on the surface."

She finally returned his gaze and did her best to not pretend his obvious deep interest in the answer had anything to do with her. "I'd try."

* * * *

Boston sipped coffee from his spot on the floor, his legs crossed at the ankles and his long hair in disarray.

"I'd have fit better on the love seat." Emily studied him over the rim of her mug.

His small, kind smile did funny things to her stomach. "We're nearly the same height. How do you figure? Besides, I'm a jerk, but I don't tell a lady to sleep on the couch." He absently scratched the side of his nose with his forefinger. "You had something to tell me about Ryder. Never did get around to asking about it. Wanna tell me now before we head back to The Canopy?"

Funny she'd forgotten to share her news, yet it had seemed of such paramount importance when she begged Boston's home address from Hani rather than waiting till the next day. And here it was, the next morning.

She puffed out her cheeks. "I'm tired of waiting for something to happen. For Ryder to tell me what he really wants with Kale, for Kale to show up and tell us why he disappeared. So, I played my hand last night. Well, sort of. I tested Ryder, and he failed."

Boston narrowed his eyes. "You tested him?"

"I've helped Quinn research a book or two. I bluffed and he showed his cards. During dinner last night, I suggested we get the authorities involved. I figured if Ryder wanted to protect his cousin from the Army, he'd be against it. If he planned on turning him over anyway, he'd have no objections."

"What was his reaction?"

"Ryder *lost* it. He became so upset by the idea I ended up leaving before dessert made it to the table. He has no desire to draw attention to Kale and, given how angry I made him with the mere suggestion of it, I'm fairly certain he's not Kale's cousin. I expected a refusal based on fear for Kale, but anger?"

Boston sighed and ran a hand through his hair only for his fingers to get caught in a tangle. "Hani and I came to the same conclusion a while ago. Kale owes someone money. We think Ryder's the collector."

Emily bit her lip. "There's something else I sort of neglected to mention. To be fair, I wanted to make the discovery on my own. Though, had I known about Kale's debt sooner"—she gave Boston a pointed glare—"I might've come clean a while ago, and we'd have figured out Ryder before now."

Boston waited. He sipped his coffee and watched her.

"Ryder has money. Like, real money. He didn't need to be bailed out, and he certainly doesn't need The Canopy to feed and shelter him. I'm sure he only let you do it so he'd have a connection to The Canopy and a handy reason to stick around in case Kale showed up. He's the one who pays for dinner when we go out. In fact, he paid my rent on the apartment so I'd stay, thus keeping you nearby. But it worked both ways. I knew if I told you about the money you'd send him away, and we'd have no way of keeping tabs or figuring out his motives."

Boston scrambled to his feet. Coffee sloshed over the rim of his mug and onto the carpet. Emily couldn't tell the new spot apart from any of the old ones on the dingy carpet. He'd tugged yesterday's gray ribbed tank top over his head by the time she'd gained her feet. "Stay if you want. I need to talk to Hani. I wish you'd have said something sooner, but you're right. I could've done the same. I was just trying to keep you... I don't know. Less involved." He grinned at her as he slipped his feet into a pair of brown cracked leather flip-flops. "Some vacation, huh?"

She wrapped both hands around her mug and shrugged. "Quinn's probably going to turn it into a book. I guess it's worth it to be immortalized."

"Tell her she's welcome to change my name."

"But it's the most interesting thing about your character."

He took it on the chin, mirth flashing in his eyes. "Finish your coffee. I'll see you at The Canopy later." He strode straight for her and, in the instant before his arms came around her, he stopped. A bewildered expression crossed his features, and he took a hurried step backward. His cool façade slipped back into place. He reached up and tugged the same loose curl he always did with a shy smile. "I guess I thought I needed a hug."

She found Mr. Don't Care's sudden awkwardness adorable. "Well, if you need one."

His baby blue gaze scoured her body, still clad in yesterday's clothes. "Nah, I'm a big boy."

He turned away and missed the heat rushing up to suffuse her face. Of *course* he didn't want a hug from her. If a stick like Jordan turned him on, Emily had to seem like a walrus by comparison.

He glanced back with a quick wave while his other hand worked to tie back his unwashed hair before disappearing through the doorway.

Emily tugged on a strand of her own hair, the same lock Boston found so interesting. At least one of them ought to start the day clean. She gathered her purse and hoped no one spotted her leaving Boston's place wearing last night's dress.

She paused at the door, unsure of whether Boston bothered locking the place. She eyeballed the apartment a final time. He didn't have anything worth climbing the stairs for.

"Don't bother."

Emily whipped around at the voice.

Today, Jordan wore a searing hot pink halter top and a silver nose ring Emily hadn't noticed before. Maybe she coped with her desire to drink by stabbing holes in various body parts. "He never locks up. Nothing to steal."

Emily ignored her first instinct to lock the door and gave Jordan the benefit of the doubt. Last night, she'd come to Boston for help, rather than trying to shove a bottle of gin down his throat.

"Thanks." She closed the door and slid past Jordan. With a hand on the splintering rail, she made her way down the steps, which she had less faith in upon seeing them in daylight.

Jordan followed behind her.

Emily had expected her to. She started toward The Canopy in perfect silence. If Jordan had something to say, she'd have to break the ice.

Jordan caught up to walk beside her. Her voice held a quiet, wistful tone when she finally spoke. "We used to laugh at how we both have locations for names."

"Contrary to what you may believe, I don't care."

Jordan ignored her and laughed as if to herself. "We'd lie in bed together and say we were going places."

If Emily and Boston were really dating, she'd probably be offended by the story. Turn on Jordan, point an angry finger in her face, and say something rude. Emily chose to keep her cool and her long stride. "Adorable. Makes me wish my name was Savannah. Or Kansas." She grimaced. "Or not."

Jordan surprised her by stopping her with a hand on her shoulder. "Hey. Can we talk for a minute?"

Emily whirled around without bothering to hide her impatience. "We're talking now. If something's on your mind, spit it out." Third time she'd had to ask people to say what was on their minds. Why did everyone have such trouble being direct?

"I mean *really* talk, Emily. Sit on a bench or something and have an actual conversation."

"Are you at least going to move past stories of your pet games with Boston?"

Jordan groaned and rolled her big green eyes. "*Gaaaah*, yes. I was messing with you." She shook her head. "Man, Boston has come a long way if he can deal with you. Seriously, I imagine you two playing doctor, but instead of a sexy nurse costume you're wearing an actual lab coat and stethoscope. Then you purse your lips and say something titillating like, 'Come here, you dirty boy. Let's talk about your overdue prostate exam.'"

Nothing—absolutely *nothing*—appealed less to Emily than a heart-to-heart with the train wreck standing in front of her. "What do you want, Jordan?"

She pointed to a brick storefront across the street. "To go to the deli and have coffee with you."

Emily didn't have much of an appetite until she realized subs didn't come with rice. "Fine." She eyed Jordan's prominent hipbones and bony shoulders on display in her skimpy outfit. "But you have to eat something."

Jordan scoffed and checked for traffic. "I'm counting on it, honey. I'll take the biggest, meatiest thing on the menu. Don't skimp on the veg. Oh, and a soda. Chips, too. They don't tell you this when you quit drinking, but your body cries out for those missing calories. I've been starving for weeks."

Emily refrained from giving her frail body another examination and held open the glass door. "I can see that."

Over six-inch hoagies, they came to a sort of unspoken agreement. Or, rather, they were too busy stuffing their faces to bother with snubs.

Emily couldn't wait for the real conversation to start. Halfway through her sandwich, she took the initiative. "Well, here we are. I do have plans later, so if you wouldn't mind getting on with it."

Jordan spoke around a wad of plain white bread, real classy like. "Sorry if I'm not eager. None of this is exactly easy to talk about. At least, not sober. It's been some time since I tried it." She swallowed and sat back with one hand on her belly.

Emily glowed with pride at the slight swell from their meal. She picked through her bag of chips for an unbroken one. "I assume this is about Boston and his past. I hate to kill your enthusiasm, but he's told me most of it. And some of yours."

Jordan paused in the act of taking another massive bite. It only lasted a second. "He tell you about his job?"

"You mean his position as a respected high school English teacher you helped him lose? Of course. C'mon, Jordan. I know your game. Scare me away with tales of what a terrible human being Boston used to be. Hurry up, though. Breakfast is almost over."

"I'm not trying to scare you." Jordan dropped her sub onto the crinkled wrapper and struggled to sit up from her slouched position. "I'm glad he was honest with you, and I'm impressed you didn't bail like the last one did. You straight-laced types can be so goddamn rigid. I have a brother like you."

"Phillip."

"Ah. Boston *has* told you quite a bit. In case he neglected to add it, Phillip is a prig who won't help me out."

Emily lifted a shoulder. Whatever pity she'd mustered for Jordan hadn't stuck around. "I'm not sympathetic, myself. Boston's moved on, which is something to be applauded. Years ago, in fact. Why should I hold his past against him?"

"Why hold it against me?"

Emily leaned toward her. "Because you're his downfall, not the booze. You said it yourself. If you cared about him and the life he's worked to rebuild, you'd walk away before you destroyed it."

Jordan's spine reasserted itself. Her emerald gaze bore into Emily's. "Boston and I have a bond. He's my drug as much as I'm his."

"That's the problem."

"No." Jordan shook her head, blond tips swinging. "No, it's the *cure*. Together and high, we're a mess. Together and sober? We've never tried. We'll be stronger. We'll make it. Our relationship will make it."

Either she was right or delusional. Emily sighed and tossed the chip bag onto her crumpled napkin. "I don't get it. Why'd you leave him, over and over, if you two have such an incredible, lasting bond? It kills him."

Jordan's stare dropped to the table. "There aren't a lot of people I talk to. Not about this." She inhaled deeply and, with sudden sympathy, put a scrawny hand on Emily's arm. "Boston cares about you. He truly does."

Emily's heart skipped a beat. Again, she kept her cool and remembered Jordan thought she and Boston were having a fling. It wouldn't do for her to act surprised to learn Boston had affection for her. She adopted a bored tone. "Oh, yeah?"

"I overheard him talking to Hani last night before I followed him home. But neither one of you are thinking about the future. When you leave, you think he'll keep turning me away? For how long? Or worse, something happens. Something much worse." Slowly, she pulled her hand back and regarded Emily, grief-stricken. "He'll do what he does when I leave."

Emily's eyebrows shot up at the absurd suggestion. "You're saying Boston will get tanked in order to cope with my heart-wrenching departure to the mainland?"

"Precisely."

Don't laugh.

Oh, but it was hard. At this point, Boston would be glad to see her backside waddle right onto a runway ramp. "Your concern is touching. Really. I'm so glad you care, Jordan. However, I believe Boston and I will enjoy our little liaison like two mature adults. We've got no misconceptions. You're confusing our affection for one another for blossoming love, but you can relax. Boston's not going to fall into a pit of despair and start slamming vodka shots because my vacation's over." She couldn't help herself. She chuckled as she gathered her trash. "I thought you had something pertinent to say. Still, it's been nice to see you put some food down. Let's call it a win-win."

Jordan drew herself up and gave Emily a disdainful sneer as she pushed her chair back and rose at the same time Emily did. "Since you're determined to stick around, you should probably know Boston gets violent when he drinks. The fights we had were volatile, Emily. If he does cave, you'd better be careful about confronting him. It won't be pretty." Her sneer turned into a taunting smile. "And another thing. The tattoo across his ribs? *A hui hou.*"

"I know the one."

"It's for me. Go ahead, ask him. Or has he already lied to you?"

Did it matter if Boston had been dishonest about the tattoo? He didn't owe her anything. At any rate, she refused to give Jordan the upper hand. "Anything else?"

Jordan's face grew mottled.

She must've really counted on throwing her off balance with her revelation of Boston's supposed violent streak, but Emily wasn't buying. Jordan's stash of weapons were running thin, so the low blow that came next didn't surprise Emily.

"Fine," she spat. "You know what I really overheard at The Canopy? He's only using you for your money, Little Miss Rich Bitch." She laughed, a nasty mocking cackle. "You think he *likes* you?"

No, Boston didn't like her. Not romantically, anyway. And Jordan... Well, Jordan was tiresome. "Five minutes ago you were trying to convince me he's in love with me." She made no attempt to hide her pity as she beheld Jordan in all her undone glory. "I knew about the money, too."

She gathered her purse and stood toe-to-toe with Boston's fuming ex-wife. Not so pretty with angry red splotches on her skin and a pinched mouth.

"Get help. Real help. I don't know what you have to gain from worming yourself into Boston's life, but I know one thing, *honey*, and that's me. You can't manipulate or intimidate me, Jordan. You rank somewhere between a misbehaving kid at a formal dinner and some jerk who double-parked in my spot at the office. And once I help Boston see you the way I do, he won't have any trouble dealing with you long after I'm gone."

Chapter 11

Boston struggled to concentrate on Hani's voice, despite how it boomed like thunder in the small kitchen. All his effort had channeled into getting some kind of mental grasp on his weird almost-hug fiasco with Emily this morning.

He leaned against the counter, with his face buried in his hands, as Hani moved about the room in his usual routine. Water in the pot, pot to the stove, rice into the water once it hit a rolling boil. "It's a good thing we put the word out Ryder's been sniffing around. No wonder Kale ain't come back."

"Yeah," Boston halfheartedly agreed. "But what else do we have?"

Besides a freak sense of sudden belonging compelling him to take Emily into his arms this morning, like the most natural thing in the world?

Hani's shoulders fell as he stirred the rice and added a stingy pinch of salt. One would think salt would be cheap in a place where it literally filled the air, but everything came at a premium on an island. "Nothing, man. We got nothing. Maybe if we had a safe zone, like a secret meeting place."

Boston stood straighter and peered at Hani. "Not a bad idea. Kale's gotta have an ear on The Canopy, right? He knows Ryder's here and it's not safe. What if we spread word of a meeting place? I'll be there to meet Kale if he shows. He ought to trust me."

"What about Emily?"

What *about* Emily? Emily, whom he couldn't hug for fear of tackling her and ripping her little sundress from her soft, pillow-y body?

Boston cleared his throat and wrested away the image. "She'll come with me. Where else would she be?"

Hani's eyebrows rose with deliberate innocence. "Perhaps keeping Ryder entertained and off the scent."

The suggestion turned Boston cold. "No way. What if he catches on? We can't put Em in harm's way."

His friend looked up from fiddling with the stove knob to give him a wicked grin. "Em? That's cute. You two make a real sweet couple. You got that opposites attract thing happening. She's calm and cool, you're off-the-grid and unpredictable."

Boston clapped Hani's shoulder. "Right. Because calm, cool women love unpredictable guys who work in soup kitchens and have no future prospects. Forget a 401K or any of that crap."

"I don't know, man. She seems to like you pretty good. You're an ass, so you should probably figure out what you're doing right before you screw it up."

"Drop it, Hani." Weary inside and out, Boston rubbed his forehead and tried to not ruminate on the long list of reasons he'd never be good enough for Emily. "She's a mainlander, anyway."

"Oh, yeah, brother. You're right. It'd be damn hard to convince her to stay in Paradise. People with 401Ks hate Paradise."

Hani's sarcasm often left something to be desired, but Boston received the message loud and clear. Unfortunately, his friend's hopes were so far-fetched, it almost hurt.

Because Emily was exactly the kind of woman he imagined he'd find happiness with. Headstrong, take-no-shit. But to meet her caliber, he'd have to return to his old life. A soup kitchen owner had nothing to offer Emily, but maybe she'd consider dating a nice high school teacher. He grimaced at the vision of himself in his old pleated khakis.

He didn't have it in him to go back, not even for a woman he fancied himself half in love with. Besides, no matter how he dressed, he'd still be a jagged lump of rock next to a polished gem. Maybe she'd pretend not to notice for a while, act like she didn't care, but eventually she'd meet another polished gem and that would be the end of it.

And quite frankly, Boston was tired of getting dumped.

He re-tied his loose ponytail and tried to focus on the more important problem at hand. "Forget Emily for a minute. We need a distraction to keep Ryder busy."

Neither of them had noticed Akela's entrance at first.

Boston startled as he caught sight of her form, fear leaping into his chest that Ryder had overheard their entire conversation. It didn't fade as he took in Akela's unusually disorderly appearance.

No flower in her hair. The sleek strands were bunched and twisted where she'd attempted a braid. Her dark eyes were wide, and her hands balled into fists which she held at her breasts like tiny shields.

Boston reached for her arm, concern creasing his brow. "Hey, you okay?"

She shook her head at the same time Hani brushed past Boston to wrap his little sister in his big, meaty arms.

"What's the matter?" Hani asked. "What happened?"

She stepped back from Hani's embrace and cast a nervous glance behind her. "It's Kale, you guys."

Boston met Hani's worried gaze over her head. With a hand on each of their shoulders, he drew them farther into the small kitchen, away from the open entrance. With the three of them crowded into the space, their mingled sweat and anxiety filled Boston's nose. "Did you find Kale?"

Akela worriedly licked her lips. "No, he came to me. He heard you're looking for him, Boston, and he says to stop."

Boston didn't give Hani a chance to respond. "Can you get a message to him?"

"I—I'm not sure. He tapped on my window at home."

"We can spread the word through the streets," Hani pointed out. "He'll get wind of it like he got wind we've been hunting for him. Hell, we had this much already planned."

"Right. We gotta keep Ryder from getting the message, too." Boston let out a puff of frustration. "We need a red herring."

Akela swallowed and eyed them each in turn. "I'll do it. I'll tell Ryder I saw Kale somewhere else in the city."

Hani snapped his fingers. "Kalihi! Ryder ain't gonna ignore two separate rumors of Kale in the same area."

Boston rubbed his hands together and dropped his voice. "In the meantime, we get the word out I'll be holed up somewhere nearby. Emily will be with me. A place not too far, but not so close to The Canopy he'll be afraid to come around."

Akela nibbled her thumbnail and tugged on her messy braid. "A crowded place where he can blend in."

"Okay. I'll find Emily, and we'll figure something out."

Where the hell was she, anyway? He expected her to not be far behind him. She must've gone home to shower and change.

Boston put a hand on each of their shoulders and looked from one to the other. "I'll call you when we've decided on a secure location. Hani, you put the word out. Wait until Ryder's on his way to Kalihi. Akela, practice your acting. Ryder has to believe you."

"Right. Got it."

Deep breath. They could pull this off. Maybe not with military precision, but how hard could it be to orchestrate some clever misdirection? He grinned at his two accomplices. "Go Team Canopy."

* * * *

Boston knocked on Emily's door, after playing a round of Twenty Questions with the shop owner downstairs.

Emily opened the door a crack and peered out. "Boston?"

"Were you expecting Chicago?"

She opened the door without returning his smile.

He slid inside and closed the door behind him. "You seem a little down."

Was it the hug thing? Maybe she wanted him to hug her, and he offended her by *not* hugging her. Did he hug her now to make up for it? What if her mood had nothing to do with the hug thing? What if she was just hungry? Or tired?

When in doubt, he employed the process of elimination. "You want to get some lunch or something?"

"Nope. I had a ham sandwich for breakfast, which I proceeded to eat alongside Jordan while we had a fascinating discussion regarding you."

Her name made the small hairs on his neck stand up. Jordan had mastered head games the way one might master chess. Emily was damn smart, but she'd never know what hit her if Jordan pulled out all the stops. "That sounds like the best time ever."

"A total blast." Emily's response held the usual underlying dry sarcasm he'd come to love.

The flat tone contradicted the cheery rose-pink summer dress she'd changed into. Strappy gold sandals completed her outfit, and he wished he had no more important plans for the day than to take her somewhere worthy of her adorable dress and the spunky ponytail high on her head.

He stepped closer and gave it a little tug. "You copying my style?"

This earned him a real smile. With raised eyebrows and a scholarly nod, she appraised his holy denim shorts and ribbed gray tank. "You *are* the height of fashion." More sarcasm.

"I wasn't exactly thinking of my appearance when I left my place this morning."

Emily moved to the dresser on the far side of the room and picked through a small collection of jewelry. She plucked gold hoops no larger than dimes and the thin chain of gold he'd come to admire from the pile. "You talked to Hani?"

Boston filled her in on the latest development and the subsequent plans. He had no control over how Kale's situation had gathered steam, and his own role of responsibility in the unfolding events. He expected Emily to show some disappointment, maybe even beg off from joining him.

Of course, he guessed wrong. Damn if he'd ever get it right when it came to Emily.

A smile spread, slow and wide. "We're meeting Kale today? You think he'll feel safe coming back if we get rid of Ryder?"

"To get rid of Ryder, we need to know what he's after. I guess *how much* he's after is the correct term."

She bit her lip. "Where do we go? Somewhere nearby but not too close. He's got to be on foot."

He'd thought of that. "Waikiki. Stick close to the beach side. There's enough foot traffic for Kale to simultaneously search for us and stay hidden. As an added bonus, we get to pretend to do the touristy stuff I've severely neglected."

The small gold hoops danced beneath her lobes as she tilted her head to look at him full on. "Tell me about your tattoo again."

Jordan's face popped into his mind. She had to be responsible for the sudden change of subject. No doubt about it. Boston refused to moan and make excuses for being caught in an untruth. A part of him recognized he didn't owe Emily an answer.

A louder part of him wanted to give her one, despite it. "*A hui hou.*"

"Until we meet again," Emily recited.

If they had time, he'd sit down and spill every drop. But his stage had a strict one-drama-at-a-time policy. "I'm not dodging you, Em. I promise. Once we're where Kale can find us, I'll answer any question you want."

She straightened. "Any question?"

"Any and every." He held out a hand for her to take. "C'mon. Akela's waiting until we're gone to enact the greatest scene of all time."

Emily grimaced as she took his hand. "You're sure she won't overplay it? Ryder has to buy it."

"She'll do great." He had to believe it.

During the short drive, Emily took many quick inhales like she wanted to say something, only to let out the breath in a slow exhale, without expelling a word.

Boston didn't push. He'd put a fifty down it had something to do with Jordan. He'd have to deal with it soon enough. Too soon, if his opinion counted.

He kept Emily occupied with window shopping and the excitement of Honolulu's most visited district until he ducked inside an ice cream parlor with outdoor seating, drawing Emily by the hand. Despite the impressive sensory input, she was unusually subdued and wouldn't come back to him until she got whatever was eating her off her chest.

With small vanilla cones in hand, they chose the most exposed table on the wide sidewalk of crowded tourists and commuters.

Boston tried not to gawk when she licked the curled top from her ice cream scoop. She stared right at him, almost *through* him, and he had to do something or he'd lose it, throw her over his shoulder, and make for the van. "I figured you for a chocolate person."

Her eyes refocused and met his. "Because everyone loves chocolate?"

He twirled a finger near his temple. "Because of your hair and eyes. Probably some subconscious thing."

She paused mid-lick. "What are you talking about?"

"The color makes me think of hot cocoa."

She searched his face, as if he'd said something truly profound. "This is going to sound insane, but that's an enormous compliment. I've always hated my eyes. My hair, too. They're the color of mud. My sister has my mom's amazing light green eyes. And Jack, you met him. Unworldly eyeballs. The kind that make you look twice." She nodded her chin toward him. "You, too. Cornflower blue is what they're called, but I don't get why. Even Blake has—"

Full stop. Boston almost laughed out loud. His ex-wife had wreaked havoc on Emily's vacation, but the mention of her ex-husband's eye color was a big no-no? "Surely we're past the whole 'let's not talk about our exes' thing."

"Beautiful eyes," she finished. "Hazel. Quinn says, 'like mint and honey.' It's a perfect description."

He settled forward. "Well, for the record, you have nice eyes, too. Very pretty."

She squinted. "Compliments won't make me forget you owe me answers."

He squinted back. "I'm offended you think I'd try. Ask me now." With an eye scanning the crowd for any sign of Kale, or Ryder, Boston braced himself.

Emily took her sweet time. In the end, what came out wasn't really a question. "You got the tattoo for Jordan."

"Yeah. But that's the great thing about tattoos. Meanings and associations change. It means whatever it means, and it's been some time since I let Jordan have that much of me. I got it for her, but I wasn't lying when I said I think of my parents." Well... If he was going to tell the truth, he ought to tell the whole truth. "Until her recent appearance, anyway." He bit into his cone and ignored the dribble of melted ice cream on his knuckles. "What about you, Em? Ever consider getting a little ink?"

"Me?" She frowned. "Of course not. What would I get? An Excel spreadsheet on my forearm? My company letterhead across my lower back?"

It came so close to Boston's first thoughts weeks ago, he choked on his attempt to cover his laugh. "Maybe a little flower or something. A good artist will make suggestions."

Emily dropped her gaze. "Jordan said you—"

She never had a chance to finish the sentence. Boston caught sight of Kale eyeing them from behind a large banyan tree across the road, on the beach side of Kalakaua Avenue. He stared from beneath the hood of a navy blue sweater zipped closed. It stood out like a bruise in the sea of bright tropically themed clothing and bared skin. A pair of oversized shades concealed most of his face but no hiding the full lips and dark skin of his heritage.

There weren't many black families in Honolulu to begin with. Maybe two percent of the population. Kale must've had a hard enough time staying under the radar without dressing like he was on his way to a bank robbery.

Boston pushed back his chair. "Kale's here." He didn't wait for Emily to follow as he dumped the remainder of his cone in a nearby bin and made for the nearest crosswalk.

She caught up in seconds and looped her arm into his. "You're supposed to keep your cool in case Ryder didn't buy Akela's story. If he's watching us, we don't want to look like we're making a beeline for anything—any*one*—specific."

She had a point. He slowed his stride. "What are you, a pro?"

"Merely a practitioner of the common senses."

"Some would say genius is uncommon sense."

"You sure you were a teacher? They should screen people before giving them access to our country's youth."

Together, they crossed when the light flashed white. When they started toward the banyan tree where Kale had been spotted, the hooded figure turned due south and started for the wide expanse of sandy beach and low waves, sand kicking up from his tennis shoes.

Emily leaned into his shoulder as they slowly strolled in Kale's direction and squinted against the midday sun. "Does he realize he's drawing attention to himself? I don't think you would've noticed him in one of those aloha shirts everyone's wearing."

"He's in analyst training."

Once they were close enough to converse, Kale smiled at him. His dark brown eyes met Boston's over the top of his shades. "Hey, man."

Boston didn't return the smile. Not knowing exactly what sort of danger Kale faced only made it more sinister. "Hey, yourself. I'd say you have at least five minutes to tell me what the hell is going on, Kale."

He turned appropriately sober. He licked his lips and ducked his chin after sparing a glance for the busy sidewalk behind them. "I wanna tell you the whole story. Where can we go?"

His Midwestern accent stretched out his vowels long and slow. He was from Missouri or Oklahoma, Boston didn't recall which.

"We stay here."

At Kale's disagreeable response, Boston clamped a hand on his thin shoulder. He'd always been a skinny kid, but his bones were like jagged peaks rising under his skin.

"I've got a guy named Ryder, who is claiming to be your cousin, off on a wild goose chase so we can have this meeting, but it won't buy us much time. Talk and let me figure out how I'm going to help."

Kale groaned and hung his head. "Man, you can't help me, Bos. I'm AWOL, you know that, right?"

"Yeah, Hani and I figured it out pretty much immediately."

"Ryder is the reason why."

Boston ran a hand through his hair, dislodging the rubber band. Strands fanned across his shoulders. "I'm a regular detective, Kale. Knew that, too. C'mon. Fill me in on the stuff I *don't* know. Like why you owe him money and how much."

Agitated, Kale put his hands on his head and growled. "Gah, man. Everything is so messed up. I had money. I could've paid."

"One thing at a time, Kale. How'd you end up in debt?"

Kale nibbled his lip, his head angled toward the ground. "You know how it is. Some of the guys party, but I ain't in that crowd. I like to gamble. It's no secret the locals don't like soldiers around here. Ryder said he wasn't from here, either. It seemed safer than owing money to the other guy."

Boston nodded his understanding. "You let Ryder buy out your debt from a local."

"Yeah. I had money coming from my trust. That's why I gambled in the first place. I've got funds. But then shit happened. My trust is from my dad. Him and my ma, they weren't never together. But when the money came in, I had to give it to her. She lost her job. House is foreclosing. I can't be there to help her." He topped talking, seemingly overcome with emotion. He swallowed and toed the sand.

Boston didn't blame him. He'd put himself in a hell of a pickle.

Once again, it boiled down to money, the one thing Boston didn't have to give. "Why'd you go AWOL?"

"I caught Ryder snooping around the base. Look, I don't know what they do to people here, but I know it ain't no game. I owe serious money to serious people, and I can't pay it back. I went into hiding and fell off the grid. I can't believe they tracked me to The Canopy."

A plan formulated in Boston's mind. A stupid idea at best. At worst, a dangerous one.

"Let's walk a minute." He left Emily's side and put an arm around Kale's slim shoulders. With a bob of his head, he indicated to Emily to give him a minute alone with the kid. He wanted to talk one-on-one but not because Kale needed a man's advice—more like Boston didn't want Emily to object to the plan.

He had to do it. Of the two of them, Kale had a real chance at a future. Hell, he was, what? Early twenties? Far too young to screw up his life. "Here's the deal, Kale. *The* plan, do you understand? I'm explaining, and you're going to do exactly as I say because there's no other way for this to turn out okay. I'm going to take on your debt from Ryder."

The sunglasses dipped low as he jerked to look at Boston. His dark brown eyes were as round as half dollars. "You can't—"

"I can. You're running on an *island*, brother. Think about it. Forget about Ryder, okay? He's my problem now. You're going directly to Schofield to turn yourself in. You tell them everything, Kale. Then you pray for leniency. It's not ideal, but it's the only shot you have at undoing any of this."

Kale issued a grieved sigh and searched Boston's face. "Ryder is a dangerous dude."

"He won't be once he gets his money. One way or another, he'll get it."

Hani was going to shit bricks.

Emily was going to berate him all the way back to The Canopy.

As for Jordan, this might be the trick to getting her to disappear once and for all. Why bother with a dead man?

* * * *

Boston's grip on the steering wheel turned whiter with each of Emily's dodges at conversation. She said nothing but gazed from the passenger side window of the van with a steely silence Boston had no defense against. He'd told her what he'd done for Kale, and her response had been no response. Total shut down.

She jumped from the van at the first opportunity and made for the jewelry shop.

Boston stopped her before she'd crossed the street. "See you later?"

Her lowered gaze met the asphalt at his feet. "I'm staying in for the night. I'll grab a plate from Hani later if I get hungry."

"I can bring one up if you like."

"No." A bloated pause, filled with something Boston couldn't understand, let alone put a name to. "It's fine. I'll see you tomorrow."

He watched her go, the short skirt of yet another little dress trying to drive him nuts with the hem flitting and dancing across the back of her thighs as she bounded across the road in a sort of half-walk, half-run to beat an oncoming car.

Boston let it pass. In truth, he was in no hurry to take on Hani in what promised to be an epic battle of wills. Hani believed in helping people when possible. But he believed even more in keeping The Canopy alive.

And Boston might've just done it in.

The dining hall practically burst at the seams with an early dinner crowd. It happened for two reasons under normal circumstances. One, the weather had turned. Monsoon season pushed the beach park panhandlers to The Canopy in droves. Given the nice blue skies outside, Boston guessed reason two—Hani had served up something besides Spam for lunch. His educated guess proved correct as he wove through the room, waving and smiling at a few of the men who took note of his presence.

Thompson sat closest to the hallway leading to the kitchen with a plate of stir-fry.

"Hot damn, someone got their hands on some peppers." Emily might be impressed if it didn't still come with a side of rice. "Thompson, do me a favor. Keep the hallway clear, will you? I need a word with Hani. It might be a loud one."

The mute nodded and scanned the crowd, simultaneously forking another mound of rice and green pepper into his mouth.

Boston patted his shoulder as he walked by. "Good man."

Hani had the kitchen working like a machine. Steam rose from several pots on back burners, and woks sizzled with the hiss and crackle of hot oil. The sweet smell of fried onion and pepper permeated the air.

His stomach growled. The ice cream cone had been a damn poor substitute for lunch. He helped himself to a plate and let Hani do his Jedi thing with the food. No chance of talking to the guy now. He'd have to wait until the rush passed.

He settled into the nook of his office desk and ate while he caught up on admin tasks he'd avoided the last week. He had a stack of messages to return, most of which were the longhand letters preferred by several of their older benefactors. Not that Boston could operate by e-mail if he wanted to. The bills, one for gas and two for light, he flung into the trash without opening.

No point. Without a sizeable donation—as in several grand—there'd be no paying the bills.

Emily had stayed the two extra weeks. The money Quinn sent had already been spent on last month's bills and the usual stock—rice, Spam, fuel for the van, various outings with Emily. None of it came free. Everything cost something. The small amount he'd held back to help Kale with his debt seemed like a sad joke. Boston pushed his half-eaten plate aside and dropped his head onto the desk. He stayed there until Hani prodded him in the ribs.

He came to with a start and rubbed his eyes.

"Hey, man." Hani poked him again. "Ain't Emily waiting for you?"

"No, she's taking the night off. Finally got tired of my lesser company."

Hani crossed his arms and leaned against the doorjamb with a sly smile. "You're wrong about her, I keep telling you. She's always watching you. Calm and cool. Not looking like she does at me or Thompson. *Watching*. She's hung up on you, and I bet the pretty little thing don't even know why." He shook his head like it was some great shame.

And he'd be right if it were true. A damn shame. Boston blinked the sleep from his eyes and sat up. "And I suppose you know why? You got some kind of ancient Hawaiian fable to explain it?"

"Nah. Intuition, my man. You're both dancing around this crush like you're gonna live forever or something. I wish one of you would pony up. The denial has to be exhausting."

"Yeah, well, we have better things to argue about than Emily's imaginary crush on a loser beach bum." His hand shot up to cut Hani's smart reply. "I'm serious. I found Kale."

A deep *V* formed in Hani's thick black eyebrows, and his compressed lips gave away his anxiety. He waited.

Boston wished for once he had good news.

One day, he'd like to walk in The Canopy and say they'd received a five-figure government grant, or some rich dude discovered their worthy cause and donated half his fortune. Or a real estate guru with a big heart had taken pity on their dilapidated home base and given them a bigger building to operate from, one not built before the 1930s.

He rubbed his cheek like he always did when things got uncomfortable. "Money, money, money, like always. Kale got into gambling, lost to a local. Ryder, being the friendly, helpful dude he is, offered to buy out the debt. Kale, being the dumb kid *he* is, decided he isn't paying anyone. Then he ended up not having the money anyway because he gave it to his mom when she lost her job."

"I guess it was too much to hope we had it wrong."

Boston sat forward and leaned his elbows on his knees. "Here's the thing, Hani. Kale's a kid. He's, what, twenty? He's on the brink of getting himself thrown in jail, which will do a lot more than destroy his military career. He's going to mess up his whole life over this. Compared to him, I'm practically a geezer. I've got no big future riding on the line. Hell, I'll be forty this year—"

Hani stood erect. He tilted his head to the side like a dog straining to hear a high-pitched whistle. His dark eyes narrowed and burrowed into Boston. "Nah," he said, slowly. "You ain't gonna say what I *think* you're gonna say, *haole*. See, because I know you'd never do anything to jeopardize The Canopy."

Nothing like menace from a giant Hawaiian to get the hairs on one's neck to do a jig, but if Boston let fear dictate his actions, he'd have never gotten sober. "You mean I'd never take on Kale's debt and urge him to turn himself in before shit got real? I damn sure would. I'll pay Ryder, okay? Somehow."

With a slow shake of his head, Hani took a step back. "I can't believe this. I said we'd try to help, but you might as well burn this place to the damn ground. We struggle every day for the things we need to fulfill our purpose, which is to give these people something to eat daily, man. You think Ryder's gonna send you a pink slip in the mail when you miss a payment like he's the damn phone company or something? He'll come after you like he hunted down Kale. Tell me, *haole*, where the hell are you gonna hide?"

Roxanne Smith

Boston came to his feet in such a rush, he hardly registered Akela entered the kitchen and came to a dead halt with a tray of dirty plates.

Disappointment stirred with anger and lack of sleep. "You'd have let him ruin his own life? Why'd we bother finding him?"

Akela set down the tray and backed out of the room. Probably for the best.

Hani pointed a meaty finger at Boston's face. "Kale has means. These people don't. *We* don't." He went back to the counter and moved Akela's stack to the sink. Then he gazed around the room like he'd never see it again.

It might be the case if Boston didn't come up with a plan for paying Ryder. "Hani, c'mon, man. We'll come up with something. We always do."

"No." He shook his head, resolute. "Bail money ain't the same as a real debt, Bos. A guy like Ryder doesn't track down an AWOL soldier— something the freakin' Army can't be bothered to do—for a couple bucks."

"I'm telling you, Hani—"

"No, Bos. I'm telling *you*. I quit." He breathed in, and his nostrils flared. "Monday I'm looking for a real job. A real, paying job. You wanna risk your future, you go right ahead. I didn't drag my ass off the streets only to be homeless again when Ryder takes this place right out from under us to satisfy Kale's debt."

The floor came out from under Boston. He gripped the desk to keep himself steady. Shock made it impossible for him get a proper breath. "Hani..."

"Thompson loves to cook. He's always bugging me to plan the menu. You ain't even got to look for my replacement." He strode past Boston.

"You're just quitting?"

He kept his back to Boston. "Nah, man. I ain't no quitter. But I ain't no captain, either. I'm a rat like the rest of them, and I can't go back to the streets. Not even for you, Bos."

Boston caught up to him as he plowed down the narrow hallway and tugged on his shoulder. "Don't do this. Don't walk away from me."

A grunt was the only acknowledgement of his efforts.

A desperate laugh escaped Boston as he scrambled after his friend. His big, stupid friend. "You won't even wait for me to fail? You're gonna walk out before the movie's over because you know how it ends, huh?"

They'd made it into the dining hall when Hani turned around. Thank God, it had cleared. Dinner was over, and their drama could play out in privacy. Hani bumped into one of the long tables as he whirled on Boston.

"You're asking me to wait until I'm homeless to look for a job? As if we don't both have personal experience with how impossible that is? I can't afford the risk." A thick finger jabbed Boston in the chest. "Neither can you."

Boston had expected anger. Hell, he'd expected Hani to be livid. Maybe hurl some shit, throw a tantrum, and stomp away with dire warnings and steam shooting from his ears in plumes. But he'd also counted on his support. If Hani didn't have his back, *no one* did. He was doomed to fail.

Why did the most important people in his life, the people he needed, always think it was okay to walk away when it suited them? To abandon him when he needed them most?

He studied Hani's face. Beads of sweat collected at his temples. "You're no different from Jordan at the end of the goddamn day. Shit gets tough, money's gone, hard times ahead." He shrugged. "You bail."

He stalked away from Hani's stunned face. The overgrown bear wasn't the only one who could turn his back.

"Boston, that ain't fair—"

Boston kept moving. "This is why people like me get drunk. Because people like you and Jordan leave us nothing else to fall back on."

He walked out of The Canopy and into a storm he hadn't known was brewing. *Gotta love Paradise.*

He turned first in the direction of Emily's apartment. He stopped abruptly upon recalling her sudden disassociation. She'd made it clear she didn't want him around. He started in the opposite direction, toward home, and stopped a second time.

He didn't want to go home.

Nothing there. No one waiting.

He let the rain pelt him. Why did humans have emotions without any good way to iron them out? He couldn't outrun his fear of the future, the hurt of Hani's decision, his anxiety over Jordan's return, or his weird mixed-up feelings about Emily.

In times like these, only one thing had ever done the trick.

Chapter 12

Emily did her best to hide her anxiety as she tossed her purse onto the dresser. She affected a careless bearing and a bored tone. "How'd you get past my landlady?"

Ryder didn't grin. Not his style. "It should offer you some measure of comfort. Wendy knows you aren't alone up here. I'm sure if you yell loud enough, she'll come running. Maybe even bring over your boyfriend from next door."

"A small measure, yeah." No harm in admitting she didn't appreciate a position of vulnerability. "I'm glad you got my text message, but you're not so great at following instructions."

He shrugged and moved away from the bed, where he'd been sitting in waiting for her. "I'm better at issuing directives than obeying them."

Her nerves danced. Knowing Ryder's true identity as an enforcer poked some holes in her armor. She had no experience with negotiation outside of her office, let alone with someone potentially dangerous and as silky-smooth as his wrinkle-free slacks and glossy black hair.

A smart man. A smart *criminal*.

I can work with smart. "You have something against meeting publicly?" The text she'd discreetly sent after Boston confessed his intention of taking on Kale's debt had suggested they meet at the outdoor mall near the Alo Moana beach park.

He gazed around the room, doing a much better job of appearing bored than she did. "I like you, Emily. We'd make great partners."

That surprised her. She kicked off her sandals, again going for relaxed and unconcerned. "You're not my type, Ryder. My job involves helping people and their businesses become successful. You, on the other hand, prey on people who've made mistakes."

He tsked and gave her a sad smile. "Prey isn't the right way to think of them. I don't put them in debt. I don't make them borrow money they can't pay back. I didn't force that young soldier to take my loan and the added interest. And I certainly have no hand in his inability to repay me. See, my specialty is handling communications."

She quirked a brow. "Communications?"

His dark eyes and lashes looked the same as ever, but she no longer dismissed the granite beneath them. The night they met, he'd reminded her of a lion. She'd been wrong and right—Ryder was neither strong nor noble, but definitely a predator.

"I'm very good at sending messages. Clear and precise."

She made a show of studying her fingernails. She had what Ryder wanted. His attempts to intimidate her grated, but she didn't want to push her luck, either. "Since you're here, I have to assume you never went to Kalihi."

"Do give Akela her dues. She did a wonderful job. I nearly fell for it. However, I've noticed Boston's distrust. He read through me, and I knew he'd try to hide it from me if he ever had contact from Kale. So, I stuck to Boston. I watched your little meeting on the beach today." His dark eyebrows came together, and he cupped his chin. "Then Kale did the most astonishing thing. He went to a nearby policeman on patrol and turned himself in. Unfortunately, getting rid of the debtor doesn't vanquish the debt. You have the misconception the money I loaned Kale came from my personal store. Like you, I answer to someone."

She smirked. "So, what? You're going after Boston for the money?"

"No, actually, though I owe him a thank you for flushing my mark down the drain. Our pal, Boston, is a hell of a guy. So noble. He's got scruples, but you know what he *doesn't* have?"

Money. Of course she knew. It was why she'd texted Ryder in the first place.

Emily sighed and dug through her suitcase for a pair of pajamas. Silk or cotton? She dropped the silk gown and folded the cotton one over her arm. "Did you know Boston duped me to get you out of jail? He used my money. Well, my sister's money."

Ryder didn't feign interest in her story. He sauntered closer to her with his hands at rest in his pants pockets. When he spoke, his voice was quiet. Quiet but intense. "You're intelligent. Most intelligent people wouldn't put themselves so blatantly in the path of trouble. I'm here because…" He paused, and though she knew it was for effect, chills still broke out over her flesh. "Well, I was here when I got your message, Emily. Waiting for you. You do the math."

She closed her eyes. It had been one hell of a day.

Jordan's spiteful words at the deli this morning hadn't given Emily a moment's rest.

You really think he likes you?

No, she didn't. He'd like someone *similar* to Emily. But not Emily. Never Emily. She'd been entertaining a tiny, niggling iota of hope because she was human, after all, but those words only grew louder and louder in her mind until they were an angry shout.

Angry and familiar.

No one ever wanted Emily.

Blake wanted Quinn. Boston wanted Jordan—he wouldn't be so terrified of losing his grip on sobriety if he didn't. A part of him believed she was worth the trouble and the pain. A part of him wanted Jordan more than he wanted clarity. A small but powerful part.

Emily scowled at Ryder. Someone to take it out on. How convenient. "I've had one hell of a long day, and your company is wearing thin. You're no more frightening than one of my office pages, deathly afraid of pissing off someone a few floors higher. You're an errand boy, and I'm the one with the goods. Drop the intimidation act or I can make your job a lot harder."

Ryder backed up slowly. He did everything slow, as if he needed time to think about each move before he made it. "Be careful, Emily. Be *very* careful with the next words you say to me."

"Yeah?" She stalked to where she'd dumped her purse on the dresser upon entering her apartment and dug around inside. "Can I assume 'Do you accept out of town checks?' works for you?"

* * * *

Emily returned to her room late. Too late for Akela to be sitting on the steps in front of the jewelry shop, with her legs crossed at the ankles and her arms gently folded in a Zen-like pose.

"It's an odd hour for yoga." She paused in front of her, blocked from the shop's front door.

Akela's eyes popped open. She didn't bother checking the wristwatch she wore as she clambered to her feet and allowed Emily access to the door. "It's an odd hour for you to be out on the town."

Indeed, the last clock she'd checked near a bank on the way home had read a few minutes past midnight. It certainly felt like midnight, the dastardly hour when everything turned to a pumpkin.

A surprise rain shower had ruined the flouncy skirt of her dress. It flattened embarrassingly against her legs and butt. She might as well have gone out in granny panties and a bra. Ryder had insisted on late night sushi in order to conduct their transaction as business associates, rather than passing a paper sack of cash between them like common criminals. She recognized it for an excuse, but half their meal had passed before she'd figured out why.

Ryder genuinely liked her. He'd taken her on a *date*, an actual date. Then again, why did it surprise her? She was doomed to get relationships wrong. She'd loved Blake, a man incapable of loving her in return, seemed to be inexplicably falling for a man fundamentally unable to abide her station in life, and a criminal had taken her out for a lovely dinner.

"I had a hot date." She ignored Akela as she unlocked the shop and went inside. Akela followed her up the stairs and into her room, where Emily kicked off her shoes and tugged the hoops from her ears. "I can visit you in the morning if you want to talk, Akela."

She didn't respond with words but a choked sniffle and a heavy breath, slowly and forcefully exhaled.

Emily forgot her wet clothes and clammy skin and came back to Akela. "Hey, it's okay. Come on. Come sit on the bed and tell me what's happened." She had no desire to spend the next hour patting Akela's back and cooing, but she didn't have it in her to turn away her only friend. Not when she'd been so kind and helpful.

Emily rubbed Akela's shoulder while she sat on the edge of the bed. It sagged beneath their combined weight.

Akela ran her hand across her nose like a child and kept her gaze low. "I sat at the top of the stairs in The Canopy the whole time Boston and Hani argued. I hate it when they do that. Everyone acts like fighting is such a childish thing, but adults are the worst."

Emily agreed wholeheartedly. "What'd they argue over?" She had a good idea, but Akela needed to get it off her chest. She left her to sniffle and went for the pajamas she'd picked out earlier, the warm cotton beckoning.

"Money. What else?" Akela sniffed again and studied her hands balled up in her lap. She looked at Emily with moist, red-rimmed eyes. "Emily, we can't let Boston do it. We can't. He'll lose The Canopy, and it's one of the only things protecting him from Jordan. Without it…"

Too tired to force a smile, Emily worked her body out of the wet, clinging garment and tried to give Akela an honest answer. "Boston is a fighter. The Canopy may rely on him, but he doesn't need The Canopy for a reason to say no to Jordan. I've witnessed firsthand what lengths Boston will go to in order to protect it."

Akela shook her head. "What if there ain't a Canopy to protect? Don't you get it?"

Emily did, all too well. Which is exactly why she'd done what she had. "Akela, I—"

"That's why he needs you."

"Okay, but the thing is, he doesn't know—"

"He does, though."

That brought Emily up short. "He does?"

"He knows but chooses not to *see*. But I do."

Emily slipped the gown over her head, then joined Akela on the bed.

The young woman turned her knees toward her and reached for Emily's hands, taking on the role of comforter as she gave Emily an encouraging nod. "I came here to give you my blessing."

"B-blessing?"

"You're the other thing, Emily." She closed her eyes and sagely nodded. "I know, I know. I got this big, stupid crush." Her eyes opened again, revealing a resolute hardness. "I'm not dumb. Boston won't ever look at me like he looks at you. And you're right. He don't need The Canopy, either. Not if he's got you."

Talk about miscommunication.

Emily pulled away from Akela. "I paid Kale's debt. That's how I meant he needed me. Financially, Akela, which is how he's needed me from the beginning. Since we became sort-of friends along the way, I try to not take offense, but I'm no more a dummy than you are."

"Oh, *great*." Akela's black eyes rolled inside their sockets. "You, too, huh? Gah, you guys are just... *Ugh*. So frustrating." She inhaled and spoke in a sharp tone new to Emily. "Boston cares about you."

Funny how everyone seemed so convinced of this, yet, the one person Emily hadn't heard it from was Boston.

"I'm glad he won't lose The Canopy," Akela went on. "I love being there and helping people. I love seeing Hani every day and seeing him happy. But it won't last. Not with Boston in charge. Not because he'll fail, not because he don't care—because he *does* care. One day he'll overextend himself like he's done helping Kale. Like he nearly did to help Ryder, even. Imagine, Emily, if you were anyone else and found out about the money he took from the Hilton? Who else would overlook what boils down to theft?"

"How do you know about the Hilton money?"

Another youthful eye roll. "The boys talk like Hani's little sister ain't got a pair of ears or something. But you hear me, Emily. Hear me good. If

Boston had tried that on the wrong person, it would've ruined everything. Boston doesn't have a 'no' button. And if Hani's serious about leaving…"

Her mind spun despite exhaustion. So much in one day. "Hani's leaving where?"

Akela sighed and her shoulders fell a little. "It don't matter. What matters is The Canopy won't always be around."

Emily stood. Maybe it was the blend of weariness and anxiety, or the strange blessing from Boston's crush, or the small fortune she'd given away to a criminal in the interest of saving a grown man from himself. Regardless, Akela needed an education.

"Akela, you're a sweetheart. You really are, but understand something. I won't always be around, either. You talk like I live here, but my home is a thousand miles away. I'm on vacation." She paced across the room. "Some vacation it's turned out to be, huh? I've spent most of my time in a soup kitchen with addicts and drunks, people for whom I have little to no sympathy. I'm the worst kind of person for this type of environment. Plus, I'm still trying to figure out how Jordan became *my* problem. She's stalked me, conned me into buying her a hoagie, and gotten me to suffer through her nasty attitude and pointless insults. And for what? For Boston to tell me I'm *like* the one, but I'm not the one? I'm kind of what he wants, but maybe in a different color. I'm the style he wants, but the size is wrong."

"So, you *do* know what I'm talking about."

The fight left Emily. She slumped back into her spot on the bed and managed a quiet response. "You've got the right idea, Akela, but the wrong person. However, I appreciate the blessing. It means a lot you'd consider letting me move in on your territory."

"It wasn't easy to do." Akela patted her hand. "But you're worthy, Emily. A little *too* worthy, if I'm honest about it." She gave Emily a sideways glance and a small smile.

"I've had my fill of honesty. It only ever gets me in trouble. In fact, you'd be doing me a huge favor if you kept my secret about paying Kale's debt to yourself for a while. I don't want Boston to spend our last week feeling indebted to me. I'll let him know when I'm ready."

Akela's head-bobbing had a decidedly sarcastic manner to it. "Sure, Emily. Because what this whole mess needs is another secret."

Nothing was ever so wise as youth.

* * * *

Emily's terse note had seared itself onto Boston's retinas.

Not feeling well. Staying in tomorrow.
-Emily

He didn't buy it. Especially given how Akela had brought it to him without hardly looking at him, then yawning and explaining how Emily had a late night.

And now Ryder had disappeared. The two were conceivably connected. Emily didn't owe him a damn thing. Not her company and not the truth about how she might feel about Ryder, despite anything and everything she might have said.

Boston gripped the van's steering wheel and fought the urge to yell at someone, *anyone.* Hell, he'd shout at the dash if he thought it'd make him feel better. He'd spent the whole day hunting Ryder. The man had vanished. None of Boston's contacts had seen him sulking around downtown, either. At least a call to Zachary at the army base had put Boston's foremost fears to rest—Kale had made it safely into military custody, however safe that might be.

If Ryder hadn't caught Kale, where was he and why wasn't he banging down The Canopy's door to collect?

Emily's poised face popped into his head. Right about now she'd drop some smarty-pants logic to make him feel better, and he'd argue against it for the sport. He had more urgent concerns than Emily's sudden disassociation, but it bothered him.

He didn't have the words to fix it, though.

Please hang out with me. I miss you.

Sorry I've ruined the only vacation you've had in three years.

I think I love you.

He glanced at the dashboard clock's dim green glow. Already after six. An entire day gone without seeing neither hide nor hair of Emily. Or Ryder. Boston put the coincidence away for later rumination. He pulled into his spot across the street from The Canopy and got out of the van. His line of vision instantly went to the upstairs window of the jewelry store. Too much to hope she'd be daydreaming out the window, see him, smile, and wave.

To hell with it. He crossed the street but didn't head for The Canopy.

Wendy greeted him with a small smile.

"Hi, Wendy. I'm just headed up to visit with Emily."

The woman let out an un-amused puff of air. "If my shop got half as much traffic as my tenant does…" She let the sentiment trail off as though the possibilities were too numerous to name.

Boston tipped his head and bounded up the steps. He knocked. No answer.

Wendy came bustling to the foot of the narrow staircase. Her palm smacked against her forehead. "I'm so sorry, Boston. She stepped out a little while ago. I was doing the books and hardly noticed, but now I recall."

"No biggie." He thanked her and left. Taking the time into account, his shoulders relaxed. Emily would be next door getting a plate from Hani. Of course.

A moment later, he stepped into the busy kitchen of The Canopy. Hani and Akela bustled around in an efficient harmony, marking the occasional bump against one another with a soft curse under their collective breath. Man, this place needed a bigger kitchen.

He glanced at Hani.

Or a smaller chef.

"You guys seen Emily today?"

Hani ignored him like he had since their argument last night, but Akela glanced up from piling rice onto a plate with a big metal spoon. "She came in late this afternoon. Eyes puffy. Told you, Bos, she didn't get no sleep last night. Then she left and, before you ask, she didn't say where." She handed the plate of plain rice to Hani.

He topped it with a healthy serving of vegetables and what might've been chicken.

"The weather," Akela said by way of explanation. "Storm's been bringing in more than usual. They're having a hard time out there."

Like it wasn't hard all the time. Boston understood, though. Difficult to sit on the corner and beg for change in a downpour. Some did, and some sought refuge instead.

He chewed his lip. Where would Emily go?

He left the business of feeding people to Hani and Akela and worked his way through the maze of folks in the dining hall to exit The Canopy. The silence outside was stifling compared to the crowd inside. Darkening clouds off to the east appeared to be considering Oahu for a little evening fun, which meant the dining hall might do more than offer a dry place to eat, but one to sleep for as many as they were legally able to capacitate. He almost went back inside.

Instead, he turned toward home. Boston paused on the landing outside his front door and grasped the knob to hold it steady while he inserted the key, only to find it turned easily in his hand.

Strange. He stepped inside and froze at Emily standing in the middle of the room. Not alone. Had it been only Emily, he'd have smiled. Hell, he'd have probably gone for that hug because he'd been stupid not to before.

But it was Emily and, inexplicably, a half-empty bottle of whiskey in her hand.

Indignation hit him hard and fast. "What in the hell are you doing with that?" He closed the door behind him and didn't dare get any closer. She might as well be waving a handgun.

Her large brown gaze fixed onto his.

She continued to hold the bottle aloft. "I suppose you should tell me." The words came out flat and struck him worse than if she'd sounded suspicious or angry. She looked at him, but her gaze kept traveling back to the bottle.

"I'd have to know first, wouldn't I?" He swallowed. Why the hell was *he* nervous?

She gave it a slight shake. The liquid sloshed inside the glass. "I found it. Right here, wedged in between the couch cushions."

She could've said the ocean had been swallowed by a giant octopus and Mars had descended from the heavens to high-five Earth and he'd have been less stunned.

"That's not—I haven't... Are you out of your *mind?* I don't even drink—haven't drank." He sputtered and stammered and knew it made him seem guilty. "Emily, please. That's not mine."

"Well, I certainly didn't bring it here. I drink beer. Don't do whiskey." She laughed, a small snort as she studied the bottle. "Let alone half a pint."

Boston clamped his teeth together to keep them from grinding. Of all the low things she could accuse him of this ranked damn near the top. "You believe I'd do it?"

She shook the bottle. "It's called evidence."

He dragged his hands through his loose hair and stomped past her. "Screw you, Emily. I didn't even stay here last night. Ask the boys at The Canopy. I spent the night there, waiting for Ryder to show."

"Akela said you argued with Hani and disappeared."

"You checking up on me? I came back late and slept in Kale's bed because I assumed Ryder would return and I wanted to be waiting when he did." Slowly, he faced her. "I haven't been able to find him, and I'm not the only person Akela likes to talk about. I heard you had a late night yourself. Could be Ryder found another bed to sleep in."

Her shoulders, bare from the strapless dress she wore, squared defensively. Her words were strictly offensive, though. She hadn't taken the bait. "Who said this bottle's from last night? Jordan was here the night I showed up, and maybe I took in the scene wrong. Maybe you didn't turn her offer down after all."

Even last night, as pissed off as he'd been at Hani, his vision hadn't gone red. But it damn sure did now. The pieces came together like a twisted puzzle.

An unlocked door.

A spurned ex-wife.

Somehow, Jordan was responsible for this. He'd never prove it, but he shouldn't have to. Not to anyone who mattered.

He came face-to-face with Emily and snatched the bottle from her hands. With every ounce of indignant anger burning inside him, he hurled it against the far wall. It shattered into a thousand fragments. Droplets of liquor flew into the air and landed like sprinkling rain on his arms and Emily's shoulders, but most of the liquid soaked into the carpet beneath the remnants of the smashed bottle.

"That's how much I care about your goddamn whiskey."

Emily had a hand over her mouth, and she stared at him with huge eyes. She took a step back.

He took one forward to match it. "You want to believe that's who I am after I've worked so hard to leave it behind, that's fine. But who said it matters what you think? How much is your snooty opinion worth to a guy like me? You think I *care?*"

Despite his anger, the lying killed him. He did care. The unfairness of everything burned him like fire—Jordan's assault, Hani's abandonment, and Emily's doubt.

He didn't realize until now what it'd meant for her to call him a fighter. She had claimed to believe in him. It meant something different when Emily said it because she wasn't one of the people sitting on his shoulders, relying on him. She respected him, and it had given him a measure of pride he'd lacked ever since losing his place in the classroom.

It pissed him off to care.

He glared at Emily. "Jordan had a hand in this. I don't know how, but she planted the whiskey. Maybe it's some test of your trust." A dry laugh escaped. "Man, did she know exactly how you'd react. It's a thing of beauty, that level of manipulation. The usual scare tactics didn't work on you, so what could she do? Plant a damn bomb, that's what."

Emily's hand fell away from her mouth. She didn't look horrified anymore, but strain pulsed in the veins on her neck. "Jordan snuck into your apartment and put a half-empty bottle of whiskey in your couch so this would happen? How could she know when I'd be here? What if you found it first?"

Boston rubbed his forehead. It sounded lame when she said it out loud, but nothing else made sense. If only Emily knew Jordan the way he did. "Ask her. Or, hell, don't if you've made up your mind."

"I-I don't know." Her voice grew quieter. "There's other stuff."

He nodded. Nothing surprised him now. "Stuff that makes you wonder about me?"

She nodded. "A little. Yeah."

"You gonna share?"

She'd been small there for a minute. He'd acted like an insane person, and Emily had shrunk beneath it.

Now, her back straightened, and she came to herself as if suddenly recalling she wasn't the type to shrink. "Forget it. But at least we've discovered one thing we have in common."

"What's that?"

"I don't care, either."

Boston gritted his teeth. He wished she had the stones to yell it and scream it in his face like a mad woman, like Jordan would have. But not Emily, Miss Poised and Proper. Oh, no. She merely *said* it, flat and without a trace of inflection or emotion.

She stopped when she reached the door and pulled it open to let herself out. "By the way, your deduction is correct. I was with Ryder last night."

He gaped at her. Everything inside seemed to collapse until the air wasn't filling his lungs completely.

With her next words, she both saved and condemned him. "I paid Kale's debt. You'll never see Ryder again, and The Canopy is safe." She searched his face while hers remained passive. "Until you find someone else to rescue, anyway."

Chapter 13

"Where is she?"

Ginger Stacey hadn't aged a minute. The seamstress looked up from her sewing through a thick pair of glasses and squinted. "Boston?" She slowly removed the spectacles.

"Hi, Ginger. I'm looking for Jordan. I need to speak with her." He'd been sitting outside her mother's small shop in Chinatown for the last hour, waiting for her assistant to flip the *Open* sign and unlock the door.

The older woman—she had to be in her sixties by now—gave him a warm smile. "It's good to see you, too."

He reined in his impatience. Ginger had always liked him, even at his worst. He had no idea why. Jordan had claimed her mother knew who influenced who in their relationship, which made more sense these days. "I'm sorry. It's good to see you, too. You look well."

She shrugged and returned her glasses to their perch on her nose. "Eh. Arthritis eating up my bones, but I suppose I do okay." She eyed him keenly. "You ain't been drinking."

A matter-of-fact statement deserved a matter-of-fact reply. "Sober two years."

She nodded and began sewing again, not surprised. She must've known. "What're you chasing her for? She's as sober as you are, but not for long." There was only sadness and weariness in the remark. No condemnation. "You ought to walk out of here the way you came in."

"I should. But I won't."

He found Jordan at her mother's new house in Makiki. He tapped on the screen door, even though Ginger had given him permission to enter the house.

Jordan came to the door. Not dolled up but wearing oversized gray sweatpants and a baggy T-shirt, her long hair piled onto a sloppy bun high on her head, her faced scrubbed clean of makeup.

This had been his favorite version of her, once upon a time. The sleepy, next-morning Jordan. She'd sleep off the booze and be too tired for anything except coffee and snuggling on the couch to watch crappy television. She looked young, vulnerable, and sad, blinking at him through the mesh screen.

"I figured I'd see you today. Didn't know it'd be here, though." She opened the door.

Boston stepped inside and followed her as she padded into the kitchen. She held up a carafe. "Coffee?"

He didn't intend to hang around long enough to finish a cup. "Nope. I'm here—"

"Oh, I know why you're here." She poured herself a mug and beckoned him to the living room. She curled herself into a big chair and left him the couch. "Your girlfriend found your liquor stash."

Ah, sweet confirmation. Too bad he hadn't been clever enough to bring some kind of recording gadget along. "I want to act shocked. I really do."

"I know Emily's type. We both do, Boston. She's like my brother. I swear, if Phillip wasn't already married, I'd match-make the hell out of those two." Jordan blew on the hot coffee and took a cautious sip. "I had to show you how little faith she has."

For a minute, his temper slipped. He grabbed the arm of the couch so hard he wouldn't have been surprised had it come off in his hands. "Where do you get the nerve?"

"Not nerve. Desperation. What if you slip up, d'you think of that? She'll drop you like a rock. At your most vulnerable, she'll walk out and turn her back on you." Jordan set the mug down on the coffee table between them and leaned forward. "A woman like Emily will *never*— can't stress it enough—*never* understand the struggle like I do. Without some measure of understanding and forgiveness, no one succeeds. Hani forgave your slip two years ago, but would Emily?"

"Why are you so convinced I can help you?" He'd rather keep asking questions than answer any of hers.

"Because, look at you!" Jordan came to her feet. "You're sober, stone-cold, and for two years. Two years. I can't fathom it. Show me, Boston. Take me through every step, every day."

Did she think he had some magic pill? "There's no secret to it." He paused. Well, maybe there had been *something*. An idea hatched. "Actually, I couldn't have done it without The Canopy. If there's a reason for my sobriety, it's the shelter."

She gave him a flat stare. "No way it's that simple."

He scratched his chin. Actually, it was. "Homeless and with nothing to lose, Hani and I begged and saved for three years to buy that place, all while simply struggling to survive. It had a busted out window. No kitchen sink, no working toilet. But it was ours. Once we had it running, I couldn't afford to stop trying. I had to get real work to subsidize donations." He shrugged. "A lapse would spell the end."

"All right." Jordan settled back into the chair. "Okay, so The Canopy. That's brings me back to Emily. Some fancy-pants loafer-wearing lady like her will keep dating the CEO of a soup kitchen for how long, ya think, before the novelty wears off? Couple months?" She scoffed. "Get real, dude."

Boston drew in a breath to reply and stopped.

A fair point. How long would Emily find his management of The Canopy charming? How long before she suggested he get a *real* job?

But that wasn't the heart of the question.

The real meat came down to whether or not he'd do it—quit The Canopy and go back to a squeaky clean life in order to appease Emily.

Jordan had honed in on his doubt with uncanny precision. "Your clothes are all wrong. You gonna take her out on the town dressed like you can only buy half a pair of pants at a time? Or is she supposed to whittle herself down to your level?" She reached across to him and grasped his wrist. Her eyes, more remarkable for their lack of makeup, pleaded with him. "If you say The Canopy is the answer, I believe you. Because I'm not like her. I want to be your partner. I want to be beside you. You're good enough for me, Boston." A small smile. "Probably too good."

He blinked. "Never thought I'd hear those words emerge from that mouth."

"Well, *this mouth*"—a small, secret smile blossomed on her full lips—"is serious about this. I want to change. I want to be like you. Mostly, I want to show you how strong I can be. Stronger than *her*."

* * * *

Emily left The Canopy after breakfast.

No sign of Boston, but it was more a blessing than a curse. She didn't return to her apartment. Instead, she went to the beach. She purchased a beach towel from the grocer inside the Hilton Hawaiian Village and nestled into a spot beneath a lone palm offering enough shade to allow her to read the screen of her cell phone.

She stared at the contact name and chewed the inside of her cheek like a ferret on No-Doz. When Quinn had been living in London three years ago, her love affair with Jack had been front-page news. Not in

America, not internationally, but definitely as far as England had been concerned, since Jack Decker was involved, and he had something of a tabloid presence long before Quinn showed up. All Emily ever had to do was plug her sister's pen name into a search engine and she learned the latest gossip.

Disappointment sat heavy in Emily's gut. Either Boston had slipped up, or Jordan had pulled off some high-level sabotage. She held her breath and dialed Quinn, who answered on the third ring, sounding not the least bit distracted with writing. Small blessings. "Hi."

"Hey, you! How's the vacation? Are you orange from tanning oil yet? I'm *really* looking forward to seeing you orange."

Emily's breath caught. Suddenly, it seemed like too much to bother with, too much to unload. And, at the same time, nothing at all. She burst like a dam, and poor Quinn couldn't get in a single question without Emily verbally rolling over her—from the appropriated Hilton funds to the bottle of whiskey in Boston's couch, Emily laid everything out.

Quinn made several noises, none of which were actual words. When she finally spoke, what came was so unexpected, Emily nearly dropped her phone in the sand. "So, you love him."

"What the hell—did you hear anything I said?"

"Of course I did." She paused for breath. "I also heard what you *didn't* say, Em. Let's not fart around the issue."

Emily rolled her eyes. Didn't matter whether Quinn could see it. "Your English is on the downslide. I hope it's not transferring onto the page."

"It is, actually, but it makes for less stiff dialogue. And, honestly, you'd be surprised at what a well-timed fart joke can do for a scene. Now, listen to me. I am, of course, the foremost authority on unexpected love affairs. First, I'll say what you obviously can't. You love Boston. I can hear it in your voice, Em, and I have personal experience with the special brand of denial you're in."

"He's an alcoholic. I don't know if I believe—"

"You don't believe it for a second, like I never bought Vickie's allegations against Jack. But you have to do that job thing where you try to see every possible angle, but you can't apply yourself in real life the way you do in a boardroom. In reality, we have to put faith in the people we care about. There's nothing more important. Don't let doubt wriggle into a secure area."

Emily ran her fingers through the sand near her thigh, her legs stretched out in front of her to where only her toes escaped the shade of the towering palm. "I don't feel like myself out here. I'm weird and emotional. Nothing makes sense. Blake—"

"No, don't tell me. Let me guess. Blake is like the sand, right?"

Emily studied the sand on her fingers. "Yeah?"

"Pretty from a distance. Annoying in most close-up circumstances."

"Well, compared to Boston, he's—"

"Oh! I know this one. Compared to Boston, Blake is a saltine cracker—a little plain and too salty."

Emily abandoned the sand and cradled her face. "You see what I mean? I'm not myself. I'm losing perspective."

Quinn's voice turned sad. "No, Em, you're gaining it. As for the whiskey, you can't know. But you can choose what to believe."

"I guess I believe him. I mean, I want to. It feels right. But evidence is evidence."

Her sister turned exasperated. "I write crime scenes for a living. Evidence is only as good as how it's interpreted. You have to tell him how you feel, Em. You really do. If I'd have done so with Jack from the get-go, I'd have saved us both a lot of heartache and needless turmoil."

Frustration bubbled inside Emily. If only she had more experience with this kind of thing. "Jack was a sure thing. You knew it, even if you didn't trust it to begin with. You *knew*. The signs were there whenever you were brave enough to read them. Boston isn't like Jack."

Quinn huffed. "Thank God. This family can't handle two of him."

"Boston's like…" Emily peered out over the ocean and for once tried to find exactly the right words. "I guess he's like me. He plays it close. At the first hint of confrontation, he tucks himself away and it's all sarcasm and rudeness. It's like a door slamming in my face, and I realize I'm vulnerable, too, and I do the same thing. We're both afraid, so we both shut down. The whole whiskey fiasco was something, Quinn. He flew off the handle and smashed the bottle."

"No one likes to be doubted, Em," her sister gently reprimanded. "Although, that's something you two will need to discuss. He can't break stuff when he gets upset. You've got some really nice pottery at your place."

"I love how you're assuming a future."

Quinn's attitude ran a little too close to amused for Emily's liking.

As if hearing the thought, her sister grew serious. "And I love how you're fighting it like I did. But the stakes go up, and it stops being cute. You're going to screw up and lose it all. So, Emily, here's what you do. You take some time to yourself, put your heart into decisive action—don't let that big, think-y brain of yours get in the way—and figure how you *feel*. Then, for the love of everything righteous and holy, do something about it. Break the cycle of fear between you and Boston. One of you has to be vulnerable."

Why does it have to be me? Why did she always seem to be the one who changed or sacrificed for someone else? "He should come to me. Jack came to you."

"Boston's wounds are deeper than yours. You can be the damsel or you can be the hero, but not every damsel gets rescued. This ain't no fairy tale, sweetheart. Don't prescribe to the rules of one."

Of *course* it wasn't a fairy tale. It wouldn't be, would it? Not for Emily. "And if it goes wrong?"

"I'll be waiting at LAX with a five pound container of ice cream."

Emily slumped against the rough bark of the palm tree. At least she had something to look forward to, either way.

* * * *

She breathed in through her nose and out through her mouth. Eyes closed. In and out. In and out. Over and over. Emily dropped her chin to her chest and wiped her sweaty palms on the frayed denim shorts she wore. One last deep breath and she raised her knuckles to Boston's door. She hadn't seen him since they argued yesterday. No telling what sort of greeting she'd get, so she tried to not expect anything.

When no answer came, she tried the knob. He'd have to get over her inviting herself inside.

Emily stepped over the threshold and froze at the sight of Jordan lying on the love seat, clad in a damp bikini, her wet hair fanned around her head.

Her eyes popped open. She lifted her head. "Oh. It's you." She closed her eyes again and laid her head back.

Emily refused to be shaken by the scene, but doubt crept into her mind. Nothing she'd come to disclose were things she'd willingly say to Boston in front of his ex-wife. "I came for Boston. I suppose he's not around?"

Jordan groaned and sat up. "So much for a nap. Boston's in the shower." She stood and stretched, displaying her lithe body, ribs poking out like they were trying to escape. "Wanna leave a message?"

"You got the couch wet." Of all the inane things to pop out of her mouth, that probably took the cake. "You could've at least put a towel down," she added for the sake of having something to latch onto. As if it were her couch and she had any right to be concerned.

Jordan gazed lazily at the damp spot and shrugged. "Surfing is wet work."

"Surfing, huh?"

She stretched again, this time side to side. "Me and Bos went this morning. Man, the waves are great after the storm we had. It's been such a long time, too. Before the drinking got heavy, we would go around the clock." She dropped her arms to her sides and smiled at Emily, a cruel, knowing smile. "Looks like we'll be able to pick up the old habit."

Obviously, something had transpired between Boston and Jordan in the last twenty-four hours. What had Emily missed?

Jordan studied her openly. "There aren't enough cut-off shorts in the world to hide what you are." The statement accompanied a head-to-toe perusal. "You're all pencil skirts, support hose, and low-heeled pumps. You're neutral tones and fresh flowers at the breakfast nook each morning, ten dollar gourmet lattes and organic veggies. You 'do lunch' and drink cosmopolitans."

Emily's face grew warmer with each tick off the list. Yeah, she drank designer coffee and purchased daisies to brighten up her apartment. She purchased organic when possible. However, she favored an old-fashioned beer over a fruity cocktail. It gave her a small boost of confidence— Jordan knew about Emily. But she didn't *know* Emily. "It's called having taste, Jordan. You should try it some time. I'm not ashamed of what my money buys me. I didn't grow up wealthy. I worked for it."

Jordan scoffed. "Gee, I'm *so* impressed. You think Boston cares? You know what you are to people like us? A reminder of our failures."

"I don't think Boston's a failure."

"Are we making this about you now?"

"No, I—"

"Emily." Jordan pinned her with earnestness in her emerald glare. "There's too much wrong about it, and you know I'm right."

Funny how it began as a head game. Emily had deliberately poked and prodded at Jordan by pretending an interest in Boston. Now, here she was, with a genuine interest in Boston, and Jordan was still fighting to put an end to it. She said the truest thing to come to mind. "There's enough right about it."

"Let's tally it up, shall we? For fun's sake. We've got a minute before Boston comes in here and tells you himself." She sashayed over to stand in front of Emily until she had nowhere else to look.

"Number one." She held up a bony finger on her bony hand. "You're a cement wall. Completely unforgiving. Lapses happen. We slip.

Sometimes, we go back to square one. You don't have what it takes to forgive him when it happens."

Emily wanted to argue but couldn't.

Jordan held up a second finger. "Two. You're stuck up. Own it, okay? Boston doesn't have fine clothes and styled hair. You prepared to take him to a corporate dinner in his shredded khaki shorts and a faded T-shirt? Can you see yourself showing off your little beach prize to your high-flying friends?"

Emily called to mind the last corporate dinner she'd attended. Formal dress. Five-star catering. Peers from all over the southwest in attendance. Blake had been at her side, and a perfect match. Her reaction to imaging Boston at her side shamed her. He wouldn't fit in. She'd die of embarrassment before they ever made it to the entrée course. The doubt had to be gleaming from her face like a fine sheen of sweat.

Jordan smiled like she saw it as plain as day. "Three. "A third finger went up. "Money. He doesn't have any. At some point, you'll ask him to give up The Canopy—to give up *himself*—to change for you. You'll say things like 'meet me in the middle,' and maybe he'll do it. But then, he won't be Boston anymore. He'll be bits and pieces of himself, and the rest will be shades of you."

"Have I missed something?"

Emily's head jerked toward where Boston stood near the bathroom door.

He wore nothing but a towel wrapped around his torso low on his hips. She licked her lips.

Jordan gave Emily one last smirk, hidden from Boston's view, and slinked into the bathroom.

Emily had no clue what was going on behind Boston's pretty eyes, but something like a grin lurked at the corners of his mouth. "Something funny?"

"A little." His smile grew. "You're kind of staring at my chest."

"Am not."

"You were." He stepped closer and lowered his eyes. "I'm glad you stopped by. I wanted to apologize for yesterday. The bottle thing. Sometimes you just need to break something, right?" The small grin fell away at her lack of response. "Jordan admitted to stashing it to mess with us. I guess it worked."

Emily nodded and bit her lip. Quinn had it right, after all. Emily should've trusted her instincts. "You went surfing this morning, huh? How was it?"

"Good." He paused and glanced at his hands, as if he couldn't say what he needed to and meet her eyes at the same time. It didn't bode well for the conversation she hoped to have. "I know it's weird and maybe dangerous, but I think I can help Jordan. She's for real about getting sober." He peeked at Emily long enough for her to note the vague apology in the drawn line of his mouth. "Her antics are crap. You didn't deserve to put up with it for trying to have my back. But what can I say? She's motivated."

Hmm. Trying to have his back and failing because here Jordan was despite it. "Surfing helps?"

"Being active helped me get through some of my tougher times, yeah. It's a start, anyway." Another pause, this time to examine the wall behind Emily and rub his freshly shaved cheek. "I have a plan, Emily. Don't think I'm diving into this without a care for what happens next. This... Jordan... It's not a *thing* like you might imagine—"

Jordan popped into the room. This time, she wore only a towel wrapped tight around her body and held in place by a knot in the middle of her breasts. She stepped between them while wringing out the long strands of her wet hair. "Know what? No. I've had enough of you two." She waggled her fingers between them and regarded Emily with a stone-cold glare. "I won't make it without him. Can you say the same?"

Over her head, Boston's blue gaze burned into Emily as though he'd asked the question. When she said nothing, he groaned and turned on Jordan. "Why are you so damn dramatic? I'll help you, but on my terms."

Jordan pointed a finger at his bare chest. "You love me, Boston Rondibett. Say whatever the hell you want to your little girlfriend, but you and I—"

He leaned into Jordan's face with a menacing stare. Emily was glad not to be on the receiving end of it. "I mean every word I've said to you, Jordan. Every. Damn. Word."

Jordan's face contorted with rage, and her arm flew up.

Boston caught her arm in its downward arc inches from his shoulder, snatching it mid-strike with a quickness that belied his lazy beach bum veneer. They glared at each other.

In the bubble of silence, no noise existed to cover Emily's gasp. "You." She pointed to Jordan. "*You're* the violent one. You lied."

Boston's glare turned to disdain as he peeked at her from the corner of his eye. "Ya think?"

Jordan cut in with a growl and glowered at Boston as she wrenched her arm free. "Don't act like some kind of victim. You broke my mother's picture frame, the nicest thing I ever owned."

His arms shot out in a defensive stance, and his voice came out a near-shout. "You mean the picture frame *you* broke throwing at me?"

Emily took a step back. The entire scene disgusted her. This life, these people, resolving to destruction and pain when there were a million words to communicate feelings. She didn't belong here, and maybe that was the lesson. In another life, if she and Boston had met under different circumstances, maybe they'd have a chance.

She made for the exit.

"Emily! Don't do it. Don't leave."

Boston's desperate demand brought her up short. She faced him and swallowed her disappointment and hurt. She'd forget his face in time, but probably not his eyes. She'd remember the clear blue color until her last moments. "I only came to say good-bye."

His eyebrows drew into a sharp V. He approached Emily with his palms up as though she were the unpredictable one. A small breathy laugh escaped him, but his eyes weren't laughing. "We aren't done. It's not time. Don't go."

"Boston." She sighed. "I know about the money."

He froze. She might've pressed the pause button on a recording.

"The Hilton," he mumbled.

She nodded. "Hani told me. I've known for a while. Funny, though, how it didn't make me angry. Not that you took the money, anyway."

He rubbed his forehead like he had a headache coming on. "Emily, I practically stole from you."

"No, you *did* steal. From Quinn, not me. She understands, too, by the way."

Boston's face started to turn green.

"It's okay. Really. She gets it. We both do."

He licked his teeth and eyed her. "Then what are you angry about if not the money?"

"I recall my first day here and can't blame you a bit. I'm not mad, but it hurts a little. You tolerated my snobbery in the interest of helping someone else. It's a lesson I won't soon forget, but it's one I needed to learn. I needed to see myself that way—the way you see me."

No words, only his arms coming around her like a cocoon.

She closed her eyes and tried to memorize the moment. His soapy smell from the shower. The damp ends of his long hair caressing her shoulders. "You can't possibly believe that. Emily, I—" He stepped away abruptly, and one arm dropped away so he could rub the nape of his neck. "Damn, girl. In another life, I'm good enough for you, you know that?"

Her jaw fell open. "What?" *Good enough* for her? Since when had that been a concern?

His blue eyes turned pleading. He gripped her hands and shuffled. "I mean, I'd try. I'm going to try. I told you, Em. I'm ticking off boxes, not swinging blind. Still, it's hard to imagine how I could make someone like you happy."

Right. Because, as Jordan so kindly pointed out, her lofty expectations would be the end of them. She swallowed the lump in her throat. "Boston, it's not a matter of being good enough. It's a matter of practicality."

His gaze went hard. It was like watching ice form. "Practicality? I shouldn't be surprised it comes down to mechanics with you."

Every last item Jordan had pointed out ran through Emily's mind with a sudden clarity. "This isn't a fairy tale. A little feeling isn't the answer to every small concern. Our differences are real. They matter. And Jordan's right, I don't have the empathy it takes to forgive the kind of mistakes you might make. And you helping her. It seems like a bad recipe. The kind that might get someone hurt."

Someone like me.

The proverbial door slammed against her. His face shuttered, impossible to read. "So, it's a trust thing?" Nonchalant as royalty, Boston backed away from her. "Eh, I don't blame you. You've got reason enough."

Maybe he meant the money. Maybe he meant Jordan. Didn't matter. The answer depended on the question, and the real question was how could it possibly end between them?

Boston sulky and resentful in an Armani suit. Emily burning with mortification when asked what her significant other did for a living. One or both of them stranded in a place they didn't want to be. Only desperation, Emily's old and dear companion, could compel her into yet another relationship with no promise of a future. That, she kept to herself.

Boston shook his head as she started for the door again. "Why is it so much easier for you to doubt me than to believe in me? I have a plan, Emily."

She almost stopped. Almost. "And I hope it works." She walked out and blinked fiercely against the emotion building in her throat. Was this the needless torment Quinn had put herself through before realizing she and Jack were meant to be together?

Because it sucked. And realization wasn't dawning.

Chapter 14

Jordan trailed behind him like an abused puppy.

Boston didn't care. She could sulk until the damn moon fell into the ocean. He wouldn't sleep with her. Sex wasn't part of the healing process—and it definitely wouldn't help him with his plans for the future. In fact, the very absence of sex, which was damn hard to come by as a homeless man, had helped him stay focused and on point during The Canopy's rough birth.

If he'd been out chasing women, how would anything have gotten accomplished? And if he were going to pursue it, a more worthy partner came to mind.

He wouldn't take Jordan out for breakfast, either, or lunch or dinner. No dates. They weren't playing a social game. They were untangling life and reweaving it into something simple, firm, and reliable. She'd eat at The Canopy like the rest of them.

I have a plan. I have a plan.

It'd become his new mantra since Emily stormed out of his apartment two days ago. He hadn't seen her since. Not at The Canopy, nor coming and going from her place over the jewelry shop. He had a plan, and if time were on his side, he'd carry it out in baby steps. The same way he'd saved money and bought The Canopy. Time didn't allow for small, careful steps, though. He had to go all in, cash in every chip, and pray to God it worked.

He *needed* it to work.

They entered The Canopy. Akela, serenely scouring the dining hall for empty plates amid the morning's guests, glanced up with a smile of greeting. It morphed into a scowl when she saw who sauntered in after him.

He padded over to her and leaned in to speak quietly. "How's Hani? Does he have time to talk?"

"He's in the back. Crying," she added. "So, maybe knock about a bit and give him some notice."

Boston pursed his lips. "Is he devastated or piss drunk?"

He expected a sharp retort or an angry question. Akela didn't normally approve of drinking jokes. Instead, she gave him a sideways smile and went off after another plate. "He's happy."

He thanked Akela and nodded for Jordan to stay put.

She huffed but took a seat at one of the empty tables.

He paused at the end of the narrow hallway and tapped on the wall. "Hani? You in there, brother? I need a word."

A sniffle sounded from the office. Hani pushed open the door and shuffled out. "Come on back."

"What's going on, man?"

"Mama came to see me this morning."

He didn't need to say more. The implications rang loud and clear to anyone familiar with Hani's history with his family. They'd disowned him when he took to the streets, and instead of being proud when he started working for The Canopy, they'd seen it in much the same light as Boston's parents, which was to say not good. Hani made light of it as best he could with jokes about their royal blood, but Boston knew the cut went deep.

Boston leaned against the counter and crossed his arms. "Well? What'd she want?"

Hani wiped his eyes with a beefy forearm and sniffed again, shaking his head until his braid swung over his shoulder. "You know how it is when you got twenty thousand cousins, man. Word got around I started looking for a job."

He'd actually done it. Boston shook his head but smiled. He hadn't doubted Hani meant it.

"She came in here with an offer. Guy who runs the buffet across from the Hilton is leaving." He lifted his shoulders and his eyes went a little wider, like he could hardly believe it. "The job's mine if I want it."

Part of Boston wanted to rejoice for Hani. Clap him on the back, shake his hand. Because, hell, wasn't that the next step up? Was Hani supposed to work in a soup kitchen for nothing but a bed for the rest of his life? Another part of him felt like something important was being ripped away. He went with his first instinct and clapped Hani on his shoulder. "Damn, man. Congrats!"

Hani took a deep, shuddering breath. "Boston, I—I don't want to abandon this place. I love The Canopy. I love helping people. I love putting food in empty stomachs and offering a warm, dry place on miserable, rainy nights. But I also know I've been leaning on you. More than you ever did me."

"That's not true."

"It is, brother." Most of the emotion had cleared from his throat, and he looked at Boston with eyes that were red but dry. "We've *all* counted on you, and it wasn't right. Not with everything else you had weighing on you. I hide in my kitchen and make demands and expect you to pull magic out of your behind like a damn party trick." He blinked, an apology in his wide, dark gaze. "I'm taking the job, Bos. I'm gonna... I'm gonna get a house. Pay my own bills. Put the pressure on myself, where it ought to be."

Boston ignored the tightness in his chest and hugged his best friend fiercely. Hani's massive arms seemed to swallow his entire body. They stepped away from each other with a couple of small coughs.

"Good for you, man." Boston grinned, rocking back with his thumbs hooked into the belt loops of his red shorts. "I'm happy for you. And maybe it's a good thing you're moving on. I've got plans for this place, and I've been scared shitless of what you'd say. Now, Akela and Jordan are the only two people I have to convince."

* * * *

Akela's glower was a thing of beauty.

Jordan's disdainful sneer nearly matched it. "You're saying I'm the new *maid*?"

Akela snapped her head toward Jordan. "Is *that* what you think I do around here? You don't know anything. See, Bos? I trust you, I do, but this idea of yours is nuts."

Boston sighed. He could be right back in a classroom dealing with children. Which, soon, he hoped he would be. "Akela, your heart's in this place. No one is better suited to take over. Thompson has the kitchen on lock, right?"

From the far end of the dining table, Thompson nodded vigorously.

"See? Food is covered." He pointed at Akela. "Management is covered." He swung his no-nonsense gaze to Jordan. "You're going to do the things Akela does around this place. She's not the maid, either. She's a crucial gear that's kept this place functioning for years. Without her...." He shuddered to think. "Look, Jordan, you can't ask me to put The Canopy in your hands. You have a hell of a road in front of you. You asked me how I did it. This is how. Akela's earned it. She'll teach you the way so long as you're willing. Now or never. This is my program, and you're in or you're out."

She studied her thumbnail for a long minute. Moment of truth. How bad did she want it? "All right. Fine. I'm in."

"Great." He nodded resolutely and switched his attention back to Akela. "I was just like Jordan when you met me. You remember? Angry, down, one foot ready to hit the pavement again. She needs a chance. You can give up on her anytime you like, but do me a favor and think of what might've happened had Hani given up on me. I'm not saying Jordan won't give you a reason at some point."

"Or several." Hani's grunt sounded loud in the empty dining hall. It was the first time in recent history Boston could recall setting the *Closed* sign in the window.

"In the morning, we'll head to city hall and get the deed switched to your name. In time, when you're ready to move on, you bequeath it to someone you trust to continue the legacy—a brand new legacy we're starting today, right now."

Hani rubbed his temples. "Jus' where the hell do you think you're going, *haole*?"

The other half of the plan. "Bottom line, guys, The Canopy doesn't need me. And I don't need it." He looked at each of them in turn. "Not anymore."

"Ah," Akela nodded sagely.

Jordan rolled her eyes.

"Whoo," Hani teased. "I see, I see. You found something else to save you from yourself, eh, brother? Does Emily know you're putting that kinda weight on her shoulders?"

Boston crossed his ankles and chewed the inside of his lip. *Emily.* Hell, he didn't even know where she was. Maybe already back in L.A. by now. "Not her, actually."

A pregnant pause followed.

Akela's keen sense of the situation, which Boston had long ago recognized as one of her special powers, led her to stand abruptly. "Jordan, let me show you around upstairs. Thompson, can you get a start on prepping the papaya we got this morning for Hani, please?"

Eagerly, Thompson popped up and made for the kitchen.

Jordan sluggishly followed Akela as she started up the staircase on the far side of the room. Akela talked, mentioning the cleaning schedule she kept—the same one neither Hani nor Boston could every recall asking her to create or adhere to—and how often she dusted the handrail and redid the screws that kept it attached to the wall because they liked to come loose.

A twang of anxiety whipped through Boston as he watched them. God, he'd miss this. With parents as old as his had been, The Canopy was the closest he'd ever come to having a normal, lively family.

Hani's stern expression brought him out of his nostalgia. He twirled his fingers in the air. "What's this about, Bos?"

Something was up, and his friend knew it. Boston shook his head. "Not Emily. I think that ship has sailed."

"You're an idiot. I want it on record."

"Duly noted."

"No, I mean it, man." Hani shifted to sit forward. "You're dumping Jordan on my sister, and not even for Emily's sake? What's wrong with you?"

Boston sat back and ran a hand through his long hair. He should probably cut it. He was cutting everything else, why not? "You said you were too dependent on me, Hani, but when haven't I needed something? I needed you to save me from the streets. I needed The Canopy to save me from booze. I needed Emily to save me from Jordan. I can't do it anymore, either." He lifted one nonchalant shoulder, but the words stung nonetheless. "I'm going home. *Home* home," he clarified before Hani could mistake him. "To Mesa."

Hani took a good minute to soak it in, a deep frown creasing his big, brown face. He toyed with the end of his braid. "I was hoping you meant in a metaphorical sense. Does your mama know yet?"

"Yeah, we've talked." An incredibly uncomfortable conversation, but in the end his mother had cried and his father had grunted something unintelligible but happy sounding. Boston scratched his cheek. "I was never charged with anything for the incident at the school. I mean, I was the talk of the administration for about a year, but nothing official. I can teach."

Hani's slow headshake held the essence of awe. "You ain't messing around. You're really going back. Not just to Mesa, but back to everything."

"Everything I had before I met Jordan. I got another confession for you, too."

A thick black eyebrow went up. "Can I handle it?"

"I went to the bar the other night. After we argued. I sat at the bar, I ordered a beer and a shot of their finest tequila because Emily had me asked to hold the change from our ice cream cones earlier that day, and I was feeling like an asshole. She shut me out, and you turned your back."

Hani slumped back and ran a hand over his hair, much as Boston often did. "Aw, Bos, c'mon—"

"It's okay, man. We're past it. Anyway, I ordered my booze and I sat there staring at these two drinks in front of me. And nothing. No burning desire, no drool dribbling down my chin. I finally ordered an iced tea to-go and got the hell out of there."

A long, rumbling laugh started low in Hani's throat. "You're gonna be all right, brother. You screwed up with Emily, but you'll be okay."

They sat together in contemplative silence. An assortment of images flickered through Boston's mind like an old movie in the cozy silence wrought with nostalgia. The Canopy, Arizona…and Emily. Mesa wasn't too far from L.A. Maybe he—

Hani broke the spell with a quiet moan as he hoisted himself from his seat. "Well, brother, I'll miss you. I don't know how the hell you're gonna handle that desert heat after living in the tropics so long—"

A figure waltzed into The Canopy.

Boston glanced up and the moment suspended in time.

Emily looked back at him with bright eyes and a barely concealed smile like she had a secret in her pocket. "You get used to it."

* * * *

Her life was about to take a glorious turn toward a future she hadn't believed herself worthy of, or plummet to a level of pathetic, known only by lonely old crones and crazy cat ladies. Emily prayed for the former and smoothed down her rough curls.

Hani and Boston stared at her.

Nerves hit her, hard and fast, and she used an old boardroom trick to sooth them. Not the old gambit of pretending they were naked—generally speaking, nudity was never the answer. During presentations she simply pretended everyone in the room really, really liked her.

Normally, it worked.

But these nerves were altogether different than the ones she handled on company time. This was no presentation, and she had to squelch the dancing loons in her stomach before they killed her resolve. "Hi."

Hani acted first. He barreled toward her and, for an instant, she considered what to do if he tackled her. Thankfully, he stopped shy of mowing her down to wrap his huge arms around her and lift her entirely off the ground in a smothering hug. He murmured low in her ear. "About those red shorts of his. If you love him, you'll—"

"Learn to love his shorts, too?"

"Burn them when he isn't looking." He released her and stood back with a big, dumb grin, his massive hands gripping her arms. She'd miss him. She'd never met anyone who'd made her feel tiny the way Hani did. "Man, y'all gonna have some cute kids. Your dark curls and Boston's big ol' blue peepers."

Emily's face heated.

His deep, bellowing laughter rang out at the same time Akela and Jordan came down the stairs.

Emily deflated some. Of course Jordan would be at The Canopy, but Boston had claimed to have a plan. Nothing to do but trust him.

Hani patted Emily's arm, gave her a secret wink, and shuffled over to Akela. He put a beefy arm around his sister's shoulders and guided her away from them, bantering as they went in the comfortable way of close siblings.

Emily didn't have it in her to look at Boston—she was still gathering her courage—so she regarded Jordan expectantly.

The hurled insults never came. Jordan toed an imaginary spot on the floor and, after a shuddering breath, squared her shoulders and met Emily's wary gaze.

Her deep green eyes were always amazing. Not quite like windows the way Quinn might poetically describe them, as a view into one's soul or some nonsense, but certainly windows in the sense that Jordan had the power to dress them however she pleased. Sultry, indignant, uncaring, disinterested, flat, lively, sparkling, glittering, and hard as stone. She'd mastered them all.

For the first time, they weren't adorned in some kind of window-dressing. "Emily, I'm sorry." Okay, so the window-dressing might have fallen away, but Jordan still had an edge to her voice, one that would never apologize for anything.

Emily had to admire her grit.

Jordan pushed a strand of long, dark hair behind one ear. "I guess I work here now. I don't recall drudgery in a soup kitchen being part of the twelve-step program."

Boston spoke for the first time. "Why take twelve when you can do it in one?"

Emily wouldn't so easily disregard the program, but... "So long as you want it, Jordan, I think the steps can vary."

"I do. Just...so you know. I do."

An awkward moment passed. No one seemed to know what to say next. Jordan mumbled an excuse to venture toward the kitchen with a limp-wristed wave and a toss of her hair over her shoulder.

Emily faced Boston and caught him examining her. "What?"

"I didn't know if you were still around."

"You could've found out easily enough."

He shifted in his plastic chair. "I suppose, yeah. I guess I assumed you knew your own mind and you'd already said good-bye, Emily. I'm tenacious when it suits me but not stupid. Chasing someone who doesn't want to be chased is called *stalking*. Trust me, I'm an English teacher. I'm awesome with words."

"You're right. I made myself pretty clear." She let the sentiment settle and glanced around the barren dining hall. "Maybe we can take a walk?"

Boston lifted a shoulder. Not in agreement. "Or you could have a seat and listen for a minute. Last time we spoke, you did all the talking. But like I said, English is kind of my thing, and I have a few thoughts of my own to share." Another shrug, the nonchalant kind she knew he used to cover other emotions. "Or, hell, maybe you don't care. Did you come to say good-bye to the others? Or did you leave something behind?"

She had, actually. But not what he imagined. "That's a crappy way to ask me why I'm here. But you're the one talking this time. So, talk." She settled into the chair next to Boston's.

He squinted at her. Even narrowed, his eyes were round and bluer than ever. "Why is it we're always so combative? What gets our hackles up?"

"My hackles are fine, thank you." She crossed her arms and fought to keep a grin from stealing over her face. He was defensive and contrary as usual. She'd let him get whatever he needed to off his chest before she came down on it with a mallet, crushing his excuses and reasons with the only force on Earth with the power to do so.

Love.

Boston sat back and did his cheek-smoothing. "Someone had to shove me. Someone has to shove Jordan. *But*... I realize it doesn't necessarily have to be me who does the shoving."

Emily cocked her head to the side. "May I?"

A smile threatened, but Boston fought it and won. "Emily, it's really, really stupid for a woman to look twice at a guy like me. You're the kind of woman I see with certain guys, guys like me, and I say, 'What is she thinking? Why that loser?' *I'm* that loser."

Her heart constricted. "Boston—"

He closed his eyes like he needed strength, and they popped open. "No, I'm going to say this if it kills me, and you're going to let me. We're not dancing around it anymore. If there's one thing you and I excel at, it's getting real, am I right? With Jordan, the answer isn't me. It's this place." His gaze briefly trailed the ceiling. "I can't be her Hani. Hell, even Hani can't be her Hani. Now that he's leaving, too."

Too? "Who else—"

A finger went up along with the compressed lips of a reprimand.

"Sorry, *Mr. Rondibett.*"

"As for me, I'm tired of being that loser. I wasn't always a loser. I've never been like you, never sat at the top of the food chain or anything. But once upon a time, I liked myself. I *respected* myself, and I'd have never been okay with becoming a loser." He adjusted so his elbows rested on his knees. "What I said about being good enough for you, having a plan. The plan is to be good enough, Em. I'm unpacking my wrinkle-free khakis, getting it 'together,' because if I can run this place and help other people, why can't I run a classroom and help myself? Fear's kept me tied down for so long I think I forgot I've known the escape route all along. Jordan can only take from me what I let her have, but you reminded me—*showed* me—that power is something each of us has. We only need to be willing to wield it." Finally, a sad smile formed. "I'm going home to Mesa."

Her hands flew to her chest. "But you love Honolulu! You can't walk away like it's nothing, like it won't haunt you every day. You told me yourself you wouldn't go back to Arizona unless God himself tugged you by the ankles."

"Or," he replied quietly, "my mother said please."

It sunk in. Boston was really leaving Hawaii. "Your parents."

His lovely blue eyes seemed to stare at nothing. "I knew I'd have to one day. They didn't ask me to, but I can't hide out anymore, afraid of real life, afraid of facing them and the inevitable."

Emily couldn't take it anymore. She stood and reached for Boston, taking him by the hands and pulling him out of his chair. She put her arms around him and laid her head on his chest. "I'm sorry, Boston. I'm so happy for you, but I'm sorry for what you have to lose."

It took him a stunned minute, but he finally embraced her with the care of a man cradling glass. "Mesa won't be so bad. It's close to a few intriguing places I've never been and wouldn't mind investigating. Places like Vegas. Lake Tahoe." A pause. "Los Angeles."

Her pulse skipped. "I had no idea you were so interested in travel," she murmured against his chest.

"Yeah, well, once I'm different, more like you—"

Emily stepped back from his embrace in a sudden, jarring motion. "You can't be different. You can't try to be like me. That's ridiculous."

"Oh, please. Look at me." He held his arms aloft and even managed a small circle to give her the full view of his attire. "You said Jordan was right about our differences, and she is. You can't take me anywhere."

"Boston, I swear, if you try to adjust to me, it won't work. You can't just *change*. I mean, fine if you want to wear decent clothes again and go back to teaching, but I like this." She ran her hands over his chest and tugged on his shirt. "I like you, and you'll ruin everything if you become someone else. I'm not changing, why should you?"

He made up the distance between them and fingered the curls on either side of her jaw. "I won't become someone else. I'll be the same jerk I am today." He gave her a bright, winning smile. "I might have to cut my hair, though."

The horror! Her eyes must've popped out of their sockets. "The hell you will. You can tie it back if the school administrators take issue. I know a fantastic lawyer in L.A., and she'll be all over that reverse sexist nonsense like Spam on rice."

Boston tugged on one of the curls twisting around his finger and grew sober. "I don't have the gall to ask you to wait for me, Em, but I'm gonna come find you eventually. You wait and see."

She let her head fall back and laughed with abandon. "If you think for one minute I'd let you out of my sight for some other woman to come along and snatch up a good-looking teacher with sexy beach hair and eyes like soft denim, you are out of your ever-loving mind."

She shook her head, another soft chuckle escaping as she took several steps back and turned around to show Boston her back. She pushed the straps of her thin bathing suit cover down to her waist, revealing two string bows holding her bikini top in place. In one quick motion, she swept her hair from her neck and over her shoulder to expose the skin.

Boston's sharp intake of breath made her smile. "Holy shit. Are those... You got *tattoos*?"

"*Kulia* on my left shoulder. It means 'effort' or 'try.' And on the right, *kalele*, which is supposed to mean 'trust.' Of course, I had to take the tattoo artist's word for it." She let go of her hair and faced him. "I got them to remind me of what's important. This—" she pointed to Boston and herself in turn—"I trust this. It feels right. It feels like home. And it's worth the risk of trying, isn't it?"

Boston's smile blossomed slow and wide. He cupped her face with his hands and, without any further warning, kissed her, equally tense and tender. She came away breathless, and his gaze held a promise as it swept her face, from her parted lips to her eyes and back.

"I swear, Em, one day I'm gonna deserve you."

"You already do."

He lifted a doubtful eyebrow but didn't push the issue. "You got any more surprises for me?"

How had he known? She bit her lip. "Well, I did get a pink hibiscus, but I thought we'd make a game of you finding it."

He dropped his chin to his chest. "I'll be damned. I'm in love with a yuppie."

"Pfft. That's nothing. Born and raised in southern California, came all the way to Hawaii to fall for a beach bum."

"Talk about expediting."

She shoved him playfully but took in a heaving breath. "There's, uh, one more thing you probably ought to know."

"Yeah? Is it another tattoo? I swear they're like potato chips."

She tilted her head. "No, but I have given my next one some thought. Something meaningful, interesting, and eye-catching. A reminder of my time here."

"Like the Spam logo?"

"You're hilarious."

He crossed his arms and set his feet wide apart as if bracing himself. "So, if not another tattoo, what's the big secret?"

She sucked in a breath, rubbed her hands together, and took solace in the fact Boston would be the easiest person to tell. The impending conversation with her family was enough to give her hives. "You're not the only one who felt a little change was in order. I've learned as much from you as you have from me, the most important thing being that… Oh, damn, I *do* get wordy when I'm emotional. I quit my job. There. I said it."

Concern washed over Boston's features. "Are you okay?"

"Yes, actually. I'm great. It's just, well, you know what happens when you quit your job, right?" A nervous giggle escaped her. "Boston, I'm pretty sure I'm homeless."

He *laughed*. The jerk laughed, picked her up, and swung her around in a circle. He returned her to her feet with a gleeful grin. "Well, hot damn!" He cupped her face a second time and kissed her again with a fierceness that floored her. "Do you know what this means, Em? We finally have something in common."

Epilogue

"It took you guys long enough."

Quinn's groan traveled through the airways, and Emily swore her cell phone vibrated from the sheer force of her sister's misery. "I'm old, Emily. Women my age have to think about it before they commit."

"What could you possibly need to meditate on for three whole years?"

"You know, *stuff*. It's not like I can take maternity leave. I attend conferences every year, from Phoenix to Perth, Australia. Do lectures and whatnot. How can I do all that and tote around an infant?"

Hell if Emily knew. All she knew was how amazing any child of Quinn and Jack's was bound to be. His charm, her poise. Her natural litheness, his piercing teal eyes. "So, how's your first trimester coming along? How do you feel?"

Another groan, this one distinctly pitiful. "Like my stomach is working part-time hours."

"Ew." Emily grimaced. "Barf city?"

"In Barf County, south of Barfville, home of the Hurling Barfers."

"Well, as much as I hate to steal your thunder, I might have some bigger news than you do."

Quinn's tone turned flat. "I'm *pregnant*, Em. How can you possibly one-up me?"

"Yeah, but who didn't see that coming? As I've mentioned, you're actually behind schedule."

"All right, spit it out."

Emily cleared her throat and promptly forgot the poised speech she had prepared. She even had a bullet list around Boston's apartment somewhere. "Okay," she breathed out. "All right. So. Okay. Most shocking, I suppose, is I quit my job. I'm unemployed for the first time since fifteen. I haven't worn pantyhose in at least a month, and I can't fathom wrestling into a pair. Ever again, in fact. And I'm moving. So, there's that. Boston and

I are going to Arizona, but I've got to get my stuff from my apartment before my landlady sells it off."

An amazed murmur bled through the line. "*Wow.*"

She swallowed. "That's not all. I got a few tattoos. Well, several. Okay, I have five. I have five tattoos."

A grave silence descended. No "wow" this time.

"I'm gonna get a job, Quinn." She scoffed. "I mean, obviously, right? Eventually. I have to figure out what I want to do, that's all. I've been busy lately, what with learning to surf and everything."

"Emily—"

"I know, I know. It's kind of crazy. *Me* of all people. Not the most athletic, am I?"

"You need to—"

"Quinn, please. You have to trust me. Boston's worth it. I know what you meant now, all that needless torment stuff. And I came so close to screwing it up. Once we're in Mesa, we'll be back on the grid. Jobs and a nice home and probably no more tattoos." She paused and gave it a second thought. "Well, maybe the occasional tattoo."

"Emily, I can't believe—"

She closed her eyes. She knew they'd be disappointed in her. "Quinn, please just… Tell Dad I'm happy, okay? That's the only explanation I have for any of it."

Quinn's voice was almost shrill. "Oh, sure, you're *happy*. Okay, yeah. I can see where quitting a man-centric corporate job from hell and shacking up with a sexy, long-haired surfer dude would make you happy, Emily. That's obvious. I'd have suggested ditching that crap job years ago had I thought you'd have listened for a second."

She blinked. "But…"

Quinn's voice dropped to a shrill whisper. "A *tattoo*, Em? Five. *Five* tattoos?"

Emily released the breath she'd been holding. It came out as a strangled gasp of relieved laughter. "What can I say? They're like potato chips."

"Dad's going to freak." Her sister's voice went even lower. "Is it one we can look at? Or did you get one of those naughty ones only you, Boston, and God will ever see?"

Emily smiled to herself and lovingly studied the band tattooed around the base of her ring finger. "You could say I've got a variety."

THE END

Meet the Author

A Florida native, Roxanne Smith has called everywhere from Houston to Cheyenne home. Currently residing in Asheville, North Carolina, she's an avid reader of every genre, a cat lover, pit bull advocate, and semi-geek. She loves video games, Doctor Who, and her dashing husband. Her two kids are the light of her life and provide ample material for her writing

http://smithrox.blogspot.com/
https://www.facebook.com/roxannesmith.author
https://twitter.com/ThisSmithRox

Keep reading for a special sneak peek of Roxanne Smith's novel

Men Like This

Can she trust a man who pretends for a living?

Horror author Quinn Buzzly knows all about the dark side, but when she meets actor Jack Decker, she's moved to explore something completely different—at least on paper. With his sexy good looks, intriguing manner, and charming Irish-tinged English accent, Jack is the perfect model for her next hero. Quinn decides to spend one year in London writing a historical romance inspired by him. Until real life butts in…

Jack's jealous ex-fiancée sparks a media storm when she accuses him and Quinn of having an affair. But Jack knows how to play this game. At his insistence, Quinn agrees to go along with the faux romance until the chatter subsides. Then they'll stage a quiet breakup and go their separate ways. Yet Jack is a shameless—and irresistibly convincing—flirt, and Quinn has to remind herself it's an act. Or is it? If Jack means business, he'll have to find the words to convince a wordsmith that their love is the real thing…

A Lyrical e-book on sale now!

Learn more about Roxanne at
http://www.kensingtonbooks.com/author.aspx/31647

Chapter One

Quinn gaped at Richard as if he'd grown an extra appendage in front of her eyes. He might as well have. He was alien to her, despite having known him for many years. "I'm giving you about three seconds to explain."

He had the nerve to smile. It showed off the large glaringly white teeth inside his too-perfect mouth on his too-perfect face. "You don't like it?" His dark gaze wandered, his approval apparent. "I really thought you would."

They were at a nightclub called Sabini's in Hollywood—Quinn deplored Hollywood. A small treasure of a private bar hid deep in the bowels of the rowdy club: quiet, classy, and far from the maddening *wump-wump-wump* of the dance floor down the hall. Yes, she liked it.

No, she wasn't going to admit it.

She crossed her bare arms, partly from the chill but mostly to show Richard she meant business. "Our relationship demands trust. Why would you lie to me, Richard?"

He spared a quick glance at her defensive posture. "Cold?" When she didn't respond, he waved off her concern. "All I've done is taken you out. Is that so bad?"

A jolt of agitation shot through her. Had he lost his mind? Had one too many cocktails earlier? "Yes, I'd say it was! You dragged me across a nasty dance floor wearing a silk ball gown and diamond brooch worth more than your house. You said my sister planned this. I want an explanation, and I want it now."

Richard continued to scan the bar, unruffled by her outburst. "I brought you through the front because I left my key to the private entrance at home. I apologize." He sat on one of the backless cowhide bar stools and lifted a hand for the bartender. "Bottle of champagne, please. Two glasses."

The busty young woman who could've still been driving on a learner's permit smiled. Her gaze roamed freely over Richard before she dashed off to fulfill his glamorous request.

Quinn fought the urge to stick her finger down her throat. Champagne? Who was he kidding?

He turned back to her and patted the seat beside him as if beckoning her to join him like she were some wayward, spoiled child. "Your feet must hurt." His eyes were kind, and his smile knowing. "Angie has excellent fashion sense, but you shouldn't have let her talk you into those heels."

He spoke the truth.

Quinn's feet throbbed from the towering stilettos she had no business wearing. She planned to set fire to the outrageous instruments of torture the very day they lifted the burn ban in L.A. and fight harder for the ballet flats next time.

She scowled at Richard for being right but sat anyway. The blood rushing back into her feet made her woozy with relief. With some effort, she refocused on Richard. "Quit stalling and tell me what we're doing here, or I'm walking out. If I have to call a cab to get home, I swear, I'm taking my next project to someone else."

Richard's dark and impeccably shaped eyebrows shot up. His mouth fell open. Finally, a dent in his smooth surface. "You wouldn't."

He didn't sound so certain.

Quinn smiled at having the upper hand. "I damn sure would. Like I said, this is a trust thing. It was odd when you told me Emily wanted to get together in Hollywood, but I told myself you wouldn't do anything weird. Then you go and order champagne. It keeps getting weirder, and you refuse to tell me what's really going on. You don't own a white windowless van, do you? Or have duct tape in your suit pocket?"

He didn't appear amused. In fact, he managed to appear unaffected, his impenetrable feathers were back in place. Her show of humor must've left him with the incorrect impression she'd be easily managed.

"You're over thinking this. We had a successful night at the fund-raiser. You're gorgeous. I wanted to have an after-party drink with my favorite client. There's nothing *weird* about wanting to prolong a nice evening with a friend."

He couldn't have mocked her any clearer.

She couldn't have cared any less. "Except for your conniving, I'd agree. Why didn't you simply ask?"

"I wanted to surprise you." He smiled his horse-toothed smile. It ruined everything he had going for his face. "Surprise."

The champagne arrived. He handed her a dainty flute. "Drink this." The sweet condescension in his voice nearly undid the frail threads holding Quinn's temper in check, but she kept her grip on the reins—until she glanced at her glass.

It practically brimmed over with the sparkly wine. A sudden burst of insight hit her. "You're trying to get me drunk."

"Now, Quinn—"

"You used my sister to lure me here knowing I'd never come willingly. Real classy." Quinn came out of her seat, disgusted and angry. She growled at the sharp jabs of pain shooting through the soles of her feet.

Richard must've taken the growl as meant for him. "Quinn, calm down, please. Yes, I'm attracted to you. Yes, I thought this was the only way I'd ever get a date with you."

"This is not a date!" Despite her pain, she stamped her foot. The small *click* of her heel failed to make the desired impact.

Richard placed a hand on her arm. "Obviously."

Her fingernails dug into her palms as her hands formed angry little fists at her sides.

Richard didn't notice. His primary concern seemed to have shifted from her to their audience. "You're causing a scene. You asked for an explanation, now allow me to give one before you get us kicked out."

Quinn seethed but didn't interrupt this time. A lift of her brow invited him to continue.

He cleared his throat and straightened his black silk bowtie. Since they'd come from the prestigious city fund-raiser, he was in a tuxedo jacket and slacks.

They'd been a striking pair. Quinn wore a black strapless gown and styled her long blond hair into an elegant chignon that displayed the diamond drops in her lobes. They matched the cluster pinned to the front of her gown.

In this casual setting, they looked like a bad joke. Overdressed and ill behaved. "You have to understand, Quinn. We work together closely. We talk every day. It's not strange I'm attracted to you. Asking you out seemed unprofessional."

Quinn nearly choked on her unspoken reply. This *wasn't* unprofessional? Her jaw practically unhinged at Richard's startling lack of self-awareness.

"I figured if we went out casually and had a few drinks, things might take their natural course."

A shrug accompanied the statement to show how big of a deal it wasn't, but Quinn saw red. She jabbed at his shoulder with an accusing finger.

"I'm not stupid, Richard. You celebrate with a glass of champagne. There are completely different motives at play when you order an entire bottle. You weren't hoping for slightly tipsy. You were going for totally sloshed. Then what? You'd take me back to your place and pretend it got out of hand?"

"No, I'd never—"

Quinn turned away. She braced her hands against the bar in an effort to stay on her bruised feet and tried to breathe. "You sure as hell would. After what Blake did, there's nothing I'd put past a man."

He had the audacity to scoff. "Blake is an idiot."

The comment acted like flame to tinder—instant ignition.

She whirled on him. He was no better. He was probably no worse, but at the least, he and Blake were exactly the same. "Oh, and you're some genius? Do you even realize what you've done? I should fire you." She shook her head to dislodge some of her anger, but it wasn't going anywhere. She trembled. "Get away from me. Leave, now."

"Leave?" He repeated the word slowly. "I'm not going anywhere. I brought you here. I'm responsible for you."

Quinn pinned him with every ounce of fire in her green eyes. They flashed when she was angry. They must be crackling like hot coals now. "Do you really expect me to get back in your car? I'll take a cab home. I don't need your protection. What I need is for someone to protect me from *you*."

He looked like he might refuse again.

She hit him with the final blow. "Our contract is riding on how fast you can get away from me. I mean it, Richard."

Their surroundings seemed to come back to them simultaneously. Everyone stared at Richard as they waited in dead silence for his reaction. Even the bartender watched their exchange with rapt attention. Richard's face flushed a dull red. He stood in a deliberate fashion as if it were his idea to leave. "This is foolish."

His clenched jaw and piercing glare labeled him furious, but Quinn had her own store of ire to draw from. She slipped into the most condescending tone she possessed. "You need to go home and think about what you've done."

He recoiled like she'd slapped him, but she'd wager his reaction was nothing more than embarrassment at getting dressed down in a room full of strangers. Maybe now he'd understand how she felt—mortified and belittled. He'd tricked her into coming here and attempted to ply her with drink for the sake of getting her in bed. She couldn't have done anything more insulting than that.

Richard stormed toward the exit. She hoped the staring eyes of the audience, hers included, burned holes in his back as he went.

Her shoulders fell the moment he disappeared from sight. Her rage fled. She wasn't built for dramatics. She frowned at the two untouched glass flutes on the bar. One sat empty while the other comically full. She'd never much cared for champagne hangovers.

Quinn wiggled her fingers in a girlish wave at the bartender still watching her with round eyes. "Can I get a beer?"

Quinn waited until she almost finished her first drink to call Angie, her best friend, the same demon responsible for her miserable, dejected feet. She plucked her cell phone from the hidden pocket inside the bodice of her gown. She wasn't totally stupid. She'd have never let Richard leave without a backup plan up her sleeve.

Or down her dress, as it were.

Angie answered on the first ring. She sounded unfazed, like she'd expected Quinn's late-night call. "How did the fund-raiser go?"

Oh, that's right. She'd done something fun tonight. "I had a great time. In fact, I wish we were still there."

"Oh, I'm sure you'll have others." Angie sounded slightly distracted. Quinn imagined her painting her toenails or watching television. "What time did you get home?"

Quinn cleared her throat. It wasn't her fault. She shouldn't feel stupid, but for whatever reason she did. Must be some kind of male superpower. "Would it be weird if Richard wanted to sleep with me?"

"Of course not. It'd be weird if he didn't." Angie didn't seem distracted anymore. "Did something happen? Oh my God, did you go home with him?" Her voice dropped to a dramatic whisper. "Did you guys do it? Are you calling in secret from the bathroom? Was he good?"

Richard had inspired an intense lack of charitable feelings, but leave it to Angie to smooth Quinn's angry wrinkles mere seconds into the conversation. "No, nothing like that, but he did bring me to a Hollywood nightclub. Shows a little spark, doesn't it?"

"Hollywood? Does he know you?" The disdain in her best friend's voice was welcome commiseration. "Where are you?"

"A place called Sabini's." Quinn appraised the room once more. Large round bulbs suspended from the ceiling hung low and cast their warm glow over the bar, thus creating quite the snug little atmosphere. "I'm pained to admit it, but the private bar is sort of nice. It's the mosh pit of sweaty, spastic idiots in the dance room next door who frighten me. I can't believe that passes for dancing these days. I thought the first guy I saw was having a seizure. He's lucky I didn't shove my brooch in his mouth to stop him from swallowing his tongue."

Angie snorted. "A creative way to divest yourself of a fortune. I've been to Sabini's before. Your Richard's a classy one. Are you two having a good time?"

"Not exactly." Quinn explained in painful detail how her night had gone so topsy-turvy.

She waited in silence for Angie's reply. She imagined her friend working through the scenario in her mind.

Finally, a response. "Well, okay. I guess my question is why you're still there."

Quinn loved easy questions. She sucked the last drop of beer from the long-neck bottle and smacked her lips for emphasis. "To get drunk. Why does anyone sit at a bar and order booze?"

"Nice. Tomorrow you'll wake up not only divorced and homeless but with a hangover cherry on top. Way to take your power back, honey."

"I'm not homeless. I'm staying at a hotel."

"Homeless isn't synonymous with cardboard box. You don't have a home. You're homeless."

Quinn waved to the bartender. Time for another drink. "Shut up and tell me what I'm supposed to do. Am I overreacting?"

Angie clucked her tongue. "Had he taken you out for kung pao chicken, I'd say yes, but this is kind of a big deal. He dragged you to some shady Hollywood club wearing a thousand-dollar ball gown and million-dollar diamonds. Not just ignorant, mind you. Potentially dangerous. This is L.A., not Friendly, Texas. Letting him leave you there was even dumber, by the way."

"Probably." Quinn tried for a deep breath. It escaped as a depressed groan. "What do I do? Fire him?"

The mere suggestion made her stomach pitch. She mustered up a weak smile for Busty the Barkeep, who promptly deposited Quinn's second beer in front of her.

"There's only one thing you can do." Angie sounded apologetic but remained firm. "You have to kill him."

Quinn pressed the phone closer to her ear. The spectacle had ceased, and people were back to their regularly scheduled partying. "Like it's ever that easy."

Angie scoffed. "You have no problem scalping a sweet, vulnerable, and ruggedly handsome pediatrician with a chainsaw, but you can't kill Richard? You even murdered the poor doctor on the very same night he finally worked up the courage to ask that cute barista out on a date. It took a lot of courage for him to step out of his comfort zone. The guy had issues."

Quinn rested one elbow on the bar and said what she always said. "You're taking it too personally, Ang. You've got to quit falling in love with my subjects."

"What in the hell is a barista doing with a chainsaw in the first place, huh? Does she moonlight as a lumberjack?"

Quinn wanted to roll her eyes at Angie's protest but couldn't. She was too pleased with herself. Her life's work revolved around inspiring heartfelt emotion in others. More's the better if the emotions were dark ones like grief and loss.

They were sort of her calling card. "Look, if I wrote Richard into a story to give him a grisly death, I'm afraid he'd notice. He *is* my agent. And you'd understand why the barista had a chainsaw if you'd bother to finish the book."

"I can't, Quinn, I just can't." Her best friend sniffed. "You kill everyone I love."

"I'm sorry. I'll write you a happy ending one day. Promise."

Angie went from sniveling to haughty in the space of a single sentence. "The only happy endings these days are in massage parlors."

Quinn was still laughing when she ended the call and returned the slim black cell phone to the hidden confines of her ball gown.

Her silk strapless Carolina Herrera ball gown.

Every bit of good humor conjured disappeared. Quinn remembered where she sat and how she got there.

Richard, Richard, Richard. He'd really screwed up tonight. Angie's solution, while amusing, wasn't pragmatic and wouldn't solve anything. Quinn nervously rolled the beer bottle between her hands.

The idea of confronting Richard in his office made her queasy. He'd downplay the entire scene and make her out to be a dramatic prude. The smoothness she counted on for publishing negotiations would come back to bite her when she found herself looking down the barrel of it rather than grinning smugly from behind it, but what were her choices?

She had to make a stand. She needed to put him in his place, be the iron fist of the feminine movement.

Then again, there wasn't much determined avoidance couldn't patch up. Key West was fabulous this time of year. Cabanas, boat drinks, palm trees, and pool boys.

When had she last gone on vacation? Disneyland three years ago. With Blake. Quinn didn't want to think about that. She wanted to daydream about pool boys. For research, of course. She was far too old for a pool boy.

She'd need a pool *man*.

"You don't match."

For an instant, the deep voice coming from behind stunned her. Since she sat virtually alone on her side of the L-shaped bar, she had no choice but to accept the man—a pool man if her luck had improved any—intended the words for her. Some drunken fool trying to succeed where Richard failed. What had she been thinking staying here? She should've picked up a bottle of tequila and moved this pity party to the privacy of her hotel room.

He had an accent, although she couldn't place the dialect. Definitely European. Rather than turn around right away to face her new visitor, she took a long, hard look at the beer bottle in her hand. Too soon to order her third? She wanted fuzzy, not pickled.

She'd put it off long enough. Quinn swung around on the tail end of an eye roll to greet Bachelor Number Two. The smart reply she had ready died on her lips.